SLAY THREE
REVENGE

LAURELIN PAIGE

Hot Alphas. Smart Women. Sexy Stories.

Editing: Erica Russikoff at Erica Edits
Proofing: Michele Ficht
Cover: Laurelin Paige
Formatting: Alyssa Garcia at Uplifting Author Services

SLAY THREE
REVENGE

Also by Laurelin Paige

Visit www.laurelinpaige.com for a more detailed reading order.

The Dirty Universe

Dirty Filthy Rich Boys - READ FREE
Dirty Duet: Dirty Filthy Rich Men | Dirty Filthy Rich Love
Dirty Sexy Bastard - READ FREE
Dirty Games Duet: Dirty Sexy Player | Dirty Sexy Games
Dirty Sweet Duet: Sweet Liar | Sweet Fate
Dirty Filthy Fix
Dirty Wild Trilogy: Coming 2021

The Fixed Universe

Fixed Series: Fixed on You | Found in You | Forever with You
Hudson | Fixed Forever
Found Duet: Free Me | Find Me
Chandler
Falling Under You
Dirty Filthy Fix
Slay Saga Slay One: Rivalry | Slay Two: Ruin
Slay Three: Revenge | Slay Four: Rising
The Open Door

First and Last Duet: First Touch | Last Kiss

Hollywood Standalones

One More Time
Close
Sex Symbol
Star Struck

Written with Sierra Simone

Porn Star | Hot Cop

Written with Kayti McGee under the name Laurelin McGee

Miss Match | Love Struck | MisTaken | Holiday for Hire

For Roxie who said
this was the best one yet
when I needed to hear it most.

PROLOGUE

THEN: EDWARD

I cupped my hand over the end of the cigarette, blocking it from the wind as I lit it. My eyes closed, relishing the first draw in. It was like sucking instant Xanax. Exactly what I'd needed. My exhale released, the cloud thicker than when it had just been CO_2 mixing in the January air, and with it my anxiety shrank to something more manageable.

It was a nasty habit, one I fully intended on kicking soon, but the foster home where I'd spent the better part of the prior year had been full of smokers. It was easy to become addicted. Four months out of the environment, and I was still spending more than I liked to admit on cancer sticks. New Year's wasn't far behind us. Quitting had been among my list of resolutions. I planned on revisiting that tomorrow.

Today, I was grateful I still had the crutch.

I peered down the row of graves until my eyes landed on Camilla, kneeling on the cold ground, her hands clearing the leaves that had gathered over the base of the headstone. Even after spending the last several weeks with her, I still hadn't got used to how much she'd grown.

Or how young she still was.

She'd been six when we'd been separated. In my mind, she'd stayed six as I'd grown. I'd filed for custody as soon as I'd been old enough, on my birthday in September, but the paperwork had been slow, as everything government run was, and it had been late December when she'd finally been released into my care, a present just in time for Christmas.

I hadn't recognized her at first. All the same characteristics were there—her deep-set hazel eyes, her sharp nose—but they were on a girl who was nearly twelve years of age. A girl who didn't beam like a ray of light the way my sister had. A girl who'd had that light beaten and burned out of her.

It had taken everything I had in me not to go to the man who'd abused her and kill him right then and there. I could have strangled him with my bare hands. And those who put her in that environment—I could have killed them too, without an ounce of remorse. My cousin and her husband. My father, if he weren't already dead. The man responsible for my father's death as well. All I needed was the opportunity, and I would fill a graveyard with their bodies.

But there had to be an order to these things. Roman Moore had taught me that. It was a vital lesson for someone as eager as I was for outcomes. A lesson I had to remind myself of repeatedly.

And so Camilla's foster father would wait. They would all wait. Dealing with them made up the bulk of my resolutions, resolutions I would not break.

I took another puff before flicking the growing column of ash on the ground and glanced at my watch. It was twenty minutes to Victoria Station from Kensal Green Cemetery. We'd need to leave soon if we were to make Camilla's train.

My chest tightened at the thought of parting with her so soon. Was it the right thing to do?

This wasn't the time for doubts. I'd made my decision. I'd started down this path, and I wouldn't look back.

With a burst of resolve, I stalked over to her. She didn't look up when I reached her, but the stiffening of her back said she was aware of my presence.

I gave her a beat to finish up her farewells, taking a long drag on my cigarette while I waited. I flicked again and the ash fell at her side.

She glanced up, her expression smug. "You could show some respect, you know."

Her bitter tone wasn't new. It had cycled in and out over the last several weeks, then had remained permanently the last day, as her departure time neared.

I wouldn't let it change my mind.

"Sorry," I said, unapologetically before grounding the butt out on the left side of the headstone. "That's father's half of the grave," I explained when she peered at me in horror. "He doesn't deserve my respect."

Her frown deepened. "He was still your father. You can't know all the reasons he did what he did. Are you going to hate him for it forever?"

"Probably," I said with a shrug. "And I know all I need to know. He chose her over us. He chose death. Over us. Whatever his reasons are doesn't matter." I shifted restlessly from one foot to the other, and I had to shove my hands in my pockets so I wouldn't be tempted to light another cigarette. "Come on. We're going to be late."

She sighed, a long expelling of air that made my insides feel hollow just observing. She stood, brushing the wet leaves from her knees, her eyes never leaving the grave. "I don't understand why I have to go."

"Fuck, Camilla…" My head throbbed. "We've been over this."

"Go over it again, then, because I still don't get how you abandoning me is any different from him abandoning us."

Zing. Right to my heart.

She was good at that already, at knowing where to hit. It was possible she could be as ruthless as I needed to be, possible that she could be an ally on the journey I had to take.

But I didn't want that for her. I wanted her to be warm and whole and good, and maybe it was too late for that, but if there was any hope for her, it wasn't with me.

This was how it had to be. There was no other way.

"Hampstead Collegiate is the finest boarding school around. It's a privilege that they've accepted you. They don't have to take all legacy students, and on scholarship, at that."

"Ya da ya da ya," she said, rolling her eyes at the spiel she'd heard enough to have memorized at this point.

"You know we can't afford anything else."

"I'd be perfectly happy in a state school."

"A state school doesn't cover your room and board. I would have to feed you and clothe you. Hampstead will even cover the cost of your therapy. It's the best option for you right now." I delivered the speech as if it were the truth, and it was, but it wasn't all of it. I wasn't concerned about the money. Roman would help with that until I got back our family fortune, which would be soon enough.

And that was why she had to be gone. I couldn't have a little girl with me on that road. This wasn't her burden to carry. Resent me if she must, but I had to take this on alone. This was *for* her. This was for both of us.

"Therapy is fine and all, but have you considered that what I really need is a family?"

I had considered it. But what the fuck did I know about family? She didn't need an angry single-minded brother. She needed a parent. How could I be a father when I didn't even know what a father was?

"I have my own schooling to pursue, Camilla," I said firmly, doubling down on my decision. "I don't need to be saddled with an unstable pre-teen with obvious daddy issues."

I knew where to hit too. I saw the blow land in the flinch of her eyes.

"I know what you're doing. You're being cruel on purpose. You're trying to push me away." She met my stare. Held it for several long seconds. "Fine. If you can't handle the responsibility, then send me away. I don't really have a choice in the matter."

I closed my eyes for a long blink, wishing I could change who I was. What I wanted. What fueled my blood and filled me.

But I couldn't.

And when I opened my eyes again, she must have seen the situation for what it was because she shook her head in resignation and turned her gaze back to the grave.

I scanned the names along with her. *Stefan Fasbender and Amelie Fasbender.* He'd died so soon after her that there had still been time to change the engraving. According to Roman, anyway.

"I don't remember much about her," Camilla said, softly. "I only know what she looked like from pictures, and beyond that, it's snatches of memories that have no order. She was always humming. I remember that. And she'd let me brush her hair sometimes. I can't recall the last time I spoke to her or hugged her or anything important she said to me. It's all just vague."

I didn't need to check my watch to know that we didn't have time for this. But I owed her something, didn't I? Something real. Something honest.

I inched closer so that our shoulders were touching. "I don't know if it was the last conversation we had, but I remember one of the last things she said to me very clearly." She'd been riddled with cancer, hooked up to machines. Her shoulder-length beautiful hair long gone, her cheeks sallow, her bones thin. "She said, 'When I'm gone, you'll have a hole in your life, Eddie. You have to find something to fill it.' She made me promise I would." Thirteen years old, and I hadn't had any idea what I was promising, but I'd made the vow all the same.

And if there was anything that I believed in firmly, it was that a man had nothing without his word. Honesty. Authenticity. Truth. What else did I have that was meaningful after losing everything?

I made another promise now, silently at my sister's side. *I'll bring you home soon, Camilla. As soon as I establish a home to bring you back to. As soon as the wheels for our future are in motion.*

"And have you?" she implored. "Have you found

something to fill your life with instead?"

I nodded once.

"What is it?"

She was young and it was impulsive, but if this was for her as well as for me, then she deserved to know. Or maybe I was just tired of being completely alone.

Whatever the motive, I answered sincerely. "Revenge."

ONE
NOW: CELIA

"Wait!" I stopped suddenly, forcing Edward to halt as well since his hand was laced in mine. "I need a minute. I'm not ready."

"You're not ready to go into your own home?" he asked with more than a hint of impatience.

He wasn't the only one who was frustrated with me. I was too. Weeks of preparation and hours of therapy should have made this easier, yet here I was, stalled at the garage entrance to the house, my heart pounding like it was going to burst from my rib cage.

"It's not my home," I said, voicing the anxious thoughts racing through my head.

"Yes, it is."

"It's not." I hadn't lived in Edward's London house in more than a year, and in the handful of months I'd spent there prior to that, I had never considered it a place I would one day actually live. I'd been there under false pretenses. The situation had been a ruse.

"Celia," Edward said sternly, the subtext in the simple utterance clear. He'd already given me time. He'd given me six weeks. He'd wanted to bring me here immediately after leaving Exceso, but I'd insisted on going back to Amelie. I'd needed to work through the avalanche of emotions he'd released in me before I could return to a normal life, and though he'd hated leaving me again, I'd convinced him it was the best thing for me.

And it had been. I'd needed the space to process. I'd changed fundamentally when he'd broken me down. I was no longer the strong, confident woman I'd once been. I'd never been that woman, to be honest. That woman had been built on lies and secrets. Who I was now was authentic and new, and just like a baby, my skin was delicate and thin, and I had to learn all over again how to function in the world.

It fucking sucked.

I loved the freedom that my new identity had brought me, but I hated being weak and vulnerable. I hated being unsure. I hated not knowing how to be real.

"I don't know how to do it, Edward," I said earnestly. "I don't know how to belong. I don't know who to be here." It wasn't the house itself that had me apprehensive, but everything associated with it. Edward's sister, Camilla, who'd been living here for several years, hadn't approved of my presence, though hopefully that had changed, and the servants had never looked to me as their employer. The expectations of my role as the woman of the Fasbender home were still unclear. I didn't have a job. I didn't have a purpose. On the island, my days had been prescribed by my husband, and that had made living manageable. My relationships with the islanders, which I'd grown to cherish, had been chosen for me.

And there was my relationship with Edward. In many ways, he was still a stranger to me, and yet he was the man who ruled my world. What sort of wife did he expect me to be? Could I be the woman he wanted? Did I want to be?

His features softened, though his eyes remained hard. He took my free hand and brought both together in between us. "You belong here, bird. You don't have to do anything to belong because this is your home, and you are my wife, and you are mine. That's all you have to be for now."

"But..."

"The rest we'll figure out in time," he said, cutting in before I spoke one of the dozen objections on the tip of my tongue. He stepped in to me, forcing my chin to tilt up to keep his gaze. "I know you think you aren't ready, but you are. *You are.*"

"You just wanted me here for the holidays because of appearances," I said baiting him for more reassurance.

"That too," he admitted with a smirk. "What would people think if my wife spent another Christmas without me?" His expression grew serious as his eyes traveled to my lips. "I want you with me, Celia. Come inside and be with me in our home."

I managed a single nod before his mouth claimed mine. It was a comforting kiss, though relatively chaste and much too short, interrupted by the opening of the door. It was Edward's house manager. *Our* house manager.

"Pardon me, Sir. Madame," he said, averting his eyes. "I came to get the luggage. I can return later."

Edward's sharp raise of an eyebrow was my cue. "Of course not, Jeremy. We were just headed inside," I said, feeling somewhat bolstered by taking command. "You can have our bags delivered to our rooms, please. I'll see to my own unpacking."

"As will I," Edward added.

"Very well. May I take your coats?"

I turned to let Jeremy help me with mine. Edward had brought it to the island for me, thankfully, as the weather in London had been quite rainy and cold when we arrived, much different from what I'd left behind. I'd boarded the plane the night before wearing a light sundress, an outfit that had been quickly shed once my husband and I were in the air. When I'd woken this morning, he'd already left the bed for the main cabin, but in his place, I found leggings, boots, and a sweater laid out for me to dress in. The clothes were a bit more casual than my usual taste, but they were comfortable, and comfortable was what I'd needed today.

He'd known that. Better than I had known it for myself. As he always did.

No wonder I loved him. We might still have a lot to negotiate, but that was one thing that was sure.

"We'll need nothing else until lunch is served," my husband said when our coats had been taken, his own command much more natural than mine. "Thank you, Jeremy."

Without letting me think about it another second, he pushed past the servant, pulling me along with him through the mud room to the back staircase. "See? You know your place," he said, his hand squeezing mine as we climbed the steps. "You fit here like a long-missing, last piece of a puzzle."

"Is that your way of saying I complete you?" I asked, as we reached the main floor.

He hesitated, turning to look at me, his mouth half open, his tongue silent.

The pause was bothersome. Why was there a pause? Sure, he hadn't ever come out and directly said he loved me, but he'd inferred it in a myriad of ways. He left little doubt of his feelings for me. This should have been an easy comeback. What else was there to say but yes? *Yes, Celia, you* do *complete me.*

Though...could I say that about him?

The oncoming rush of something small and boy distracted either of us from having to answer.

"Uncky!" Freddie said, throwing his arms around my husband's legs.

Edward swooped his three-and-a-half-year-old nephew up in the air, causing the boy to erupt in laughter.

It was impossible not to break into a smile at the sound. At the sight. Though deep inside, at the core of me, my womb pulsed with its emptiness. It was an ache that had become recurrent. One that knew I had to learn to ignore. Edward was already in his forties, a decade older than me with two grown children of his own. He'd told me before we married that he didn't want more children. That he *wouldn't* have more. It hadn't been an issue when I hadn't planned to stay married to him.

But now?

The rest we'll figure out in time, he'd said. It wasn't something I had to address today.

Camilla Fasbender Dougherty, however, was something I had to address today.

"Oh, for fuck's sake. Really, Eddie? You brought her back here?" She stood at the door to the salon, her arms crossed indignantly. Apparently she wasn't any more tolerable of me than she had been the last time we'd been face to face.

It probably didn't help that she hadn't known I'd be here. Which was as much of a surprise to me as my appearance seemed to be to her.

I turned to stare down my husband. "You didn't tell her I was coming back with you?"

"And no wonder that he didn't since he knew how I'd feel about it." The remark was addressed to me, but it was meant for Edward.

Suddenly it was clear that he'd kept more from her than just my arrival.

"You didn't tell her about my uncle, either?" I was incredulous. Maybe it was my fault for assuming he would have told her already, but it was an important tidbit of information. Why wouldn't he have cleared that up with her before now?

Because he was a sadist, that was why. Because he got off on others' discomfort, and while I couldn't speak to how Camilla felt, I definitely wasn't comfortable right now.

Edward's sly smile seemed to affirm my suspicions. His eyes danced gleefully from the venomous gaze of his sister to the equally venomous gaze of his wife. "I thought it would be a better conversation had with the three of us together."

"Then you should have told that to *me*," I said, angrily. "Edward," I added, using his name as he preferred, but with contempt.

His eyes narrowed and his lips drew into a firm line. He'd told me more than once that he wouldn't tolerate disrespect in front of others, and, for the most part, I found a certain satisfaction in obeying that rule.

But bringing me into this situation without any warning was disrespectful to me, and he needed to know how I felt about it.

"Sheri," he called out, flagging down a member of the household staff as she walked by. "Could you please take Freddie to Anwar?"

Once he'd passed off his nephew, he wrapped his hand possessively around my waist and drew me tightly to his side. "Camilla, let's go sit, shall we?"

She sighed reluctantly, then turned toward the salon. Though the invitation had only been extended to his sister, Edward guided me behind her, directing me to sit on the sofa across from the one Camilla sat in. I expected him to sit next to me, but he put distance between us, perching on the arm.

I didn't know if the distance was for Camilla's sake or his own, but it was probably a wise choice. There was a good chance I would have clawed his thigh with my fingernails if he'd chosen to be by me. He definitely deserved it.

"So...?" Camilla's eyes darted from me to her brother, her expression pointed. It was obvious she preferred to have this conversation without me present. It was also obvious that she expected him to be the one filling her in.

It was probably most respectful for me to let him do just that.

But he'd had his chance to tell her, and he hadn't, and since he'd chosen to leave it for my attendance, then, as far as I was concerned, that meant I had permission to step in.

More accurately, I didn't *need* to have permission. I was his wife. I wasn't his submissive.

Was I?

Another thing we had to work out later.

"I'm just going to dive right in and say I'm truly sorry to be sprung on you like this, Camilla. It wasn't fair to either of us." I glared at my husband whose expression was unreadable. "But it particularly wasn't kind to you."

"Don't be insolent, Celia," he warned. "That isn't called for."

I scowled at his rebuke, but he was right. Passive-aggressive digs in his direction weren't going to help my relationship with either of them.

I got to the point. "Edward has told me the circumstances surrounding your parents' deaths, and I understand completely why you harbor such animosity toward the Werner name. You've both been through a lot, and I'm sure that I would feel the same way if I'd been in your shoes."

It was bad enough to have a parent die from cancer. To have the other commit suicide right after was unimaginable. Edward's father had taken his own life, not only because he'd lost his partner, but also because he'd lost his company in a hostile takeover. To a company my father owned.

"That said," I continued, choosing my words carefully. I didn't want to diminish her history, but it was important she knew the truth. "My father is not the Werner that was responsible for Accelerate being bought out from under your father. Yes, he was the head of the company at the time, but it was my uncle Ron who ran everything that happened in the UK. He took over several media businesses here, dismantling all of them. He had one hundred percent autonomy at the time and was later kicked out of his position because of the poor decisions he made and the direction he'd taken that branch of the company, which was in no way retribution for the things he's done, but the fact is, it wasn't my father. Warren Werner had nothing to do with the fall of your family."

She'd listened stoically as I'd spoken, her attention solely on me. But now Camilla's focus flew to her brother. "Is it true?"

"Yes," I said, though I knew it wasn't me she was asking.

"It's all true," Edward confirmed. "I verified it."

I swung toward him. "You verified it? You didn't trust me?" He hadn't given me any indication that he'd doubted me when I'd told him. It bothered me to hear now that he had.

He shook his head. "It wasn't about trust. It was about needing to see the proof."

If there was a difference, I couldn't see it.

"How do you feel about discovering this, Ed?" Camilla asked. The tone of the question was personal, and it made me feel like an intruder. Like maybe the conversation would have been better without me.

Worse, it felt like this was a question I should have asked myself and before now. He may still have been a stranger, but I knew how important his vengeance had been. Changing course this far into his plans had to have been a huge loss. It had to feel devastating, and I hadn't acknowledged that.

"Honestly?" He aimed his response at the person who asked. "I feel relieved."

I blinked in surprise.

"Yes," Camilla said, looking us both over. "I see."

What did she see? I didn't see. What was there to see?

"Then the two of you are…?" She trailed off, and thank God she wasn't asking me, because I wasn't sure I knew the right answer.

But Edward did. "We're married, Camilla. We intend to stay that way. Happily."

Ah, now I saw. He was relieved because, now that my father wasn't the bad guy, I wasn't either. Which meant he no longer had to resist the pull between us.

I was relieved about that too.

"You should know we have no secrets between us," he continued. "Celia knows what my goals are and what lengths I'll go to in order to see them to the end." Lengths like marrying a woman with the intention of killing her to get the shares she owned of her father's company. I wasn't convinced that he would have been able to see that to its end, the evidence being that I was still very much alive even before he'd found out the truth about my uncle.

But Edward wanted to believe he would have done anything, and it wasn't the worst thing to let him have that.

"And you're still with him," she said, finally acknowledging me.

I looked to my husband with my answer. "Very much so."

"She also supports whatever actions we need to take next," he said. "Or so I believe."

"I do," I said. It was the first time we'd made our declarations of devotion in front of another person, even though we had made similar ones to each other in this very room, when we'd exchanged rings.

This time we knew we meant them, and the difference sent a bolt of warmth through my chest and heat down between my legs.

The moment wasn't appreciated by my sister-in-law. "Your family loyalty runs thin," she scoffed.

"No, no. It's not like that." I scanned her over quickly, trying to picture how she must see me. How she must see herself in comparison. Though she was the one sitting in a designer jumpsuit, I'd grown up far more privileged than she had. I hadn't seen them personally, but from what I had been told, I was sure there were burn marks on her skin under her long sleeves, permanent tattoos from an abusive foster father. After surviving that, she'd gone on to lose her husband quite young. Besides her son, Edward was the only family she had, and he had bent over backwards to care for her, not only raising her after he'd been old enough but also taking her in again after she'd been widowed.

That sort of bond bred loyalty I likely couldn't understand.

But it didn't mean I didn't feel my own version of devotion. As misguided as it often was.

"I'm loyal to my parents," I went on. "And Edward knows the lengths I'd go to—*have* gone to—for them." My own lengths included marrying my father's rival with the intent of ruining him in order to win my father's love. Not a healthy loyalty by any means, but I wasn't sure any of us in the room knew what a healthy relationship was.

"Ron is another situation entirely. He's…" I searched for the words to describe his sins, how he'd groomed me and treated me like his doll. How he'd sold parts of my innocence to his rich friends. "Let's just say he's not a good person. And whatever wrath Edward plans on unleashing on him, it is likely only a portion of what he deserves."

Camilla met my eyes, and though it was tempting to put up my guard, I forced myself not to. She kept my gaze for several beats until her features eased and her head nodded, and I wondered if she saw what I had wanted her to see. Wondered if she understood how much we had in common. How we'd both been hurt by the very people who had been tasked to care for us. How we both loved a man who had tended to us in unorthodox ways.

"It's a shift in the narrative, I know," Edward said, the tenderness in his voice wrapping tendrils around both me and his sister.

"It's a huge shift," she agreed. "Forgive me if it takes me a minute to get my bearings."

"Take your time. But understand that Celia is part of my life now. She is my wife. This is her home, and I expect that to be appreciated."

"I know how to be respectful, Eddie." Her retort was soft, full of affection despite her words. "I never interfered with the arrangement you had with Marion. I can behave. As long as you can assure me this relationship is in your best interest."

"She's not Marion," he said firmly, and though I didn't understand the meaning of the remark, it whipped into my new baby skin. "But she's not Frank either. And neither am I."

The next few comments whizzed by me as I tried to find a thread I could follow.

"Glad to hear it, but I've never thought you were," Camilla said.

"You haven't?"

"I don't know. Maybe I did."

"I'm that despicable, perhaps, but the malice I feel is always earned."

They shared a smile. Whatever had transpired in the exchange, they'd reached some understanding. An understanding that I felt very much left out of.

"Who's Frank?" I asked, hoping one of them would loop me in.

"It doesn't matter," Camilla said, her head turning to peer out of the salon and down the hall toward the bustle at the front door. It sounded like someone arriving or a delivery maybe. Nothing half as interesting as the conversation she'd dismissed.

Before I could make another attempt to pursue it, she stood. Her height when standing was intimidating, to the point that I rose too. "As I said before," she stated, "this is a big alteration in my thinking. Since Eddie took me in, hatred of the Werner name has been drilled into me."

She'd spoken to me directly this time, and the words lashed as harshly as the mention of Marion. I knew and understood where she came from, but I was still who I was.

Or maybe I wasn't anymore.

Because Edward really had torn me down to nothing, and what was left in my place was still unknown.

But this newbie did have a name. And it wasn't the one I'd grown up with.

"Good thing I'm not a Werner then, isn't it?" I said, the comeback a beat late but true enough that the hit landed.

"Yes. Exactly right." She smiled earnestly and held out her hand, which I took without pause. "Welcome to the family, Celia. I look forward to the new war ahead of us. I hope you don't find the burden of being a Fasbender as heavy as those before you."

It was a strange thing she'd said, and I opened my mouth to ask what she meant, but before I could say anything, Edward's children were in the room, greeting us enthusiastically.

"We're not too early, are we?" Genny asked as she hugged her father. "You didn't say what time to be here for lunch, and we wanted you to have time to settle."

"No, not too early." Edward beamed at her.

I smiled as well, despite wanting to kick the man. If I'd known he'd invited his kids over, I would have insisted on changing into something more presentable as soon as we had arrived. Had that been his plan with the clothing he'd laid out? I'd thought he'd chosen my outfit so I'd feel good in my surroundings. Now I wondered if he'd intended just the opposite.

"It's good to have you home," Genny said when she turned her greeting to me. "Father's been miserable without you." She embraced me and I was surprised both by her words and the warmth of her welcome.

"I'm not sure he isn't just as miserable when I'm around."

"Well, that's true enough," she agreed with a laugh that both Hagan and Camilla shared with her.

When their amusement died down, I excused myself to change, though somewhat reluctantly. There was a pleasant aura in the presence of Edward with his children. It was an aura I wanted to feed on like a vampire, as though their bonds could nourish the empty parts of my existence. As though it could complete me like I longed to be completed.

But it was a false completion. It was a puzzle piece that looked like it fit, but didn't quite, and as I paused at the foot of the stairs to gaze back at the bunch, I ached for what they had. Could I ever truly belong to that? Would Edward ever truly let me in?

I wasn't sure.

I wasn't sure I should even accept it if he did. There was too much lacking between us that I wasn't convinced would be fixed with time. Too much uncertainty.

It wasn't just the clothing or the way he could never say outright how he felt. It was also the way he'd set me up with Camilla. The way he hadn't prepared me for his children's visit. The way he said I fit in but continually made me feel like I stuck out. Was his behavior natural hesitation around a new relationship or was it part of his constant need to keep me on edge?

That was the thing with Edward—it was impossible to know if the way he manipulated my life was for my benefit, or his. I suspected it was often a combination, but how could I be sure? To borrow Camilla's concern, how did I know what he did was always in my best interest?

I loved him, no bones about it. I was his, and he owned my heart entirely. That flag was planted as firmly as my feet were planted on the bottom stair.

My trust, however, was still up in the air.

TWO

EDWARD

I t wasn't that late when I retired for the night, but with the jet lag and the time change it felt late. Celia had managed to sneak in a nap after lunch, excusing herself when Genny left to work on her studies. Hagan remained to talk business and ended up staying through dinner. He'd worked at Accelecom even before he'd graduated from university, and I'd always had the intention of training him to follow in my footsteps. It had been convenient having him around the past year when I'd made frequent trips to Amelie to visit Celia, and he'd handled the tasks I'd given him quite well.

That didn't mean he was privy to everything.

I had inherited the mistakes of my father, but I would not pass them onto my progeny. Thus Hagan was involved with my company, but he was not involved with my revenge. And right now that was the business that was front and center in my mind so his visit had walked the line between tedium and productivity.

"Young Mr. Fasbender is gone?" Jeremy asked from

the doorway of my office, likely wanting to lock the house up and prepare for the night.

"He is." I shut my computer down and stood. "My wife has already gone up. I'm headed now as well."

"Don't forget you promised Master Freddie you'd check in on him."

My nephew was often more attached to me when I'd been away. He'd come into my office, despite the rule that it was an off-limits space, begging for a bedtime story. It had been tempting to give in. *The Little Engine That Could* was more entertaining than discussing television market opportunities of the Czech Republic, if only barely, but Hagan needed my attention. Freddie wasn't the only one more attached when I'd been away.

I'd managed to mollify the little boy by promising to peek in on him before I retired.

"Thank you for the reminder," I said, though I hadn't forgotten. "I'll head up there first."

I took the stairs two at a time, continuing past the floor that held my bedroom space to go to the top level of the house. These rooms had belonged to Hagan and Genevieve when they were younger, but for the past several years, Camilla had resided in them, and now I thought of them as her apartments. As such, I rarely ventured up there, and it felt somewhat like trespassing as I stepped onto the landing.

Quietly, so as not to disturb my sister, I walked through the playroom to the door ajar on the far end. Ghosts of the past hovered in the corners of the space, bidding me to remember other trips to the nursery, long ago, when I'd had a different wife and a different life. Then, the days had remained hectic, even after I'd left the office, the energy of corporate doings replaced with the energy of small children. There had been no such thing as downtime, and when I looked back on it now, it seemed like they must have been the primary occupation of my existence.

But I didn't have any evidence to back that up.

In fact, the evidence that I did have—the business I'd built, the instances of justice I'd carried out, the woman I'd chosen when I'd remarried—all pointed to an existence that was quite the contrary. Had my children been as frontmost in my life as they should have been? Had I given them the time and attention they deserved?

They certainly were smart, competent, well-adjusted young adults, but the plaguing doubt that I'd been a subpar parent might have been what drove me now to be so attentive to Freddie, even though he wasn't my own.

The boy was fast asleep, as I'd known he would be. I retrieved his ragged bunny from the floor and tucked it under his arm before pulling the covers up. Then, after sweeping two fingers gently across his forehead, I switched off the bedside lamp and crept back out, shutting the door behind me.

"Oh, good. I caught you." Camilla stood in the doorway on the other side of the playroom, where the hallway led to her bedroom suite.

I cursed under my breath. Eventually, I knew I'd have to talk to her, but I'd hoped to put it off, at least until I'd had a good night's rest.

Perhaps I still could. "Shh," I said, using Freddie as my excuse. "You'll wake him."

She shook her head. "He sleeps like the dead, and you know it. You can't use him to get out of talking to me."

The problem with being close to my sister was that it

was very hard to get away with anything.

"Would you prefer to come into my sitting room for this?" she asked, knowing she had me completely where she wanted me.

I preferred not to be doing this at all.

"Here will be fine." Standing would be easier to insure it was quick.

"Have it your way." She folded her arms over her chest, clearly not pleased with my choice. "Now, don't get cross with me for asking, because I'm only looking out for you..."

I'd found that the most irritating conversations began with "Don't get cross," and I had to take a beat before urging her on. "Go ahead."

"So it wasn't Warren Werner who brought down father's company. If you're certain of that, then I can be too. But how can you be certain that Celia isn't in this marriage to help him take you down now?"

It was a reasonable question, and one that had merit considering how little Camilla knew about the situation and my relationship with my wife. "Her father is no longer in control of Werner Media," I explained. Even though he was no longer my target, this fact still stung. "He's acting CEO, but his power is limited. He doesn't have the ability to make a move on me in his current position."

"Okay," Camilla processed the information faster than I had. "Then what about the uncle? How can you be sure she isn't going to warn him of any of your plans?"

"I can be certain." It could have been enough. Camilla would drop it with my assurances, but I wanted her to know more. I wanted her to understand, not just the predicament but Celia.

So, at the risk of betraying my wife's confidence, I gave Camilla what she needed to put the pieces together. "Let's just say she feels about him the way you felt about Mitch."

Mitch Ferris, the man who'd physically abused my sister when she was in his care through the foster system.

"Ah." Her features softened as her body wrapped more tightly. "I thought I recognized...something..."

It had been nearly impossible to see the effects of Celia's abuse when I'd first met her, but the woman she was now was much more transparent. She would hate it if she realized she no longer masked those secrets as she once had, but I was glad that she'd revealed enough of herself to possibly start a bond with Camilla.

Now my sister just needed to be decent about it. "Then you'll be nice?" I prodded.

"I'll be nice." She took a deep breath and exhaled slowly. "I should move out."

My reaction was immediate. "No. This is your home. This is Freddie's home."

"It's your home. And now it's her home, and we're only intruders."

"You are not." But even as I insisted, I knew she was right. If I had any intention of making a marriage with Celia—and I did—then it had to be a real marriage. There wasn't any place for in-laws in the home of a real newlywed couple.

"It's for the best to do this sooner rather than later," Camilla continued. "Easier on Freddie when he's young."

I looked behind me at the closed door, thinking of the child beyond it. Thinking of his mother and the circumstances that had brought her pregnant and alone to my house.

Hideous circumstances. Circumstances that tended to have a long-lasting effect.

"It's too soon," I said, suddenly intent on protecting her, no matter the cost.

"Too soon after Frank?" Her tone said she thought the idea was rubbish. "It's been four years. Do you really think me that fragile?"

"I didn't mean that." I didn't know what I meant. It wasn't as though she still needed protecting. We were long past that.

She smiled slightly. Knowingly. As though she understood my meaning even if I didn't. "There's a bond between people who share a secret, Eddie. We won't lose ours just because I have a different address."

Was that all this was? Me, afraid that we'd somehow grow apart?

Perhaps that was some of it. But there was more, and she seemed to sense that as well.

She crossed the room midway then stopped. "I'm all right with it. With what we did, okay? I've never said that, I realize, and I should have way before now. Honestly, I try not to think about it very often because I hate to think of myself as someone who has ambiguous morals, but I'm all right with it. I don't regret that it happened, and I know you don't either. So let's put it behind us, once and for all. All right?"

I had already put her husband and the details of his death behind me. It had been easy. But I was a man who'd built an identity on seeking justice. I'd lost my soul to that devil long ago. Camilla still had hers, and I feared that if she actually did put Frank behind her, that would be the day that she lost it.

Then again, that might be the cost of learning to live again.

It wasn't my road to walk, and as much as I wanted to preside over her journey, I could see it was time to let those reins go. "Do what you feel you need to do," I said, finally. "But let it go on record that I didn't push you out."

"What, Edward Fasbender? Push his little sister out of his life? Never." She laughed and so I chuckled too, despite the painful reminder of what I'd done to her in the name of vengeance in the past.

The worst part? I'd do it again. Every time.

The bedroom was empty when I got there. Even though the lights were off, I checked the closet and the bathroom before opening the door that adjoined mine and the one Celia had slept in before we'd married. Marion's old room.

I found her sitting on the bed, rubbing lotion onto her long limbs. Instantly, my trousers were uncomfortably tight.

"What are you doing?" I asked, wondering why she'd chosen to primp here instead of in our bedroom.

"I'm getting ready for bed."

"In here?"

"In my room, yes."

"No, no, no." I shook my head vehemently. We'd been

sleeping together regularly for the last couple of months, whenever we were together anyway. It was possible she'd assumed that being in this house meant returning to the previous arrangement, but it was more likely that she knew that wasn't the case and just wanted to hear me say it. "You can keep this space as your sitting room, if you like. I honestly don't care, but you will sleep with me."

"That wasn't what was negotiated before we got married." Her smirk gave her away.

I hated being manipulated, particularly being manipulated into displays of affection, and I was tempted to leave her where she was and retire alone, simply so she'd understand that I wouldn't play her little game.

But the truth was, I would play her little game. I liked it, even. Playing her little games meant she'd play my much more significant games, and that was where the fun really happened between us.

I gave her a stern scowl instead. "Those terms are null and void, and you know it. Now, unless you prefer sleeping in here—in which case we'll have quite a row about it that I will win—"

"I don't prefer it."

"Then get your pretty little ass over there where it belongs. Speaking of, I believe I need to turn it red after the way you spoke to me in front of my sister earlier."

She stood and moved toward me and the door leading to our bedroom. "So the separate bedroom terms are null and void, but the respect you in all instances term is still valid? Who says I'm on board with that?"

My jaw clamped tight. There could still very well be a row in our future. Several, even. We'd come into our arrangement under false pretenses, but we'd shared a lot in our time on the island. I'd hoped that what we'd established in our time there would be easily transportable. Part of me had believed we might be able to come home and just be who we were together without any fuss.

But not only was that an overly optimistic scenario, it wasn't the one I honestly preferred. I enjoyed setting boundaries. I enjoyed even more when they were somewhat confining. Mostly, I enjoyed pushing them until she saw how much she appreciated that they'd been set up for her in the first place.

That's when things got interesting.

"Tomorrow night, we will set new terms," I said, allowing her the illusion that she would have room to negotiate. "That doesn't get you out of what happens tonight. No matter what you thought about the terms of our relationship, I know you were fully aware that I would be displeased when you voiced opposition to my method of handling Camilla."

"Was I fully aware?" she asked, her lips puckering into a taunt. "Hmm."

She sashayed past me into our bedroom, drawing my attention to the ass I meant to have under my palm soon. I followed with a stiff cock, half from anticipation and half from the sight of her. The nightshirt she wore invited the most improper thoughts. It was pink and girly and made her look young. So, so young. I felt indecent even looking at her.

Her sauciness only added to the need to dominate her.

"I guess I was being naughty then. The question is, what are you going to do about it?" She sat on the bed, her arms braced behind her.

Her flippancy was adorable and irritating both at once.

Consequences for lack of respect was not something I ever treated lightly, and I didn't intend to now. It was possible to take advantage of the sex kitten while also reminding her of her place. I just had to get her ass bare and bend her over my knee.

But then she gasped, her face suddenly going pale.

She stood, her eyes wide and drawn to the far wall. As though she couldn't believe what she was looking at, she went closer, her expression more aghast with each step.

I kept my own gaze glued to her, not needing to see what she was looking at. I already knew. I'd been the one to put it there. I'd even known she'd likely have a reaction when she saw it, which was the reason I'd put it up in the first place.

What I hadn't known was what kind of reaction she'd have.

Yes, this was where things got interesting.

"It was with your belongings when I had them sent from the States," I said, my eyes never leaving her. This painting had been wrapped differently than any of her others with more care and attention. The assumption could be that it was important to her, but when I opened it up and discovered what the painting depicted, I guessed it was more complicated than just being important.

"Blanche Martin gave it to me," she said, her voice raw. "I'd been trying to convince her that I was going to get her art in some rich guy's house. It was a stupid scheme, and anyway... She brought this one to show me personally. I didn't want it, but I could hardly give it back to her. I should have thrown it out. I don't know why I didn't."

I glanced at the country garden scene, at the path that wandered off into the distance, at the swing that hung from the branches of the centermost tree.

"It makes you think of your uncle," I said. It wasn't a question.

She nodded, her chin trembling.

I'd supposed as much. She'd told me that was how he'd begun his grooming of her at the age of seven. He'd built her a swing large enough for him to sit with her on it. He'd referred to it as their special place as he'd held her inappropriately on his lap.

"It's confusing, really. Because the memories of being on that swing were actually quite good ones. I was too young to understand what his end goal was or that the way he treated me wasn't right." She swallowed then turned her gaze to me. "It's only with what happened in later years that the garden memories soured, and they didn't sour in the way they should have. I should see this and feel nothing but rage and horror, but I don't. I see that swing..." She shifted to stare at the painting again. "And I remember what it felt like to fly, what it felt like to be free. And then I feel guilty and wrong because it's all associated with him and he made my life a mess."

My little bird was wounded. She had been for so long, her wings damaged and torn, but she'd kept it hidden until I forced her to let it be seen. Now, she needed to learn to fly again, and she would. I swore to it with every passing breath.

She turned all the way around, putting her back to the painting. "I know you couldn't have known. But could you please take it down?"

I paused, even though I knew my answer. I'd had the painting before she'd told me the story, but I hadn't opened it until I'd been preparing for her to move back with me.

As soon as I'd seen it, the words of her story had come back to me, and while I didn't know why she had the painting, I couldn't imagine that she'd be able to look at it without similar thoughts.

But she'd still owned it. Which meant she wasn't ready to let it go.

And if she wasn't ready to let it go, then she was damn well going to look at it. Even if it made her uncomfortable. Especially if it made her uncomfortable.

"No," I said after several beats.

Her head jerked up in surprise. "What?"

"You heard me. I won't take it down."

"Then I can't sleep in here. You can't expect that." She started back toward the door to the adjoining room.

But I was in her way, and I caught her as she tried to pass. Bending her arms behind her, I held her wrists at the small of her back. "I do expect you to sleep here, and you will."

"Like hell I will." She struggled to escape which only led me to tighten my grip.

"Celia, Celia. My little bird." I trailed kisses along her jawline, and though she was hesitant at first, she began to melt into my caress. "You remember what you are to me, right?"

Her brows creased as she tried to figure out what I was after.

"Everything. You're everything to me. And I will do anything to protect you, to keep you safe from the monsters in your past. Whatever needs to be done."

"But…"

"No buts. I will take care of you. You're mine, no one else's." The words wouldn't be enough to change her memories alone, but right now they served to distract her. I took her mouth with mine, reminding her physically how much I felt for her with my lips and tongue.

After a bit of coaxing, her resistance fell away, and she gave into my kiss completely. I devoured her then, swallowing her raspy mewls and bracing her body as it shuddered with pleasure. I let go of her wrists and her hands flew to clutch onto my sweater, fistfuls of cashmere twisting in her grip. My own hand snaked underneath the hem of her nightshirt and into her pants where I found her wet and swollen.

It only took a few rough swipes of my thumb at her clit before I could easily slide two fingers inside her, bending them to stroke without mercy against her sensitive inner wall. Her whimpers turned into ragged moans as I continued the assault, pushing as far inside her as I could, urging her toward her climax.

Good girl, I thought when she erupted, unwilling to break the kiss to reward her with the praise directly. *Be with me. Stay with me.*

It was manipulative, yes, because I had an agenda, but it was also sincere. My desire for Celia reached epic proportions. It filled me like a reservoir in the midst of a heavy rainstorm, the water pushing unforgivably at the walls of the dam. The only thing that kept me upright in its wake was the secure foundation I'd built out of control and rage.

I wanted her, wanted to touch her and fuck her. Wanted to hear her gasp my name while she came all over my hand.

I also wanted her strong and whole and resilient and mine, and I knew how to have it all. If that made me greedy, so be it. It was greed that served her best.

So when she was still spent and pliant in my arms, I acted on that greed.

I walked her backward until she hit the upholstered accent chair. Then I spun her around and bent her over the arm. She was still getting her balance as I swiftly removed her pants, kicking her legs apart when they were gone so that I had plenty of room to step between her thighs. A handful of seconds later, my cock was out and lined up at her hole, ready to drive in with one aggressive thrust.

But first, I gathered my hands in her hair and pulled back, lifting her head so that she would see the painting on the wall as I shoved into her.

"No," she cried out even as her body pressed back into me, meeting each controlled stroke.

To the side of us, the dressing mirror caught her reflection. Her profile showed her face was screwed up in an expression of pleasure/pain, her eyes closed tight against her view.

"Open your eyes, Celia," I demanded, pulling her hair so hard her back arched in my direction. "Look at it."

"I don't want to look," she begged.

"Look!" I said sharply, feeling her grow wetter at the strength of my demand.

Her eyes flew open, despite the deepening of her frown, as though she couldn't help but obey. She always responded when I got a bit mean, whether she liked that about herself or not, it was who she was, and I understood that.

I rewarded her with more thrusts of my cock and praised her with my approval. "Here you are, bird. Good girl. Keep looking. Do you know why I want you to look? Do you know what I want you to see?"

"No," she whimpered. "I don't."

In the mirror, I could see a tear running down the side of her cheek, caused by her approaching orgasm or emotional strain, I couldn't be sure, but my cock thickened at the sight, turning into a rod of pure steel. My balls tightened, too, signalling the nearness of my own release.

This was going to be over soon. I had to hurry on with it.

Pushing my free hand underneath her bent upper half, I found her clit and pressed on it slightly. "I want you to see where you are and where you are not. You're not in that place. You are not in that garden. You are not with that disgusting excuse of a human being. You are here, in my bedroom. In *our* bedroom. I'm the one who is with you. It's me who is touching you. My cock inside you. No one else's, do you hear me?"

Her eyes widened and her mouth opened, but all that came out was a single grunt of acknowledgment.

It wasn't enough. I needed more. She needed to be convinced.

"Who's fucking you?" I demanded, plowing into her so hard my thighs slapped audibly against the back of her legs.

"You," she whispered.

"Say my name."

"Edward."

Fuck, the sound of my name on her lips nearly undid me. My rhythm stuttered, and I had to fight not to lose my load right then.

With a growl, I took hold of myself, increasing the pressure of my thumb on her nub. "Who owns this cunt?"

"Edward."

"Who makes you come?"

"Edward." Her voice tightened as she clenched down around my cock, her body trying to push me out as she came explosively.

I forced my way through her grip, determined to ride her until the very end. "That's right. It's me, and I'm not going anywhere. I'm here with you now, and it doesn't matter what's on our wall or what memories are lurking in the shadows, they can't own you. You belong to me. Only me."

My words strained with the last of my declaration as my release overtook me. With my hand still wrapped in her hair, I jerked into her, shooting every last drop of my climax into the tight sheath of her cunt.

I stayed inside her while my breathing slowed, running a firm hand up and down the length of her spine, reassuring her of my presence. I watched her still in the mirror. She'd laid her cheek on the opposite armrest, her eyes once again closed. Her features were soft, her expression sated. Or tired. Perhaps, resigned.

Was this really going to work between us?

This was who I was, a man who would keep pushing her comfort levels because it bettered her, yes, but also because I liked it. Could she accept that?

Could she accept it without losing everything she was?

I pulled out of her, and she let out a soft sound of protest.

"Shh," I soothed her. "I'm not going anywhere." I reached over to the wall and turned off the switch for the light on this side of the room. The painting disappeared into darkness.

Then I gathered her into my arms, kissing her temple as I carried her to the bed. She was half asleep by the time I tucked her in, but she reached for me before I could leave her side to get cleaned up.

"I get it," she said. "And I'll try. I'll try to be here more than I'm there with him." She nodded her head toward the now unseen painting.

I brushed the hair from her forehead. "You can ask Jeremy to have it taken down in the morning," I told her. "It's your choice."

She nodded.

But she knew as well as I did that the garden and its swing was still there, whether it was on our wall or not.

THREE

CELIA

I sat up with a start, panting in the dark. My hand went automatically to my chest where I could feel my heart pounding. It felt like I'd been running, but the images in the nightmare I'd just had showed me in a confined space.

Just trying to recall more made my skin crawl. I shook the thoughts off of me with a shudder.

"Another one?" Edward's voice graveled from behind me.

My shoulders tensed. This was half the reason I hadn't felt ready to come back to London. He knew about the occasional bad dreams, but since he'd been away so much, he hadn't been aware of the recent uptick in frequency.

"I'm fine," I said, swallowing the truth. It was bad enough that I'd become so fragile in my waking hours. He didn't need to know the extent of my weaknesses.

As always, though, he could see me, even when I tried to hide.

His palm slid heavy and comforting along my bare

back, massaging the rock of a muscle lodged beneath my shoulder blade. "You won't be able to go back to sleep until you tell me."

I wanted to snap back at that, inform him that it wasn't true. I'd woken from recurrent bad dreams for years without him and been just fine.

But the truth was that I hadn't been fine. I'd been suppressing a lifetime of experiences that I'd never fully dealt with. Traumas that left me emotionless. Wounds so deeply buried in my subconscious, that most of them didn't even haunt me when I closed my eyes. In fact, the only dream I'd remembered having for the past several years had been a recurring one of a faceless man and a tightly bundled baby that I could never quite see.

Then Edward came along with his "sessions" and his constant probing into my psyche that compelled me to examine events in my life that I had wanted to never look at again, and now, along with having all sorts of feelings, I had all sorts of dreams. Terrible dreams. Fragments of memories, mostly, or variations on things that had happened to me in the past. He'd opened a gate inside of me, and everything that had been secreted away behind it refused to be shut up any longer. He'd forced me to deal, whether I wanted to or not, and now that I'd started, I couldn't stop. Even when I was sleeping, the thoughts would come, begging to be processed. Pushing them away was impossible. The only way to be rid of them was to face them head-on.

"It's a blur," I said, unable to recall any of the pieces to describe them. "But I know what I was remembering. I can see that clearly."

The bed lurched as he reached for the bedside lamp.

"Keep it off," I snapped. As if remaining in the dark would help me be able to hide. "Please," I added, softer.

He paused, and I could feel him deciding whether or not to comply before he sat up, the lamp untouched. "Something new?"

"Yes." A lot of the memories I'd been dreaming lately had been things I'd blocked out, if that was the right term. At least they were things I hadn't thought about in so long that I'd forgotten them.

"Something worse?"

I turned toward him, studying the outline of his features as if they could tell me the answer. The bulk of the pain that Uncle Ron inflicted had been cumulative. So many of his individual acts only became vile when added to the others.

But there were still moments that were singularly horrific. Auctioning parts of my innocence off to his friends had been the one that I'd considered the worst. As I began to remember more of what he'd done, other instances rallied for the title.

"I don't know if it's worse," I answered, finally. "Just... different."

"Different how?"

I groaned. I didn't want to talk about it. It was easier to explain a bad dream than to share something terrible that had actually occurred. Nightmares came without my free agency, and yes, it could be argued that I hadn't had agency when I'd been under Ron's care, because I'd been too young to understand, which was the truth. But I'd been in those moments, and they hadn't felt manipulative. It had felt like I'd actively participated. I'd let him hug me and fondle me. I'd let him bathe me and pamper me. How was I not to blame at least in part?

"Celia..." Edward pressed, his voice as hard as the

force his hand was currently applying on the knot at my neck.

"Is this a session?"

"It is now." His hand dropped, and the mattress shifted again as he started to get out.

I reached out and grabbed his thigh through the covers, stopping him. "Okay, but stay, please? I'll talk but I want you here." Next to me, instead of across the room. Where I didn't have to face him. Where I didn't have to see what he thought about me written all over his expression.

"If you think that will be easier," he agreed, settling back into the bed. But he leaned against the headboard distancing himself from me even while remaining close.

His game, his rules.

Best just to get it over with.

"It was the summer I was ten, I think." Then I knew. "Yes. I was definitely ten because Uncle Ron had made a big deal about me being finally a lady which meant I was old enough to have a 'proper date' and go to the ballet."

The taste in my mouth soured as the words crossed my lips, not only because of the sick way my uncle had referred to an outing with a child, but because of how excited the pronouncement had made me. There had been so many things I'd been left out of then because I was too young—parties and events that my parents had told me weren't appropriate for a child. It had been maddening being left with a sitter when I'd felt grown-up and independent. I'd wanted nothing more than to be treated like the adult that I knew I was.

Ron had fed on that desire. And I'd eagerly given him more of myself to devour.

"He bought me a pretty formal dress. Which had been one of the best moments of my life to that point because he'd taken me to a fancy private boutique, and I'd had all this personal attention from him and the attendants when I modeled each of the items." I shifted toward Edward. "It's disgusting when I say it now, I know, but for a ten-year-old girl, it had been the best day imaginable."

"Don't make apologies for how you felt. Those feelings were honest. The disgust is in how he manipulated them."

Right.

My therapist said that a lot too. It was sometimes hard to remember.

I turned forward again, lowering my eyes to my hands gripped tightly in my lap. I could almost picture them back then, newly manicured with bright pink polish, innocent in their movements.

I was getting ahead of myself. "Anyway, he took me to a salon too and had my hair curled and my nails painted princess pink. The whole shebang. Then he took me to the ballet. *Romeo and Juliet*. He'd told me he'd chosen it just for us. That Romeo and Juliet had a love that people didn't understand, the way that people would never understand how he and I loved each other."

"He was a monster," Edward muttered. "That wasn't love."

"He was a monster," I agreed. "And it wasn't love. But it sure felt like it at the time. The *Romeo and Juliet* references went over my head, of course. I didn't really understand the story, and I'd been a little bored because it was so long, but it was hard to really be irritable when I was dressed so pretty.

"He told me how pretty I looked too. Over and over. Every time I started to get restless, he smoothed his palm over my hair and whispered in my ear. 'Pretty girls sit still and don't fidget so other people can truly enjoy looking at them.'" I swallowed the bad taste back. "I think he probably watched me more than he watched that performance. And I loved it. I felt like I was glowing from all the attention."

Edward's fingers pressed lightly on my lower back. "It wasn't your fault," he said, guessing where this was going, and I suddenly realized why he usually sat away from me during these sessions. Across the room, it was easier for him to listen objectively instead of consoling me.

It was also easier for me to go on without the endearment.

Right now, though, I was grateful for it.

I swiveled my head in his direction. "Let me tell the story, would you?"

His lips pursed, but he nodded, letting his touch linger for another beat before folding his arms tightly across his chest.

"We didn't go to the city often, but when we did, there'd be a driver. Charles was the name of the guy who drove us that day. He was new, and I'm not entirely sure he was even really a driver. I never saw him before or after, but I liked him instantly. He'd made the outing feel special as much as anything else. The way he called me 'Ms. Werner' and held the door for me like I was important. He let me tell him all of my terrible knock-knock jokes on the drive too, which made him a pretty cool guy in my book. He joined us for dinner too at this fancy restaurant that was famous for their ice cream concoctions, and then I had both of them talking and laughing and fawning over me.

I had never been given so much attention in my life, and I remember thinking, 'This is what it must feel like to be grown-up, all the time.' It was the best."

"Then what happened?"

He was rushing me, and I almost turned to glare at him for it.

But all the expositional parts of the story had been shared now, and I was at the part he was pushing me to get to, so might as well just go there. "We drove back home. I slept most of the drive, and the Bentley was already pulled up in the driveway when Ron woke me to say we were back. I waited for Charles to open the door for me, like I'd been taught to do, but instead of stepping aside for me to get out, he got in. The backseat was spacious, but it was weird—all three of us sitting there in the driveway in the dark, me sandwiched between the two of them. I got nervous then. I remember worrying I did something wrong. I don't know why I immediately thought that after the rest of the day had been so fun. There was just a shift in the energy somehow.

"Ron asked me if I loved having Charles around, and when I told him I did, he said that was really good because Charles loved being around me too. He said that I should call him 'Sir,' because that's what grown-up girls called the men who loved them. He said I should call them both that, that it would be a special code between all of us. A fun way to express our love without anyone knowing.

"And then his voice got really sharp and he told me again how pretty I was. But that there were consequences for being so pretty, and it was time for me to address my responsibilities since I was such a grown-up girl." I swallowed, embarrassed at how much the memory affected me, at how believable his proclamation still felt.

"What did they force you to do?" Edward's tone had changed. It was softer, no longer pressing but reassuring. As though he suspected the words were stuck in my throat and needed a hook to pull them out. He would be that hook.

"They didn't force me," I said, feeling my cheeks heat. "Convinced me, is more accurate. Ron pointed to Charles's lap. I'd always been taught not to look at men's crotches, and I knew nothing about erections, but I did know that the bulge in his pants wasn't right. I'd felt Ron's pants get stiff a lot of the time when he held me on his lap, though, so maybe that clicked for me. I'm not sure what I thought, really, except that I shouldn't be looking at where Ron was telling me to look.

"But he told me I needed to look, because I'd done that to him. He said that pretty girls made men hurt there, and that I needed to fix it." The exact thing he said came to me suddenly. "He said it wasn't nice to leave men hurting, and that I could make him feel better. With my hand."

I could remember it distinctly. The sound of his zipper coming down, the sight of the red ugly baton of flesh Charles had hidden beneath. The way Ron showed me to spit on my palm before taking the other man in my hand. I could remember how his skin felt and how my fingers looked curled around his hot length. How my arm got tired, and how it smelled when the white ooze finally spurted over my fist.

The memory was so strong, I didn't notice Edward had leaned up beside me until his hand was turning my chin toward him. "Look at me, Celia," he said sternly.

I couldn't do it. I couldn't lift my eyes to meet his. "I know," I said, hoping it would be enough to acknowledge the point he surely wanted to drill into me. "It's not my fault."

"It's not. Now look at me." It took a beat before I managed to find his gaze. His eyes were intense and piercing, even in the dark, but they were also deep and warm. "Say it again."

"It's not my fault," I repeated.

"Whose fault is it?"

"Ron's."

"And this Charles guy. You don't have more of a name than that?"

"I don't." If there was more about the man buried in my head, I didn't want to go searching for it, though I could tell that was exactly what Edward wanted me to do.

I leaned away from him so I could get a better view of his expression. "You look like you're planning things. I don't like that look."

A beat passed before he smirked, a beat that confirmed he was definitely planning something. "Are my plans really that objectionable?"

In the past his sessions had inspired torturous oral sex and pretending to auction me off to a room full of strange men. "Uh, yeah, they kind of are. They're terrifying."

"You like that about them. About me. And my methods work." His smile widened.

That egotistical bastard.

Admittedly, I hadn't had nightmares about the auction my uncle had put me through. Edward had successfully "replaced" that trauma with his version, where he told me I was worth more than all the money in the world and that no price could be put on any part of me.

So, yeah, his methods did work. "It doesn't mean they're easy to endure."

"You can handle it." He reached for me.

But I leaned away. "What if I can't? What if you fucked me up forever?"

"Me?!"

He wasn't the one I was mad at, yet I suddenly felt angry, and he was there. "Yes, you. I was fine before you came along. I might not have been a decent person, but at least I wasn't visibly fucked up. You're the one who brought all this to the surface."

"And I'm going to be the one who helps you sort through it so it doesn't destroy you," he said, soothingly. He reached his hand out to rub his knuckles across my cheek. "I have a plan, bird. I'll take care of you. Trust me."

I wanted to trust him. I loved him, and I was smart enough to know that the two went hand in hand.

But the thing about him forcing me to look at myself meant that now I saw everything. I saw the ways I'd been taught to manipulate others. I saw what it looked like when people manipulated me. I recognized patterns of behavior in my relationships I'd never noticed before.

And what I saw scared me.

"There's something else," Edward said, reading me with his astute ability. "Something else you remember?"

"No." It sounded like a lie, even to my ears.

"Tell me."

I didn't want to voice it, because if I did, and if his response wasn't good enough, I'd have to reevaluate our marriage and what we could be to each other.

But if I didn't voice it, our relationship would suffer just the same. He required authenticity and honesty from me, and if I couldn't give him that, we had nothing.

I shifted toward him, holding the covers tightly against my chest like they could hide the vulnerability that my question posed. "How are we different?"

His forehead wrinkled as he worked out what I was asking. "You mean besides the fact that I have not and would never share you with another man, how is our relationship different than the one you had with your uncle?"

I nodded, once, feeling guilty that the question even crossed my mind. But also feeling bold because another Celia, the one who had been the victim of her doting uncle, would have accepted that a man's love meant blindly submitting.

I couldn't be her anymore. I was fragile from my recent breakthroughs, but I was strong enough to take this stand. I would not be groomed and molded into something someone else wanted, for his pleasure only. Not anymore.

And where did that leave me with Edward? A man who wanted to dictate my life. A man who wanted me to yield to his will.

His knuckles unwrapped to cradle around my jaw. "You want this," he said, holding me with his fierce gaze. "You want me to take charge of you. You want to belong to me. And the minute you stop wanting this is the minute I step away."

It was the right answer, and though I still held on to a fair amount of trepidation about what a healthy marriage would look like between us, I sank into his arms and submitted to his kiss, because he was right—I wanted it.

FOUR
THEN: EDWARD

"I can do it," Kofi said, decidedly. "It will take a while
to make it look believable, but I can definitely do
it."

"You'll do it little by little? Make it almost unnotice-
able at first. There can't be red flags going off with the
first transaction." There was no way this could be easily
detected if it was going to be convincing.

"Sure thing. I'll spread the embezzlements over time.
Then a larger one when you want him to be caught.

I nodded.

"I can't guarantee a long prison sentence," he warned.

"That's fine. I do want him in prison, but the more important thing is that he won't be able to qualify to foster
anymore."

"He won't be able to be anywhere near kids after prison time," Kofi promised. "Depending on where he's sent,
I can throw in a couple of prison beatings too if you like."

I thought about Camilla, about the burn marks she hid

under her clothes, about the scars that weren't visible that took longer to heal. "I'd like," I said. "Make it hurt."

Kofi grinned. "Can do. I could start this as soon as you send your payment. Half upfront."

I took a beat, as though considering, but I'd already made up my mind. I would have paid twice the price he'd quoted, now that I had money. It was well worth it.

"I'll transfer the funds first thing when I get back to London," I said, extending my hand out to shake on the deal we'd apparently just made.

"Fanfuckingtastic," Kofi said, leaning back in his chair. He pulled a joint out of his front pocket, lit it, and took a drag.

"I told you this was a place of business," Roman said, with a wink.

I hadn't believed him when we'd first arrived. He'd told me I'd find the sorts of people I needed on the island, but when we'd landed, and I'd discovered Exceso was a place of pleasure and debauchery, I'd been skeptical.

After several hours spent in a building known as The Base, he'd proven he was right. Yes, sex was the main transaction on the island, but there were other deals that were made as well. Not only had I made the arrangement with Kofi to take down Camilla's abuser, but I'd also met with a group of bounty hunters who'd assured me they could help track down many of the family items that had been sold off after my parents' deaths. It was bound to be an expensive project, but I was completely invested.

I sank back in my armchair and took a sip of my brandy. There was still a long road ahead of me to get all the justice I sought, but today had been one of progress.

"And you doubted me," Roman said, throwing back

the rest of his scotch. "Have I ever let you down?"

I should have known better than to doubt Roman Moore. He'd proven himself time and time again over the last two years. The man had been waiting for me after my graduation from grammar school.

"I was friends with your father," he had said. "Let's go get back his money, shall we?"

I'd been skeptical then too. I'd already tried to talk to the authorities about the money my cousins had stolen from us and been told adamantly that there was no case. The funds were gone, according to the investigation they'd conducted. Therefore there was nothing to pursue.

But Roman Moore knew differently.

"Your cousins hid the money in offshore accounts," he'd said. *"They've spent some of it, and there's not an exorbitant amount left, but it's enough to get you started."*

"How do you know?" He was a stranger telling me about family money that I'd never heard of. I had no rea-son to believe him.

But he had a compelling answer. *"I'm the one who set them up."*

Roman Moore wasn't exactly the most ethical person, it turned out. When he'd discovered the cousins who had been entrusted to raise us and watch over our money had filed bankruptcy and turned my sister and I over to foster care, Roman had weaseled his way into their good graces, offering to help them hide the money only so he'd be able to lead me to it when it came time.

That wasn't all he had to share. He also told me in de-tail how my father's company had been taken over and dis-assembled, sharing information I never would have been able to glean without someone who had been on the inside.

It was only with his help that I was able to add the most important name to my revenge list—Werner Media.

"You did leave Camilla and I in foster care for six years," I reminded him now. "I'd say that was a bit of a letdown."

"Pshaw." He rolled his eyes. "I've told you time and time again—I'm not fond of children."

That was Roman. Willing to help out the son of a former friend, but only if it didn't inconvenience him too much.

Though his version of loyalty was skewed, I'd grown to be quite dependent on him. He'd helped me get access to the money that should have always been mine, then he'd helped me destroy the cousins who'd stolen it, leaving them even more destitute than before my parents had died. Now, along with supporting my goals for vengeance, he was helping me build my own media company.

Three decades my senior, he'd become a sort of father figure, and I appreciated him more than I could ever express.

"Business is done for the night, got it?" Roman gestured to Stefania, the heavyset woman he'd chosen as "his" when we'd arrived. At the snap of his fingers, she came over and sat on his lap, flaunting her generous bosom in his face. "Now we enjoy the benefits of the island. The very voluptuous benefits."

I scoffed, realizing I should have kept my disinterest to myself only after I'd made the sound.

"Look, Ed…" Somehow I managed not to cringe at the nickname he sometimes used for me. "You can't be fed on revenge alone. You need to search for other things to feed you as well. Like women." Roman peeled down one cup of Stefania's bikini top. "Women taste much better than fury."

I wasn't fortunate enough to have found that to be true.

"I think I'll stick to my brandy," I said, watching as he trailed his tongue over her nipple, teasing her until it grew taut. Something hard and hot spiked in my chest. A sort of envy that didn't wash down easily with my drink.

Roman turned from his current feast to give me his full attention. "Whatever you're into, Ed, there are women here for that. I promise you."

I wasn't sure about that. I wasn't naive enough to believe that my tastes were singular, but I was experienced enough to know they were somewhat unique.

If there were ever a time that I was tempted to challenge that notion, however, it was now. We'd spent the day distracted with business, but I hadn't been immune to the abundance of beautiful women in our midst nor the sexual acts that had been performed with high frequency around us.

Still, fooling around wasn't my priority. There were more items on my list to be addressed.

"I'm good. Thank you." I finished off the contents of my tumbler in a single swallow.

"Can I refill your drink?" The words were said before I'd even lowered my empty glass, spoken perfectly but with a fairly thick French accent.

I looked up to scrutinize the woman who had asked. She wasn't even that—she was a girl. Fully developed in a dress that revealed as much as it hid, but very young. Her plump lips were lined in blood red, the color bringing out her brown eyes and olive skin.

"Are you even legal?" I asked before I could fully consider the question.

"Are you?" she tossed back, her hip thrown to the side, tauntingly. It begged to be touched, to be gripped with firm fingers while being fucked from behind.

Yes, she was young—too young for most of the men in the room. But I was young too. Age-appropriate, in fact.

I slanted my eyes, considering it. Considering taking Roman's advice, forgetting my schemes and losing myself in a woman instead, at least for the night.

Not this one, though. She was tempting, but as I'd hinted to my friend, I needed a woman who could handle me. Not a child, no matter how luscious her mouth.

"I'm closer than you," I said back, turning my gaze from her in obvious dismissal.

"Everyone's legal here. International waters in the middle of the Caribbean. What kind of talk is this?" Roman was intent on merriment and was determined that I join in.

I gave a halfhearted shrug. "I guess I forgot where we were. I'll have another cognac." I'd only recently discovered the brandy, and it was quickly becoming a favorite.

"Coming right away. Sir," she added with enough sarcasm to suggest I didn't deserve the title and enough challenge in her tone to dare that I try.

She was right—I didn't deserve the title. Compared to the others in the room, I was merely a boy. I had big confidence and even bigger plans, but I was still only an intern and grateful to those who would teach me how to carry them out.

Yet the unearned title ignited something in me, something low and primal that had my dick stirring with curiosity, and try as I might, I couldn't keep myself from watching her as she walked away. She still had baby-fat that many of the more mature women on the island had long lost. It made her appear curvy and lush, and the back view highlighted this as well as the front. Her short dress hugged her indecently, showing off the definition of her round behind, and I could suddenly imagine my face buried there, my teeth tearing at her juicy flesh.

No, no. She was too young for that. Too innocent for the likes of me.

But what was an innocent girl doing in a place like this?

A dark thought jarred my stare. I swung my head sharply back to the men. "Are the women here of their own volition?"

Stefania let out an uninterpretable laugh.

"Fuck, man!" Kofi scanned nervously around. "You shouldn't even be asking something like that."

Roman seemed less concerned with the implications of my question. "It's fine," he said, reassuring the other man. "You certainly don't want to be asking Maximillian about the women he's with, and anyone who comes with Abdul Bagher is most likely owned. But if you're wondering about our little waitress—she's definitely here because she wants to be."

I focused on the last part of what he'd said, which was somehow the most shocking. "How do you know that? She can't even have finished grammar school."

"That don't mean nothing," Kofi said. "She's obviously flirting with you, man. You should bang her."

"I know because she came with Claudette." Roman

nodded to a woman across the room, kneeling at the feet of an older man who was sitting at one of the conference tables. "Claudette often brings friends. This is the first time I've seen this particular girl, but they're all the same."

"Wannabe subs," Kofi spelled out.

"Wannabe, exactly." Stefania smirked in agreement.

"Well, they come because they believe they want the submissive lifestyle," Roman asserted. "Most just find that they don't once they've truly experienced it. Claudette loves it, though, so I think she keeps spreading the gospel, so to say, hoping to find other disciples."

I studied Claudette. She was fully naked, her eyes cast down. Her arms were twisted behind her, and the spread of her thighs looked like it had to be uncomfortable. Yet she sat motionless, even when the man reached down to stroke her head, like she was a pet.

Her discomfort was an admitted turn-on.

Except I didn't imagine myself a typical dominant. A sadist, perhaps, but I enjoyed psychological pain more than physical. I'd learned that about myself early on. I'd fucked quite a lot, despite my young age. I also fucked quite mean, and I couldn't bring myself to believe that any woman would truly seek that sort of treatment, not for more than the occasional novelty, anyway. I certainly hadn't encountered any that found it particularly enjoyable, which was why I'd come to practice a one-time-only rule with my partners. That way it was my choice not to get involved and I never had to endure the inevitable conversation about changing my behavior if a relationship were to continue.

Because changing wasn't ever going to happen. I was who I was, and I was definitely not nice.

Seeing dominance in action, though, I wondered if

maybe there were ways that I could adapt. Maybe I could be satisfied with rigid rules and doling out punishments. Maybe there would be room to manipulate sex into a game that fed my sadistic needs as well as the masochistic desires of another.

Shit, what was I thinking? That wasn't where my energy belonged. I had too much on my plate to worry about managing a complicated relationship as well.

"I need some air," I said, suddenly finding the environment stifling. Without waiting for anyone to acknowledge my pronouncement, I took off toward the main doors, swiping one of Roman's cigars from the side table on my way.

Outside, the air was heavy and thick, but it felt less suffocating than the impenetrable fog of sex and desire that hung inside The Base. I walked far enough up the path to be out of the sightline of the security guard outside the building, then, when I was truly alone, I bit off the tip of the cigar and lit the end.

I puffed on the end, reveling in the flavor of the Belicoso. I'd managed to successfully kick the cigarette habit, but Roman had turned me on to these in the process, and I doubted this form of smoking was a vice I'd ever be able to abandon. Besides revenging, I considered it my favorite hobby, an enjoyable way to draw out the flavor of my thoughts along with the taste of the cigar.

The sound of heels on the stones tugged my head to look behind me. I nearly groaned when I saw her, so irritated at having my solace interrupted, the girl from inside. The friend of Claudette's.

The twitch of my cock only aggravated me more.

"You're stalking me," I said, not bothering to hide my

annoyance.

"You left without your drink."

"And so I did."

She came close enough to hand me the tumbler, and I took it from her, my fingers brushing hers as I did, purposefully. I wasn't quite sure what I intended with her, but the fact that she'd followed after me had me pissed off enough to want to harass her, at least a little.

She jolted at the touch, her eyes growing darker, the dilation of her pupils noticeable even in the moonlight.

She thought she wanted this? From me? Well, we'd see about that.

"How old are you?" I demanded.

"Old enough."

"That's not what I asked."

"Twenty," she said, sticking out her chin with the obvious lie.

"Try again."

She licked her lips. "Eighteen."

I turned my back to her, dismissing her. I didn't do bullshit. I'd had enough of it in my lifetime. I only cared to deal in honesty now.

"Merde," she muttered. "Seventeen."

I gave her only the rotation of my head. "Is that the truth?"

"Oui."

There were only two years between us. I'd fucked plenty of women with a greater separation, both older and younger.

Why then did my attraction to this one strike me as so depraved?

It was because of what I wanted to do to her. The obscenity of which was so vivid in my head, I'd be able to use it as wanking material for months.

My pants stiffened as I thought about acting those images out.

"You're seventeen and you're so sure you want this? To be ordered around by a man who knows better than you what will bring you pleasure?" I was incredulous.

But, also, hopeful.

She tilted her head, assessing the subtext of my question. "I'm good at being told what to do. I like it. I'm old enough to know that."

That was fair. Hadn't I known for myself when I was still younger than she was?

I wasn't ready to trust it. "To be treated like a pet? Like a dog?"

She nodded definitively. "Completely cared for."

It wasn't an unappealing idea, caring for another creature, though I'd so far neglected doing so in any form. My flat was animal free. No matter how much she pleaded, I still insisted Camilla stay at boarding school. The only thing that truly had my care was the list of people who had wronged me. It was all I had room to commit to.

Yet, there was so much opportunity in what this girl seemed to want. I could see it. Could see the ways I could enjoy her, enjoy manipulating her life this way and that. The question was, could she really enjoy it as well?

On a whim, I tapped the growing ash off my cigar and threw it slightly down the path. "There, dog. Go. Fetch."

She was on her knees in a flash, crawling along the rough stones, marring the smooth skin of her knees.

And I was instantly hard.

When she reached the cigar, she bent and picked it up in her mouth, before turning to crawl back to me, her breasts swinging and straining against the light fabric of her dress. Once at my feet, she knelt back and thrust her neck forward in offering, extending her hands up my thighs like a dog pawing its master.

There was no way she could miss the rigidity of my cock. It was at eye level.

Yet, she kept her gaze on me, laser focused, and in that moment, an intoxicating kind of power that I'd never felt before surged through me like a lightning bolt.

I took the cigar from her mouth and brought it to mine, puffing on it to rekindle the cherry as I appraised her. "Do your knees hurt," I asked, knowing she wouldn't move from her position until I allowed her.

"Yes, sir." This time the title was given with respect, and the bolt of power surged through me once again.

Good. She was uncomfortable, and I was in control of that discomfort, and it wasn't exactly the way I liked to fuck with my women, and it didn't taste quite as succulent as fury, but it was bloody delicious all the same.

"What's your name?"

Her eyes stayed pinned to mine. "Marion Barbier."

I took one of her hands with mine and moved it from my leg to the pulsing rod above it. She was fumbling and inexperienced, but so willing to be instructed.

This could fit into my life, couldn't it? There had to be enough space for this. Roman was right—a man needed more than the hobby of cigars to escape the business of retribution. This could be a very agreeable hobby.

As I guided my crown between her ready lips, I already felt the beginnings of our attachment, an invisible leash from the core of my being to the core of hers.

"Marion," I said, shoving deep into her tight throat with a grunt. "I think we're going to get along just fine."

FIVE

NOW: CELIA

I'd known before I woke that it would be to an empty space beside me. Even while sharing a bed in Amelie, Edward often was up before I was. We were still new at so much of our relationship, but I'd already learned he slept very little and was an early riser, and now that we were back in the real world—the world that was supposed to be our real home—he had responsibilities and obligations that he hadn't on the island.

He was the CEO of a major media company, after all. I knew what that job entailed. Long hours at the office, rising early, late arrival home from work. I'd grown up with an absent father. I expected an absent husband as well.

The knowledge didn't curb the stab of loneliness that pierced through me as I lay with my eyes still closed, wondering about what my day would be. It had been easy in the Caribbean. Much of my time had been dictated by Edward, and as much as I'd fought it at first, I'd liked the rhythm of the routine he'd given to my days. Yoga and chess games and beauty appointments and books—not all of my time had been planned for me, but the moments that had were pillars that helped form the structure of my life around them.

Where were the pillars here in London?

I had no job, no friends, no family but Edward. What was I supposed to *do*?

Lying around in bed certainly wasn't an option. The staff would talk. The employees that worked here weren't warm and affable the way the staff had been on the island. They ran the house with formality and decorum and would likely look down on a mistress who spent the day lounging around.

With a weary sigh, I opened my eyes, planning to head to the room that had been mine. Whether or not Edward meant for me to move into his suite or just *sleep* there remained to be discussed, but for now, my belongings were still next door, including my clothes. Finding something to wear would probably occupy a portion of my morning. I'd had some seasonally appropriate items from before I'd left for my honeymoon, but that had been more than a year ago, and my body had become trimmer while on the island. I wasn't sure anything would still fit.

Conscious of the painting on the wall—the painting I would definitely deal with before the day was over—I climbed out of the warm bed, and immediately halted, my eyes caught by the armchair that my husband had bent me over the night before. My lower belly hummed involuntarily, but it wasn't the memory of the thorough fucking that had me frozen in place. It was the white and black colorblock jumpsuit draped over the back that had me riveted, along with the lacy white bra and panty set. The black pointy-toed pumps on the floor in front were nothing to blink at either.

A smile crept up on my lips as I walked over to pick up the single piece of paper laid out on top of the clothing. Sure it was possible that the outfit had been borrowed from Camilla—the long sleeves were certainly her style— or that a staff member had been instructed to set the items out, but I recognized the paper before I touched it. Edward had written me dozens of personal notes when he'd sent me clothing in the past, and the cards had looked just like this, embossed with his initials in the bottom corner.

Bird,

Wear what I've laid out and nothing more. Put your hair up and light makeup, if you wish.

I expect you to get reacquainted with the staff. You are the lady of the house now and they'll look to you for guidance. Meet with the chef early to plan dinner. I'll want it ready to be served when I get home at seven-thirty. Then speak to Jeremy about having your belongings moved to our suite. There is plenty of room in my closet for the both of us, but if you like, you may keep off-season items in the closet next door.

After dinner, we'll meet in the den to discuss our marriage going forward.

Taking care of the household should occupy a good deal of your day. You also have a manicure appointment at one. The manicurist will come here. She has been instructed to paint your nails pink. If you have time left over, I invite you to try out the pool downstairs. Or there is space in the exercise room for a yoga session if you prefer. You are also welcome to take any book from my library. I've had it stocked with several titles I think you will enjoy since the last time you were living here.

Last, but not least—call your mother.

Edward

The smile vanished and reappeared as I read through the letter. Frankly, I didn't know how to feel about it. I was irritated at being ordered around, especially in such detail. So irritated that I was ready to crumple up his note and ignore every word of it.

But I was grateful for it as well.

Thrilled about it, even.

How could I not be? I had longed for structure, and he'd known, without me ever saying a word. Not only had he known, but he'd gone out of his way to give me what I needed. He'd taken time out of his busy life to attend to me. It made me feel special in a way that I hadn't felt since Ron had doted on me all those years ago.

The comparison sent a chill down my spine.

I shook it off remembering what Edward had pointed out the night before—I chose this.

I chose him.

I hadn't chosen Ron. And the reason Ron had so easily wormed his way into my graces was because I had so badly wanted to be treated the way he'd treated me. Like I was meant to be cared for. Like I deserved it. Like I was worthy of a person's time and attention.

I still relished that sort of care. And if Edward wanted to care for me like that, without the nefarious expectations that had been attached to Ron's care, then why not let him?

Because you don't entirely trust it, I reminded myself.

Or rather, I didn't entirely trust myself. I didn't trust that I knew what was best for myself. Was this it? Or was this falling into an unhealthy pattern because I was too lazy or too weak to work out a better one?

I didn't know the answer.

And I wasn't going to figure it out standing here naked. With that decided, I scooped up the clothing and carried them with me to the bathroom, the smile back on my lips. I could accept what was given. For today, anyway. I could allow myself to find comfort in Edward's care. I could follow the orders he'd given this one time, if for no other reason than it was easier than finding any other way to approach the day.

Falling into the role of lady of the house was easier than I'd anticipated. I'd watched my mother perform the duties for all of my life, never with any particular interest in following in her footsteps, but once the job was laid out in front of me and handed to me as my own, I found it unexpectedly satisfying.

The clothing Edward had selected helped, if I was being honest. The jumpsuit was a power outfit. After having worn sundresses for so long, the pants were noticeably different than what had become my norm. I couldn't help but feel like a different person wearing it, a person who was meant to be taken seriously. A person who commanded authority.

Then underneath, the underwear, though virginal in its white color, was see-through and sexy and fit the situation so perfectly, it could only be considered what it was—a personal message from Edward. He wanted me to remember that he knew who I was, remember that I was new at the tasks I'd been given. Innocent and yet not. Without stating it out loud to everyone else, he wanted to remind me of my place. *You are in charge of this household, but I am in charge of you.*

It was strange to realize he'd given me power in my submission. I wasn't sure how to process that fact, but I couldn't deny that I liked the way it made me feel. Maybe not quite as fierce as a dragon, but definitely stronger than a wounded little bird.

As instructed, I met with the chef as soon as I'd dressed. Solene was nowhere near as approachable as Joette had been, but she was organized and polite. She made our meeting simple, giving me options rather than requiring me to come up with a menu out of thin air.

When we'd finished planning the meals, she'd sent me to Jeremy to confirm which dinnerware to set out (I chose the fancy china) and go over the calendar. There wasn't much on the schedule for the day, but there were several parties and social obligations that Edward expected me to attend with him in the near future as well as a bunch of items that were left for me to decide. I said yes to Handel's *Messiah* and no to *The Nutcracker* and held off on deciding about the revival of *My Fair Lady* in the West End until the reviews came out next week.

After that, I instructed him on moving my belongings from my suite to Edward's, and by the time we got to discussing the removal of Blanche Martin's country garden painting I was sure that I was making the decision from a place of strength. I didn't want to look at reminders of the past on a daily basis. That didn't mean I was overly vulnerable. It meant I was capable of knowing what was best for me, at least as far as what environment I spent my time in.

Besides, the whimsical feel of the landscape portrait didn't fit the rest of the masculine decor, and, even if it was no longer my job, I was still a designer at heart.

With the house taken care of, it was time to call my mother. Surprisingly, this was the hardest of the tasks that I'd been assigned. It wasn't as though I hadn't communicated with her at all in the last year—I had written her letters that Edward had passed on, though not all of them had been quite intact. He'd shown me all the emails she'd sent in reply so I was caught up on her life as well.

But I hadn't actually *talked* to her. Hadn't heard her voice. Hadn't had to wonder if she could detect the secrets that I kept in my tone.

Not that she'd ever figured out my secrets in the past.

I was making too much of a big deal about it. Straightening my spine, I sat at Edward's desk in the library, picked up the receiver from the cradle and dialed my home number.

"Edward," my mother said in lieu of hello. "I was wondering if I'd hear from you soon. It's been a few weeks."

My chest pinched at the sound of her voice in my ear. It had been so long. I hadn't realized how much I'd missed it.

I would have probably said something to that effect, but her greeting had me stunned speechless. Quickly, I tried to assign meaning to what she'd said and came up empty-handed.

"Edward?" she prompted.

"Mom?" It was the best I could manage.

"Celia? Darling, is this you? I saw the number and naturally expected your husband. Why isn't this a surprise. Does this mean you're finally back from the middle of nowhere?"

I pulled myself together. "Yes, it's me. I arrived back in

London yesterday."

"Thank God. Sending letters via email is sweet and quaint and all that, but it's such a pain to have to sit down in front of the computer and go through all the nonsense of composing my thoughts."

That was my mother. She had a smartphone but I was fairly certain the only thing she used it for was playing solitaire and calling her friends immediately when fresh gossip crossed her path. She was glad I was back to civilization because my absence inconvenienced her, not because she'd missed hearing my voice. Not because she'd wondered how I sounded.

Really, had I expected anything different?

But I was still caught on what she'd said first. "Why did you think I was Edward?" Sure his name probably came up on the caller ID, but wouldn't she assume that was me? And she'd said something about it having been a few weeks. Had he...?

No. He couldn't have.

Could he?

"Because it's usually Edward calling from this number," she said like the question was ridiculous.

Damn. He really had.

"It's been a little while since his last call," she went on. "I figured he'd be ringing soon."

"He's called more than once?" I was having a hard time processing any of what she was saying.

"Well, yes. Every time after he visited you, I think. At least it seemed that was the pattern. He always said he'd just been to see you, so I presumed—"

"Mom, wait," I said, cutting her off. "He called you

after his visits to the island?"

"Like I said, I never asked specifically. Why is this so surprising to you? Did he not tell you he was calling?"

No, he most certainly did not tell me he'd called my mother. Another incredible idea shot to mind. "Did he talk to Dad, too?"

"Oh, no, no. Definitely not. After the idea had been proposed at your wedding, your father has been hounding Edward to do some sort of corporate deal and, well, you know your husband. He wanted to wait to get past the newlywed stage before getting tangled with business. Smart man you married, honey, though your father wouldn't understand. So I haven't mentioned the phone calls to him at all. You shouldn't either."

"No, of course not." I was blown away. Not only because Edward had called my mother—on more than one occasion—but because of how he'd handled my father. Even if he hadn't decided whether to keep me alive or not, he could have certainly weaseled his way into Werner Media through my parents if he'd wanted to. Which, I would have assumed he'd want to.

I really *didn't* know my husband.

So why had he called my mother, if not for some sort of gain? "What did he say when he called you, Mom?"

"Just told me how you were doing, what you were working on. Since you couldn't call yourself. It was really sort of sweet, reaching out on your behalf. Told me how you were getting really into yoga and about all that work you did to the house there. Edward said you fell in love with the island. You must have to have stayed away from your new husband for so long. I told him I didn't raise my daughter to be so negligent of her husband's needs, but he insisted he was happy if you were happy. Not only is he a smart man, he's a good man. Amazing you were able to find him after you managed to let go of Hudson. Those men don't usually come twice in a lifetime. You better hold on to that one. You'll be a fool if you don't."

With that, my mother burst into the latest society gossip, unable to continue a conversation not focused on things that interested her.

I sat back in Edward's chair and half listened to her, my mind so caught up in her revelation I was even able to ignore her dig about Hudson. My husband *was* a smart man. He'd endeared my mother to him, which was one of the smartest moves he could make.

But what if he hadn't made the move because he was smart? What if he'd actually called because he'd cared about me and thereby cared about her? What if he'd cared about me for longer than I'd realized? For longer than he'd like to admit?

There was no question that Edward Fasbender was a smart man.

But a good man? I was still trying to figure that one out.

I managed a swim in the afternoon. The pool on the lower level was a good size and was heated, but couldn't compare to swimming outdoors in the Caribbean. Still, it was a familiar activity and put a sense of routine to my day.

Afterward, when I'd donned the jumpsuit again and

fashioned my hair the way Edward had commanded, I came downstairs to await his homecoming and ran into my first household management snag.

"They're for special occasions only, Jeremy," Camilla was stating sternly. "They always have been. You're well aware of this. So why would you suddenly pull them out for a Monday in December? It's not even a saint day."

Curious, I walked into the dining room and realized right away what they were discussing—the china set I'd selected to be used for the evening's meal.

I hadn't been spotted yet, so I considered for a handful of seconds which way to approach this. I could assert my authority, which I was sure that Edward would insist that I do.

Or I could try to make friends with the only woman currently in my life who wasn't paid to be there.

"It was my faux pas," I said, drawing both eyes to me. "I selected them because they were the most beautiful set, and I thought it was a shame to hide their beauty away. I didn't realize they were special. I sincerely apologize."

Jeremy had the good sense to stay quiet.

Camilla opened her mouth twice to say something then shut it again. It was only then that it dawned on me what an odd position this must be for her. Before I'd married Edward, I'd lived in the house for a couple of months, never considering who it was who oversaw the house. Never considering that it was Camilla.

Now that I'd returned and was Edward's wife, I certainly hadn't thought about what that might mean for his sister's role in the household. It couldn't have been easy, watching someone she'd thought of as her enemy usurp her throne.

It didn't mean I should cower to her, but I could make the situation more bearable. "Jeremy, please do as Ms. Dougherty suggests. We'll save this set for Christmas dinner."

Before he could begin to gather the dishes, Camilla stopped him. "No, that's not necessary. It didn't occur to me that you'd requested them. I apologize for interfering." Swiftly, she stepped past me and out into the hall.

I nodded to Jeremy to leave the place settings as is and then followed after my sister-in-law.

"Camilla," I said, catching her before she charged up the stairs. She paused, her shoulders rising with a visible inhale before she turned to face me. "I really am sorry. I didn't mean to step on your toes."

"I was the one stepping on toes." While she wasn't quite warm, she was direct. "They were my parents' wedding china, is all, but they are Edward's now and therefore yours to use as you see fit. And perhaps you're right—their beauty is wasted all locked up."

"Maybe we could carve out some time later this week and figure out how we can manage things together?"

She studied me with incredulous eyes. "You're joking, right?"

"Not at all. You've lived here longer than I have. You know how things work best. It doesn't make sense for me to change things that aren't broken."

She blinked in disbelief. "I'm sorry. It's just so unexpected. I had you pegged as...well. I suppose that's what Edward's been trying to tell me. That you aren't at all the woman we believed you were. It might take some time before I truly understand what that means."

"If it helps, I'm not quite the woman I believed I was

either. And it's definitely going to take some time before I figure out who that is."

Her features softened, her jaw relaxing. She moved down the steps until we were on the same level. "I know I've been cold and, at times, cruel. I hope you understand that it's out of a sense of protection. For a long time, Edward was all I had in the world. In all fairness, he's been equally as protective of me."

"I'm sure he has," I said, barely above a whisper, too afraid to break the honest moment between us.

"He believes in you, though. So I shall too." She swallowed, her throat swelling with the action. "I want you to know, I contacted an estate agent this morning. I'll be moving out as soon as I find something suitable for me and Freddie."

My gasp was audible. "No! Edward would never want that! I'm sure of it. Please, please don't leave on my account."

"I've already told him," she insisted. "You are correct that he wasn't happy about it, but let me assure you that it's not because I feel threatened by you or because I have lingering animosity but because I want this relationship of yours to be successful. For his sake. And marriages never work when there is a third party present. Trust me, I know."

My brow quirked, intrigued by her insinuation. Was she speaking about her own marriage? I didn't know enough about her relationship with her husband before he'd left her a widow, only that he'd died in a house fire several months before Freddie was born.

Before I could even consider prying, however, two members of the staff came around the corner of the stairs, the country garden painting carried between them.

"Excuse me, madam," one of them said. "The canvas was too large to fit in the lift."

Not that the canvas was all that large. European elevators tended to be quite compact.

"No problem," she said, shuffling out of their way. "May I ask why it's being removed? It was only put up just last week."

She looked at me, the subtext clear—*Eddie put that painting up, does he know you're taking it down?*

"I know," I said, trying to figure out how I was going to step around this response. "Edward was very sweet to hang it, thinking that it was special to me, but it's not, and it doesn't go with the room. I told him I'd have it removed today."

Rather, he gave me permission to have it removed. I didn't want to be that specific, possibly because I was em-barrassed to admit that I believed I needed his consent, though Camilla already seemed to understand what kind of man her brother was.

"It's such a lovely piece, though," she said, peering at it with awe.

I was half afraid she'd suggest we display it elsewhere, and after just inviting her to help make household decisions, I knew I needed to cut the possibility off at the head. "Honestly? It brings up bad memories. When I see the swing, I'm back in a place I don't want to visit again, if that makes sense."

I didn't know what Edward had told her about me or if she knew that I knew anything that had happened to her, but, as one abused girl to another, I hoped it was enough of a response to resonate without further explanation.

Again she studied me, her eyes as focused as her brother's often were and, without ever having seen any of her art, I suddenly knew she was probably a very good photographer. "I think I understand," she said after several heavy seconds had passed. "Objects as well as locations can be haunted."

"Yes," I agreed.

"Every time I see a fire poker, I'm reminded of my dead husband. Best to move it on out or at least out of sight. If you've noticed, all the pokers in the house are well hidden."

Like the thread of conversation that had been cut off by the arrival of the painting, this thread was cut by the arrival of my husband coming home from work. He greeted me with a kiss that curled my toes and made me blush since his sister was present.

Then Jeremy announced that dinner was served and the moment was long past reviving the topic.

But all through dinner—which was unexpectedly convivial, Edward at the head of the table, me at one side, his sister on the other with Freddie in a booster seat next to her—I wondered about the odd statement and the hint she'd given to an unhappy marriage. Frank Dougherty had died in a fire, and perhaps it wasn't a stretch then to believe that fire pokers upset his widow because of the association. But why didn't the fireplace itself bother her? Or candles, several of which were lit up on the dining table as we ate?

My husband was still a mystery to me, so it made sense that his sister was as well. It was only surprising that her mystery was starting to seem equally intriguing.

Six

Edward

Celia reached into the side table drawer and pulled out a coaster, setting it down pointedly before taking the cognac I offered. "There. In case I need to put my glass down momentarily," she said, referencing the last time we'd been in this room negotiating, when she'd set her tumbler on unprotected seventeenth century rosewood.

My blood hummed as it circulated lower. She learned fast and she learned well, which pleased me more than she could possibly know. "I would have thought you would be as keen to preserve old furniture as I am, considering your interests."

"Yeah, but last time the furniture wasn't mine." A smirk grazed her lips briefly, disappearing as she brought the glass up for a sip. When she lowered it again, her expression was serious. "Last night, you said you wouldn't share me."

I almost laughed, surprised by the lead she'd taken. I used the two steps it took to get to the armchair to gather myself, unbuttoning my jacket on the way. When I sat, facing her, I was composed.

"Is that where you want to start?" I asked, crossing one leg over the other then perching my own tumbler-clutching hand on my thigh.

The setting was exactly the same as the first time we'd negotiated the terms to our marriage—after dinner in my den, Celia on the sofa and I seated across from her. Both of us drinking one of my favorite three-star cognacs.

The only difference from that other night and this was that I no longer hated her as much as I wanted her, and the things that I intended to ask for would be genuine instead of passive-aggressive attempts to scare her away from our union.

Her brows turned inward as she considered how to respond. The topic made her noticeably nervous—her jaw was tight, her breaths shallow. She was beautiful like that, her agitation sending a charge to the air, causing her to fidget and buzz. I had the power to quell that anxiety, and I would.

But I'd let her linger in it first.

"It's just a complete one-eighty from the first time we were in this room," she said finally, the strength of her tone belying the lack of confidence underneath. "When you told me you'd help me find other lovers if necessary."

She took another sip then set the glass down on the coaster, the tremble in her hand barely apparent before she stroked both down her pant legs, likely to wipe clammy palms.

Breathtaking.

But she'd suffered enough on this point, especially when there were still things to discuss that would make her sweat more. "I was trying to find ways to keep you at a distance. You can see how well that turned out."

"Then you don't want other women." This time her pitch was higher and thin, almost more of a whispered prayer than a statement of confirmation.

"There will not be other women." There hadn't been since I'd slipped the ring on her finger, and the few I'd been with in the months before had all taken her face as I'd pushed them and prodded them and fucked them, only to be left wanting the real thing.

It had been the first sign that I'd fallen for her, when no other woman could come close to leaving me satisfied. When her name repeatedly fell from my mouth, ragged and angry, as I jerked myself raw.

Her shoulders loosened somewhat at my response, but her body remained mostly tight. "Didn't quite answer the question, but okay. Good." She reached again for her glass, as though she needed a point of focus that wasn't me. As though she thought she could disguise her turmoil.

As if I'd let her get away with hiding.

I could make her say it, could make her beg for the words she needed. I would have her begging for something or other before the evening was finished.

But we were only at the beginning of a conversation that mattered. So I wouldn't press. Not yet. "I do not want other women, bird. Is that better?"

Her relief was palpable. "Much."

A surge of unfounded jealousy raged through me, prompting the next commandment I issued, even more important than the first. "And there will be no other men. Which is non-negotiable."

"I suppose I can live with that." She was teasing, and it was obvious, but I couldn't help wanting to bend her over my knee and leave palm prints on her ass.

I managed to restrain myself. Barely. "How very noble of you."

Her eyes met mine and her grin widened, and as sure as I was that she rarely could fathom my thoughts, I was sure this time that she could. We held this gaze for several thick seconds, each one more taut and wanting than the last, until I moved my attention to the drink in my hand.

She took the cue to move the discussion along with it. "Then everything you said last time was just to turn me off?"

"No. Some of it I very much meant."

She knew I'd tell her eventually—that was entirely what this evening was about, after all—but she still hadn't shed her constant need to try to stay a step ahead of me, and she tried again now. "The traditionalist, man-of-the-house stuff. You don't want me to have a job."

I gave her a beat to second-guess before confirming her doubt. "Not true. I think work would be good for you. Part-time, anyway." She'd become a different person on Amelie when she'd begun her redesign projects. More alive and vibrant, and there was no way in hell I was letting her lose that. "In fact, I insist on it."

"*Insist.*" She said the word like it tasted bad. "Interest-ing."

She was a funny bird, quick-witted and wise but still completely clueless when it came to understanding her-self. She was disgusted by the idea of yielding to me, re-coiling any time it came up, and yet she submitted to me so naturally in other ways. Here she was wearing the clothes

I'd dictated she wear, drinking the beverage I'd chosen for her, discussing the topics I'd planned, subconsciously following my cues to bring up the subjects herself. And she did it all happily, with a flush in her cheeks and a glow to her eyes that shone only when she surrendered.

And yet, she still believed it wasn't what she wanted.

That ended tonight. There would be no more insinuation on my part. My command would be acknowledged. "Yes, insist. As the man of the house, I have that authority."

Her arms folded over herself defensively. "So the whole subservient wife role is still something you're clinging to. I thought you didn't want me to be like Marion."

"You aren't like Marion."

"As you keep reminding me."

Again, she was ignorant. Acting as if she'd be better favored if she *was* like Marion.

How could I make her realize that wasn't what I wanted with her at all?

Marion had been precisely what I needed at the time. She'd been uncomplicated, never distracting or competing with the goals that had taken precedence above her. It had been easy to command her, and I'd liked that. She'd handed me the reins without any struggle, and that had made me powerful. Powerful enough to dominate the other areas of my life with similar ease.

But she'd been so willing. Too trusting. I couldn't count the number of times I'd wished she put up more of a struggle. Wished that submission was hard for her.

It was hard for Celia. And that was a very big turn-on, in more ways than just sexually.

I threw back the last of my brandy, rid myself of the glass, then steepled my hands over my knee. "I do not want you to be my submissive in all things, Celia. I don't want you to wear a collar, and I don't expect you to be kneeling naked at the door when I arrive home from work. I want—"

"Were those things you expected of Marion?"

I couldn't decide if I was more irritated by her interruption or by her continued mention of a woman who was solidly no longer a part of my life. My overall annoyance was plain in my answer. "My arrangement with Marion has no bearing on the arrangement I'd like to have with you. May I go on?"

"Yes, Edward."

Her smart mouth and saucy tone was going to get her in trouble soon. My cock roused in anticipation.

We aren't there yet, I silently instructed the swelling organ in my pants. There was too much still to be made clear before bringing sex into the equation.

I lowered my crossed leg to the floor and switched it for the other, subtly adjusting myself in the process. When I spoke again, my tone was softer but resolute. "I want you to let me take care of you. I want you to let me look after your well-being. I want authority over your free time, over your income. Over your body."

Heat simmered in her eyes, which she quickly blinked away. "Why?"

"Because I think you'll like it."

She let that settle. I could imagine the argument she was having over it in her head. She knew she'd like it, but could she let herself? What would that mean about her as a woman if she did? As a person? All logical questions yet irrelevant if she simply gave away the responsibility of answering. If she gave the decision-making to me.

After a dozen or more seconds had passed, she sank back into the couch. "That's it? You want to tell me what to do because you think I'll like having you pick out my clothes and tell me what I'm allowed to spend."

It wasn't quite a question, but I affirmed all the same. "And because I think it will be hard for you. And I know I will like that."

The heat returned to her eyes, and this time she let herself hold it. She was considering it. Really considering what it could be like, it was evident in her expression.

And thank God, because now we could have a real conversation about it.

"That sets me up to be very vulnerable," she said, finally understanding what I wanted from her.

"That isn't new."

"I thought we were past that."

"Did you think we were past it because you wanted to be? Because you didn't like it?"

She didn't hesitate. "I didn't say that."

That's right, she didn't say that. Because she couldn't say that and mean it. She'd very much enjoyed the ways I'd broken her down, even though the process had been difficult. She couldn't deny that.

"It's the dynamic between us that has brought us the closest," I pointed out, in case she hadn't connected that.

She swallowed. The next breath she took in shuddered through her. "It's made me weak."

"Not at all. It's made you strong."

"It's made me unstable."

"It's made you irresistible."

A smile flickered on her lips, her cheeks turning the lightest shade of red.

A beat passed.

"It makes me have to trust you."

She delivered this last statement as though she were giving confession, so I knew the answer before I asked it. "That's still a problem for you?"

She responded with silence, her eyes unable to meet mine.

One of the reasons I was so attracted to her was because she was one of the few people who could still surprise me. Though this particular subject was not one I enjoyed being surprised by.

I wanted her to trust me. I *needed* her to trust me. All of my rules about honesty and transparency had been set specifically to build up trust between us. It would be impossible for me to care for her the way she needed without it. Our relationship required it.

After the panic subsided, I could see the situation for what it was more clearly. She *did* trust me. We never would have got this far if she didn't. She just didn't realize that she did.

"You say you love me," I challenged.

"I do." The response must have come more sharply than she meant it to because she repeated it with effusiveness. "I do, Edward."

"Doesn't love require trust?"

She opened her mouth to answer, then shut it again.

Then repeated the opening and shutting, and I wondered how much of this argument had been given to her before from the shitstain of a human that was her uncle.

"I'm not him," I reminded her. "We aren't that."

She nodded, affirming that she had indeed been thinking about him. "I think I'm beginning to know that," she said. Then, after a pause, "Maybe it's myself I don't trust."

"And that's why you want me to take care of you."

Her nose wrinkled. "I *want* you to take care of me?"

"Mm."

I could feel her temptation to argue, but she knew as well as I did how much she wanted to be cared for. The thought of it alone made her eyes shine and her body press forward with eagerness. "What would...?" She licked her lips, gathering courage to explore the desire. "What would that look like exactly?"

And now we were at the heart of the discussion, the part I'd been waiting for, where I'd lay it all out for her to accept and embrace. I took a breath, ready to explain on the exhale, but she cut me off.

"You know, it's hard to consider any of this talk different from last time when it still feels like we're negotiating a business deal."

I'd purposefully set up the seating arrangement, keeping us apart. It was the same positioning I used in our sessions, the positioning I'd always used when I played with a woman's mind. It was more of a challenge to manipulate without touch, but I'd learned from experience that it brought the most authentic results.

Then, with Celia, when physical manipulation might have given me a hand up, I'd sat away from her because

I'd needed the barrier. Because I hadn't been able to trust myself if she were within reach.

That concern had obviously been invalid. I hadn't needed to be touching her to lose myself to her. Distance hadn't had any benefit in the least.

Tonight, though, I had assumed the boundaries would help her keep a clear head. The decisions she needed to make about our relationship required it.

But I'd forgotten that she also needed reassurance. That, more than anything, she needed to feel loved.

"Come here," I said, the command abrasive with my self-displeasure.

She didn't need to be told twice. Within the space of a few seconds, she'd risen from her spot on the couch and crossed to me, where I pulled her into my lap. The chair was wide enough for her to sink down on the cushion next to me, her legs thrown over one of mine. It constantly amazed me how well we fit together like this, how her body seemed made to be melded to mine. How still my thoughts went when she was in my arms, like she was a meditative mantra that brought my focus laser sharp.

I stroked her cheek with the tips of my fingertips, glad that she'd kept her makeup light so I could feel the true softness of her skin. "There are things that you need," I said, my voice as much a caress as my hand. "And I will give them to you, but I will be the one who decides what those things are."

"What things do I need?" She looked back at me with an adoration I didn't feel worthy of, but gladly accepted all the same.

"There are your basic needs, for starters. You need to feel pampered yet important. You need to be admired for your intellect more than your beauty. You need structure to your day, but you prefer not to organize it. You need to have boundaries but you need to feel free."

"Yes," she whispered.

"I want to be in charge of your schedule so that you don't have to worry for yourself if you're taking on more than you should. I want to ensure you have the tools you need to stay healthy—physically and mentally—because you won't consider those things important on your own. You need me to do that for you. You need me to make sure you are getting appropriate exercise and brain stimulation. You need me to tell you how to prioritize your interests, because you have too many and they overwhelm you on your own.

I brought my thumb to trace the edge of her bottom lip. "You need me to care for your appearance—to dictate how to wear your hair and what to dress and how to groom your pussy so that you aren't tempted to use your body as a weapon as you have in the past. You won't be able to play games with something that doesn't belong to you. You need me to remind you that you belong to me. You need me to be sure there are consequences when you don't."

She gasp-laughed, apparently shocked that I'd called her out so bluntly but unable to refute it as truth.

I took the opportunity to slide my thumb past her lips and teeth into the recesses of her hot mouth. "Suck," I demanded, feeling my pants tighten when she did, imagining it was my cock between her lips instead of my thumb. "You need me to turn you on," I said, my voice low. "You need me to get into your head and understand the way you need to be fucked."

She hummed her agreement, sending a sharp jolt to the rigid bulge that was quickly growing beneath her.

And then, because sex was so connected with psychology where I was concerned, "You need me to force you to face your demons. You need me to put you through sessions and ensure you see your psychiatrist and that you write in your diary regularly. You need me to be sure you don't bury your hurt inside, turning you into a shell of a person. You need me to keep you present, and, trust me, everything that I demand from you—every pain I press from your body, every rule I require you to adhere to—it will all be with that goal in mind. I will keep you a full person. I won't let you be anything less."

I drew my thumb out, resting it on her chin, my fingers curling around her jaw. She swallowed, and I could feel it against my knuckles. "I would expect you to respect me, because that's what a master deserves. My demands here haven't changed. You will support me publicly in all things, and if you do decide to argue with me privately, you accept that there may be punishment. This is a tough one for you, I know, but I believe you've had enough experience with me now to understand you can manage. Am I wrong?"

She blinked, doe-eyed and nervous, her lids heavy with lust. "Are you wrong about the last thing or all of it? Because you aren't wrong about the last thing. I know I can manage it."

I chuckled. "And the rest?"

Her shoulders rose with her breath. "If that's everything...I think I could manage it all too."

"I know you can." My subtext was clear, prompting a more sincere agreement.

"I want to. I want to try."

I leaned in to brush my lips against hers. "Good girl."

I kissed her lightly, wrapping my hand around the back of her neck to hold her how I wanted her. I only pulled back briefly to issue my last stipulation for her care. "There is one more thing you need, one more thing I am prepared to give you as soon as you agree."

"What's that?" Her eyes were dilated and focused on my mouth, begging for more than the chaste kiss I'd delivered. It was tempting to give in to her desire.

But I was in charge of her well-being, and the last thing she needed to accept from me was likely the most important.

So I resisted and gave her the one word that would be the key to her healing. "Revenge."

SEVEN

CELIA

"R evenge," I repeated, cautiously, pulling back to look at Edward. "On who?"

Asking the question was a stall tactic, perhaps. I knew the answer already. He'd spent years going after my father, going to absurd lengths in pursuit of justice. He'd abandoned that quest because I'd pointed him in another direction, not because he'd suddenly decided he didn't need retribution.

Sensing that my true question was why, he answered that instead. "You can't understand the benefits of closure until you've experienced it. It may feel like life goes on. You may feel yourself get better and stronger as you accept the things that have happened to you in the past. But you can't ever truly move on until you find resolution."

A moment ago I'd felt warm in his lap, my body keening for more of him physically. Now I suddenly felt cold and guarded.

I rubbed my hands over my sleeves, trying to heat the skin underneath. "How can you know that? Since you haven't found your own resolution yet yourself. What if you finally close that door and it doesn't change anything?"

He settled back in his chair, his head tilted as he examined me. "I haven't felt resolution where Werner Media is, no. But I have experienced the rewards in other areas of my life. Trust me when I say they were worth the effort."

The hair stood up along the back of my neck.

Edward had gone to dark places trying to make my father pay for something, it turned out, he hadn't done. He'd not only married me but had also wanted to kill me, all so he could get his hands on my father's company shares. It was still hard for me to believe I'd fallen in love with a man who could be so sinister, but, in the end, he hadn't murdered me, and maybe that made it easier to overlook his thwarted plans.

I smirked thinking about that. My husband, the man I was in love with, had only *almost* killed me. That was still a serious crime, and I'd forgiven him. It was quite possible I was a lunatic.

Maybe the craziest part was that I'd never considered there may have been other plans of his that hadn't been thwarted. Other revenge schemes just as ruthless and sinister that he'd gone through with. My skin tingled with curiosity. My gut churned with revulsion.

Did I want to know?

"Let's not think about it," he said, reading my expression correctly. He ran the back of a single finger across my jawline, tenderly. Soothing my unease. "Focus instead on your own lack of closure. How much easier would it be to press forward if you knew that Ron had atoned for the things he's done?"

"You mean how much easier would it be for you to

know that he'd paid."

He dropped his hand at my acidic tone. "Yes, he owes me a debt, and I plan to collect, but in this moment, I'm thinking only about you."

His own words were stern but genuine. He really did mean to help. The least I could do was discuss it with him. "I can't try to prosecute him. My parents would never back me, and without them on my side, I'd have no chance of winning. He's a rich, powerful man. I'm sure you know as well as I do that rich men never pay for their crimes." Besides, I was sure that revealing all the horrible secrets of my past to the world would do more harm to my psyche than good.

"There are other ways besides the legal system to seek out justice."

I breathed through the shiver that threatened to crawl down my spine. Of course he wasn't just thinking of the legal system. Had any of the ways he'd gone after Werner involved authorities? Even if there had been something illegal to nail them on, I had a feeling Edward would have avoided that route.

And if the methods he wanted to pursue weren't legal, I didn't want any part of it. I should just say no and move on.

But Ron had hurt me deeply and permanently, and as I'd begun to feel again, I'd only skimmed the surface of the well of rage that existed inside me.

Did I want him to pay? Fuck yes.

Only, at what cost?

"What exactly *are* you suggesting?" I asked, unable to tamp down my interest.

His lips puckered with a shrug, as if he didn't have a long list of ideas already waiting to execute. Before I could call him on it, though, he said, "I thought I should leave that up to you."

Oh.

I hadn't been expecting that.

He took advantage of my surprise to press on. "What would you like to do with him, my little bird? You can't tell me you haven't thought about it."

I *hadn't* thought about it for a long time. I'd pushed down all the memories and the feelings associated with them until they'd formed a cement chrysalis, holding them in and away from my conscious mind.

Edward had broken through that shell, though, and now thoughts of vengeance did occupy more of my time than I liked to admit. But mostly they were rough and unformed ideas. The fantasies that had taken better shape were impossible to carry out or, at least, impossible for *me* to carry out. While I'd certainly love to parade Ron naked in a room full of rapists and sell him to the highest bidder, for example, I wouldn't begin to know how to go about making the scenario take place.

Edward might, however.

That thought scared me as much as it excited me.

"I've thought about hurting him," I admitted, vigilant that anything and everything I said to my husband was collected and stored for later use. "And yes, I want him to pay. But, short of killing him—which I refuse to do—I wouldn't even know where to begin that sort of takedown effort. I'm not that diabolical, I suppose."

God, the topic nauseated me. That I'd had to specify that I was against murder because I didn't know my husband's limits, doubly so.

His caress was back, the hand he had wrapped around my waist stroking along my ribs. "Sure you are," he said, and it took a moment to get past my indignation before realizing he had every reason to believe that was true.

That wasn't who I was anymore, though.

Was I?

"You know how to manipulate people," he continued. "You've practiced these games for years. Same thing now. Only, this time, your victim is deserving."

"You mean use my powers for good?" I asked, scornfully.

He chuckled. "Something like that."

I jumped out of his lap, the action so sudden he didn't have time to try to tighten his hold before I was up. I had to put some space between us—not between me and him, but between me and the lure of being someone I didn't want to be anymore.

I crossed to grab the brandy I'd left on the table by the couch and took a long sip, my back turned to the man behind me. It was tempting. It really was. To be our kind of superheroes. To play the game that had invigorated me for so long. To finally give Ron a taste of what he deserved. Me with the devil at my side—what could possibly get in our way?

"I don't know, Edward," I said, finally, setting the tumbler down and turning back toward him. "I did those things before, thinking it would help, and it left me cold and unfeeling and terrible. I don't want to go back to that. I don't want to live that way anymore."

He nodded once, patiently. "It wouldn't be that way,

you understand. Not with the right motive."

I threw my hands up. "And *vengeance* is the right motive? 'A man who desires revenge should dig two graves.' 'Neglect kills injuries, revenge increases them.' There's a reason why there are hundreds of quips about the futility of revenge, Edward. It's not a healthy aspiration, and I'm trying to thrive here."

"'It's every man's business to see justice done.'"

I couldn't help but smile at his comeback. I hadn't forgotten he was a worthy rival, still, sometimes he surprised me with the reminder.

"How about this?" I leaned back to perch on the arm of the sofa. "I don't care what you want to do to Ron. Have at it. He's yours. I'm not going to stop you from doing whatever you need to do to get closure on what he did to your family. But it's for you, not for me. I don't want this. I don't need this. I want to focus on healing in other ways, if you don't mind."

There. It was a solid compromise, as far as I was concerned.

He leaned forward, his elbows propped on his thighs, his hands clasped together. "What if I do mind?"

I blinked. "What?"

He stood up and stalked over until he was standing right above me, making me feel caged in without actually surrounding me. "You heard me."

Hearing him hadn't been the problem. "I don't understand why it matters if I'm involved."

"Because I believe you do need this, that you will never be able to fully heal without it, and being a passive observer is not going to deliver the same results as being an active participant. And I care about your well-being very much. In fact, it's one of my main responsibilities as your husband, as we've discussed tonight."

I bit the inside of my upper lip. Something bloomed deep in my belly, something wild and beautiful and satisfying. It was unfamiliar to feel so looked after, so protected. As frightening as it was to imagine Edward with blood on his hands, I couldn't deny how good it felt to believe he'd likely kill for me if he believed it necessary.

It was the most loved I'd ever felt in my life.

I reached up and placed my hand on his lapel, over the place where his heart drummed in his chest, and even though I couldn't feel it through the layers of material in the way, I knew the beat was steady and driven. "I'm grateful. I truly am. But we're going to have to agree to disagree. It's still a no from me."

The smile that inched onto his lips was ominous. "I could insist, you know. I have that right."

My own heart tripped, and while I felt a rush of endorphins at his exertion of alpha attitude, there was also a notable flood of panic. "I don't like that. Maybe I'm not ready for this whole submission thing after all."

He let a heavy span of silence pass before his features softened. "Settle down, bird," he said, tucking a stray hair behind my ear. "You don't need to get your feathers ruffled over this. I can drop it—for now—if you agree to at least think more about it."

My answer wouldn't change, but I could give him that. "Okay. I'll think about it. No promises."

"Thank you."

But, even with the conversation tabled, he'd made me anxious. "We should still probably talk more in detail about the submitting stuff."

"You're nervous about what I may decide is best for you."

"Uh, to put it bluntly—yes." I dropped my hand to my lap, but he stayed where he was, hovering over me.

"Let me ask you this—how did it feel today, to wear the clothes I'd picked for you? Performing the tasks I'd instructed you to perform?"

"I liked it," I said, honestly. "But—"

"More specific, please," he demanded, cutting me off.

I gave a beat to thinking about exactly what I'd liked about it, then gave up, sticking to the original addendum that he'd interrupted. "But they weren't important things. If you chose something I didn't want to wear, it won't really have bothered me to wear it anyway. The tasks were fine, too, but what happens when you want me to do something I am strongly against?" Like participating in his schemes for justice.

His arms came around me now, settling on my hips. "Then we discuss it, privately, just as we have tonight. I'm not entirely impossible, as I believe I've proven here."

That wasn't any different from any other healthy marriage. I should be able to do that.

Still, I wanted to be absolutely clear that I was not giving up my autonomy entirely. "I just wouldn't want to mislead you into thinking I'm easy to boss around. I'm not. I'm probably going to argue a lot."

"Oh, I'm well aware." The low rumble of his voice was panty-drenching. "We'll get through our disputes as we have so far. Though, I will remind you, there may be repercussions for disagreeing."

Again, my heart skipped. "Is there going to be a repercussion for disagreeing with you tonight?"

He bent in to whisper at my ear. "Oh, yes, Celia. There will be." His breath on my skin made my own breath quicken. "And you're going to like it. In fact, I think it will prove just exactly how much you enjoy submitting to me, if you'll let it."

Oh, fuck.

That feeling of fear/excitement flooded over me in a single wave. It was a dual emotion I was becoming quite familiar with. Edward always summoned the two ingredients in equal measure, had since the first time I'd met him, and it wasn't worth even trying to lie and say that I didn't find the hybrid as addictive as any drug.

"Tell me what to do, Edward," I said, surrendering to him.

With my capitulation, he took the role of dominant, immediately releasing his hold on me and stepping back. "Turn around."

I straightened then turned. The sound of my pantsuit's zipper accompanied the parting of the material along my backside.

"Take this off," he commanded. "Fold it nicely and set it on the sofa. Leave your shoes and underthings on. Come stand before me when you're done."

"Yes, Edward." I started working myself out of my outfit while he took his empty glass to the wetbar. This wasn't bad. His punishments in the past had always ended in orgasms. It was like a game, really. Like Simon Says with sexy stuff involved. What wasn't there to enjoy about that?

"One more thing," he said as he poured the cognac.

"Tonight, you will call me 'sir.'"

I froze. He knew I didn't like that term. He knew why now, too. "But you said before—"

"I know what I said. Need I remind you tonight is a punishment? You will do as I ask."

My jaw tensed. I'd forgotten somehow that he also had to dole out a certain amount of discomfort in these games.

I liked that too, in some ways. But that was harder to admit, even to myself.

"Celia?" he prompted when I hadn't responded.

It took a second before I realized what he was waiting for. "Yes, *sir,*" I said, unable to control the acerbic tone that came when the single syllable crossed my lips.

He didn't seem to mind the abrasive response. "Good. Carry on."

By the time I'd finished stripping and folding, he'd taken his drink and crossed the room to stand where the hardwood flooring turned into rough tile stone in front of the fireplace.

I walked over to him, feeling both sexy and oddly bashful wearing only heels and lingerie. This was the moment I'd thought of as I'd put the white lace items on—the moment when he'd be seeing me in them. Was this what he'd thought of as well when he'd set them out?

His eyes were dark as he studied me over the rim of his glass. He took a swallow and set it on the mantle. "Turn around for me."

I complied, spinning slowly so he could see me from every angle. He let out an appraising hiss that shot lust through my blood, made my skin flush, and almost made me forgive him for requiring me to address him as "sir."

Almost.

"You're beautiful, Celia," he said when I was facing him again. "All covered up, too—you looked quite regal in that suit—but especially like this, in nothing but the bra and pants I chose for you."

Okay, maybe he was forgiven entirely.

He kept his hands to himself, crossed over his chest, much farther from my body then I would have liked them. Whatever punishment he planned for me, I had a feeling it would also hold rewards, and I was more than ready to discover both.

My heart sped up with excitement when he suddenly dropped his hands to his sides, but instead of touching me, all he did was remove his jacket. "Hang this over the arm of the sofa," he instructed. "Give me a show when you do."

I did as he asked, practically prancing back to where I'd been, bending with exaggeration to drape the jacket on the couch and giving my hips a little sway as I straightened again. When I strutted back to him, the bashfulness was gone. All I felt was pure seduction.

"You feel beautiful right now, too, don't you?" he asked, never missing a beat. "Is it because of what I'm saying to you or because you're wearing items I picked for you to wear?"

"Both, sir."

"You felt beautiful all day, didn't you? Wearing items that I'd laid out."

"Especially the underwear," I confessed. "Sir," I remembered to add a beat late.

Disapproval knitted his features at my mistake, but it passed quickly. "You enjoyed wearing my underwear because you knew that only I'd see you like this, your nipples peaked and rosy for me."

My nipples went even harder at his acknowledgment. "Yes, sir. And also because I knew you chose them for me because you would like seeing me in them."

"That's right. I very much do," he rasped. "They're naughty, but you don't have to take responsibility for that, do you? Because I was the one who picked them."

I swallowed, realizing I did like that only as he pointed it out. In the past, when I wore risque underwear, it had usually been because I meant to use them manipulatively later. All the women who wore pretty panties for themselves—I'd never been that girl. I'd been taught early on that everything I did and wore had an effect on the men around me, and that it was my job to be conscientious of that.

I was so sick of dressing for other people. For thinking of all of my actions as moves in a chess game. It could be argued that this was more of the same because I'd dressed for Edward, but it didn't feel that way. He had chosen the items that would make the day easiest for me.

The naughty items underneath were like the compensation he got for taking on that responsibility. I didn't mind giving that to him in the least.

And when, with hungry eyes, he said, "Kneel down in front of me," I didn't mind that either. Even when my knees hit the hard stone tiles and I understood the reason he'd moved over here.

Beautiful bastard.

Reaching around, he pulled my hair from the knot at my nape. "You're gorgeous like this. On your knees. I should have had you in this position sooner."

"You did once, sir," I said, reminding him of our first session, when he'd very nearly had me go down on him then went down on me instead. "You decided it wasn't demeaning enough, if I remember correctly."

"I decided it wasn't a fitting punishment at the time, and I was right. You were much too eager. Tonight, I think it will do just fine."

I was eager now too. My mouth watered at the opportunity to finally suck him off.

With my hair down, he threaded his fingers through the strands. "Now, look in front of you. What do you see?"

I'd already been staring at the bulge currently tenting his trousers. "You're hard," I said sounding more thrilled than I'd meant to let on.

He pulled firmly at the hair in his hand. "What did you say?"

"Fuck. Sorry, I forgot. You're hard, *sir*."

"You did that. You made that happen." He let his words sink in, but I recognized them immediately.

And I understood what he meant by this now. What this was.

This was his redo of my first hand job with the chauffeur.

I'd known this was coming, somewhere inside of me I'd known. Yet somehow I was still surprised. I also discovered it was possible to feel both dread and excitement at the same time because that's what I was feeling. Like I had both butterflies and stones in my stomach.

I didn't want to relive this.

I also very much wanted to have the memory replaced with Edward.

"You're going to take care of it, the way I want you to, aren't you?" he asked, and I knew what *this* was too—my chance to back out.

Not that there was ever really backing out where Edward was concerned. If I refused to face this now, he'd make me face it again sometime else, in some other way.

There was probably a lesson in that for me about our current disagreement, but I wasn't able to focus on that at the moment. I had a hard cock to take care of.

"Yes, sir," I said, with the trepidation of the child I once was. "Tell me how, please, sir."

Anxiety threatened to seize me, but the accompanying bolt of lust was stronger.

"Undo my buckle and my pants."

I did as he said, my pride swelling with his head as it poked out over the band of his boxer briefs.

"Take out my cock."

When it was out, standing stiff and boastful at eye level, I couldn't help myself. I wanted it in my mouth, and putting it in my mouth differentiated this moment from the one that had preceded it all those years ago. At ten, I hadn't even conceived of blowjobs, let alone wanted to give one.

Immediately, Edward flicked the side of my cheek with two fingers. I released him with a gasp at the sting.

"I didn't tell you to suck on it. I'm the teacher here." Just like Ron had been then. And Charles. Teaching me things a child should never need to know.

The memory sat heavy at the sidelines, refusing to disappear from the present. "What do you want me to do, sir?" I echoed the girl I'd been.

Like Charles and Ron had been, Edward seemed

pleased with my willingness. It was confusing to recognize. As confusing now as it had been in the past. I'd hated what they wanted me to do then, but I'd still glowed in their praise.

Just as I glowed in Edward's praise now. "Thank you for asking. I want you to spit on your pretty hand." He waited for me to do it before going on with his instruction. "Now grab it, just like this."

The sight of him holding his cock made me wet. The scent of my arousal drifted up, and I swore Edward caught it, his mouth twitching as though trying to hide a grin.

I brought my hand up to wrap around his length, stacking it on top of his. The bright pink of my nails against his flesh looked so eerily similar to that day so long ago, I had to close my eyes momentarily to recenter myself.

I'm here in the present. With Edward. No one else.

When I opened my eyes again, I recognized the adult size of my hand and how differently it fit around the cock before me than my child hands had fit around Charles. Another gush of arousal pooled between my thighs. "Like this, sir?"

"Two hands," he said, letting go to make room for mine. "Yes. Just like that."

It made me dizzy, the way my head flipped from past to present to past to present again. One minute I was still barely clinging on to my innocence, the next I was desperate to be further debased. There was something cathartic about the merging of the memory with the moment. It made me have to choose between who I was then and who I was now. There wasn't room for me to be both, and there was no way I was going back to that other me.

Edward wouldn't let me.

"Good girl. Such a pretty, good girl." He anchored me like that, his encouraging tone bringing me back to him every time I started to disappear into another time. "You keep on rubbing it just like that, keep treating it real nice. Because you're the one who did this to me, didn't you?"

You did this to him, Ron's voice pierced through the fog of lust.

I shook him away, looking up at Edward's eyes to remind me where I was. "Yes, sir."

"And it's not nice to leave me hurting, is it?"

"No, sir."

As though sensing the ghosts of other men crowding the space with us, Edward acknowledged them. "I'm the only man you need to worry about, Celia. Anyone else who tells you that you make them hard, that's not your problem. Do you understand?"

My hands stuttered at the change in script. "Yes, sir," I said, absorbing his words.

"It's not your job to take care of the men who you make hurt. Say it."

I took a breath in then let it out. "It's not my job to take care of the men who I make hurt."

His dick twitched, and my gaze went back to the job in front of me. I put more vigor in the churn of my hands, sensing he was getting close. My pussy throbbed with the anticipation as though it was the genitalia being rubbed. I wanted him to release, not just because I wanted to get past this scene but because I was also fully into it.

Edward seemed not to be as concerned with coming right away. He grabbed my chin and tilted it up, roughly, to look at him. "And even though I'm hard for you, Celia, even though looking at your gorgeous body and watching you twist and writhe through our discussions tonight made me need to fuck your pretty hands, there's only one reason you are responsible for taking care of me. Can you tell me what that is?"

"Because you're my husband, sir." I swiped my palm over his crown, earning me a growl.

"Try again."

I paused, unsure what he wanted.

Then I knew. "Because I choose this."

"Say it again."

"Because I choose this, sir."

"That's right, Celia. You aren't a victim here. You choose to let me dress you like my doll. You choose to let me degrade you on your knees like this, with the stone scraping against your skin." My hands picked up vigor with the raw grate of his words. "You're going to have bruises, later, aren't you?"

"Yes, sir."

"You choose to let me do that to you, don't you?"

"Yes, sir." *Yes, yes.* And I loved it.

"You choose to let me do what's best for you, too," he said, his hips shoving forward. "Because you trust that I know how to care for you. That I'll build you up to who you want to be. That I will protect and honor and love you in every way that I know how."

My throat felt suddenly tight, like his cock was lodged inside it instead of thrusting in my hand. I couldn't speak. So I just nodded, instead.

"All right, my turn." He stepped back taking his cock

into his fist. My arms dropped to my sides, but I could barely feel their exhaustion, I was so mesmerized by the rapid tug of his hand back and forth over his steel length. "Pull out your tits for me, pretty bird. I'm going to decorate them with my cum."

I grabbed the bra cups and pulled them down, thrusting my chest forward, a willing canvas.

"Yes, yes, fuck." His words disappeared into a groan as hot liquid spurted from his tip, shooting ribbons of sticky white across the peaks of my breasts.

Yes, yes, fuck was right.

It was dirty and filthy and debasing, and I was soaring. How was it possible to be both claimed and liberated all at once? To be treasured *and* defiled? To be taken *and* given back?

I didn't realize there were tears falling down my cheeks until Edward's thumb swiped them away. After tucking his still semi-hard cock into his briefs, he pulled me to my feet and into his arms, not seeming to care that his semen was now pressed up against his chest.

He kissed me thoroughly, his tongue slinking predatorily deep into my mouth, promising there would be more generous rounds of lovemaking before the night was through.

When he pulled away, it was abrupt, and I had to cling onto his shoulders for balance, even though his arms were still wrapped tightly around my waist.

"You didn't answer me earlier—how do you feel when you submit to me? How does it feel wearing my clothes and doing what I ask and jerking off my cock and wearing my cum? How does that make you feel?"

I could sense the importance of the answer he was

looking for, and I paused to make sure I found it too, repeating his questions again in my head. I'd felt powerful. I'd felt important. I'd felt cared for. I'd felt desirable. I'd felt strong. I'd felt worthy. I'd felt horny. I'd felt new. I'd felt...

Then, there it was. The truth clicking into place. By submitting to him, I gave up all the baggage that I'd carried all these years. That peace I'd searched for in The Game with Hudson had been false, but this peace was real. With Edward, I no longer had to pretend the chains around me weren't there. They'd actually gone, because he'd picked them up for me, he'd taken them as his own like reins.

How did I feel without that burden?

My voice was sure with my answer. "Free."

EIGHT

EDWARD

"Well?"

At the sound of her voice, I turned to find Camilla leaning on the doorframe behind me. I swept my eyes once more around the guest room then gave an approving nod. "It's nice."

"That's all?"

It wasn't fair, and I knew it. I'd been a giant ass, actually. She'd started her search for a new flat as soon as Christmas passed, and while she'd given me many opportunities to be part of the process, I'd declined every step of the way, too busy nursing the wounds of her impending departure.

Of course I'd had my advisors look at the property before she made her official bid, just to make sure she wasn't making a mistake. It had been without her knowledge, which I felt no guilt about. She insisted she was ready to be on her own, and she probably was, but she was still my sister. Still the girl I'd had a hand in raising. Parental instincts didn't just turn off.

Now the deed was in her name, and she was already moved in, and the London rags were already gossiping about a family dispute between us. I couldn't delay a visit any longer without creating a great deal of animosity.

Besides, we had other things that needed to be discussed.

"I think you chose well," I said as I crossed to stand at the door beside her. From here I could see across the hall into the playroom where Anwar was tending to my nephew who was currently occupied with the Lego set I'd brought for him just this morning. It was a smaller space than the one he'd had, but brighter, giant latticed windows bringing in an abundance of natural light. "Freddie seems to like it. The courtyard is nice. Warwick Gardens is a respectable neighborhood. Not too far from the park or the office."

Not too far from my residence, either, though it might as well have been across the ocean as far as I was concerned.

"But…?"

I blew out a sigh, letting go of my stubbornness along with it. "But nothing, Camilla. I would rather have you at home is all. I hadn't realized how quiet the house is without the two of you around."

Her body sank with relief, and for the first time since I'd arrived ten minutes ago, she smiled. "It's not me, you miss. It's him. He's the noisy one."

"Mm." True, but I wasn't about to admit it.

"You could have a child of your own."

I laughed, stepping out into the hallway to head toward the stairs. "I have children of my own."

Camilla's footsteps echoed on the floor behind me. "I

meant with Celia."

A strange weight of yearning pressed against my chest, imagining the family we might have had, if I'd met her as a younger man. If my path had taken a different route. "I'm passed that time in my life."

"You're only forty-three. A lot of men aren't even starting their families until now."

"But I did start young, and now I'm done. I'm not about to start the whole process over again." I stepped off the landing onto the stairs that led to the main floor. They weren't carpeted, but there was a runner, and they were less steep than the ones on Cornwall Terrace. That was a benefit of the move, at least. Safer for the boy.

"Genny and Hagan were easy for you," Camilla said, continuing the conversation I'd thought I'd closed. "You got to be the typical man who left the childrearing to your wife. What are you complaining about?"

Ouch.

We were generally honest with each other, no matter the expense. Unfortunately, that sometimes resulted in blatant truths that I would have preferred been left unsaid.

This one had been said now, though. I turned at the bottom of the stairs to face her. "Perhaps that was exactly the problem—I wasn't the best of fathers the first time around." Not with Genny or Hagan, and certainly not with Camilla.

She reached her hand out to rest on my arm, an unusually affectionate gesture from my sister. "You were a fine father, Eddie. A bit preoccupied, perhaps. You had an empire to build. Your children understand. They weren't neglected. But if you truly think you weren't as good as you could have been, then all the more reason to give it another go."

I frowned at her logic. "All the more reason *not* to give it another go."

It was her turn to frown. For a moment I thought she meant to push the issue, but then her expression shifted. She dropped her arm and crossed it with the other over her chest, putting up the familiar wall. "Why are you here?"

I narrowed my eyes. "What do you mean? I came to see the place, now that you're settled."

"That's your excuse, but it's not the reason you came. If that were all, you would have brought your wife along. I called to see if you had left yet. She didn't even know you were coming here. She said you'd gone out shopping for Valentine's Day."

"That was what I told her," I admitted.

"See, then? Secrets and subterfuge. Are you going to at least tell *me* what you're up to?"

I glanced around the house again, wishing this hadn't been the way we'd reached the subject I'd been aiming for eventually. "I really did want to see your new place."

"I know. I'm glad you did." The wall didn't come down all the way, but it was less fortified. Which was good, for what we had to discuss.

"Shall we sit?" I asked, gesturing toward her living room.

"I'll tell Perry to put on the kettle."

Thirty minutes later, we'd drained the pot of tea between us, and I'd finished telling her the major points of my plan to go after Ron Werner. This scheme was much different from any I'd had for his brother. With Warren, I'd wanted to steal his corporation, let him experience what I thought he'd done to my father.

Ron, I wanted to ruin. Entirely. His reputation, his fortune. His life.

Since he'd sold his shares of Werner years ago, the different tactic was somewhat out of practicality. Mostly, though, it was because of Celia. Whether she wanted to be part of his ruin or not, she remained a large part of my motivation.

For the most part, Camilla had sat quietly, letting me tell her my ideas without interruption. Now it was my turn to ask, "Well?"

She set her teacup on the ottoman before her and folded her hands in her lap. "That's quite a plot, Edward. A long game. And not like you to use the justice system."

"It has to be a long game, I think. There's no way around that." I was familiar with long games. In fact, I considered myself quite good at them.

"Likely true," she said.

"And I'm only using the justice system because I think, in this case, it's the best way to completely ruin him."

"Agreed." I could see the gears shifting behind her eyes. "If you can get him to go to Exceso, why don't you just arrest him at that point?"

That was one of the early stages of my plan. Get him to the island where all sorts of debauchery played out. It would help earn his trust. Make him think that those of us who were members there were men of the same ilk, or at least were willing to look the other way.

"That would be easiest," I agreed. "But international waters. There's no jurisdiction there. It will have to be here or the US."

"It will be more devastating for him in the US, I'd think."

"I agree." I studied her, looking for any clues as to what she thought about the idea on the whole.

There were none to be found, though. She'd learned to guard her emotions as much as I had.

She clicked her tongue, a habit she'd had for as long as I could remember, and then pursed her lips together. "You usually don't tell me this much about your plans. You rarely care about my opinion. Why are you involving me this time?"

Either I was losing my touch or she could read beyond my mask better than I realized. "I think you should be the one to make the first connection," I said, realizing that trying to hold it back any longer was futile.

Her eyes widened. "You're kidding me."

"You're well-bred and polished. There's nothing that screams undercover agent with your pedigree. He'll be in town in a couple of weeks, staying at the Savoy. You could casually meet him at the bar—I'm told he'll likely spend his evenings there. You could leave Freddie with us, check in a couple of nights. It's the perfect opportunity."

She barked out a laugh. "Casually meet him and say what? 'Would you like to come to an island with me in the Caribbean where you can rape little girls without getting caught?' That's not something strangers just bring up over a drink."

"No, of course not. But I do think directness is key. You would approach him purposefully. Tell him you know who he is and what his interests are. Assure him not to worry, that you're discreet, and then inform him you have a client who is looking for a particular sort of hookup and then ask him if he might have any leads."

"And you expect him to just hand over that sort of information to someone he's never met before?"

"No. He won't give you anything." Only a fool would, and there was no way Ron Werner was a fool. He'd managed to remain untouched by gossip or speculation for at least twenty years. "He'll pretend he has no idea what you're talking about. You'll thank him for his time, give him your card, and tell him to contact you if anything changes. As you're leaving, as almost a throwaway, you'll mention that you'll reach out to him if you find another lead yourself. Then we let a few months pass before you call him and invite him to Exceso."

"You want me to be Ghislane Maxwell to his Jeffrey Epstein," she said, correctly identifying the type of role I envisioned for her.

"Only, if this works—and it will work—you'll be saving girls. Not destroying them."

She crossed her legs and clasped her hands around the top knee. "Why me? Why don't you make that connection yourself?"

"I'm married to one of his victims. He might see right through it."

"How am I any different? I'm her sister-in-law."

"Exactly. Close enough to the family to have learned about her uncle's proclivities, but not necessarily close enough to feel obligated to her in any way." I let that her absorb that before continuing. "It wouldn't be ridiculous to let him believe you aren't fond of your brother's choice in wife. You've already got the rags talking about a possible family dispute. Ride with it."

It only took a beat before her mouth opened in a silent

gasp. "*You* planted the gossip."

I shrugged then thought better of it. She deserved honesty. "It was the perfect opportunity to set up the scene," I admitted.

"Again, why me?" She leaned forward now, as if to press me physically as well as with words. "It could be just as believable with one of your hired men. Or women, if you prefer. A real agent of the law, preferably. Someone who knows what they're doing."

"You know why."

"Because you think I need this."

"Yes. As much, if not more, than I do." Also, I didn't trust anyone who wasn't blood or on my payroll. Fewer people than that, actually.

Her tongue clicked again, the wheels turning. With a sigh, she sat back and draped her arm over the back of the sofa. "What else are you working on?"

The question took me aback. "What do you mean?"

"I heard you on the phone when you got here. I didn't mean to eavesdrop, but this is my house. You were talking about someone in prison, from what I gathered. Definitely not talking about Ron Werner."

I'd already been on her doorstep when the call had come in, and while I would normally have sent it to voicemail, I'd been waiting for weeks for Kofi to call with the information I'd requested.

There was no reason to try to hide this from my sister either. "There were more men involved in Celia's assaults than just her uncle."

Her skin paled as she digested my meaning. "Jesus," she said with a shudder.

I understood the feeling. My stomach was constantly on the brink of heaving, thoughts of what she'd endured never far from the forefront of my mind. "I'm working on tracking down the ones I'm aware of. One of them, a Charles Endcott, worked briefly as a personal chauffeur for Ron. He's currently serving time for child abuse, rape, and molestation as well as several counts of possession of child pornography."

"Look at that. Justice somehow managing to get done without the intervention of Edward Fasbender." Her teasing held a bite, but it was lighthearted all the same.

I, on the other hand, was deadly serious. "He's one man, Camilla. I can't find any others either currently serving time or with records who are connected to this monster. They're smart and they cover their tracks. There are dozens of men with close ties to Ron, but none I can be certain are part of his pedophilia ring."

She sobered at that. "And Celia isn't able to help point you in the right direction?"

"She doesn't know I'm looking for them," I said, my throat tightening at the admission.

Of everything I'd said, this seemed to alarm her most of all. "She doesn't know about any of this?"

"She's given her blessing on going after Ron in whichever way I choose, but she declined to take any part in it. She doesn't know I've expanded my quest for vengeance beyond that."

"Ah. I understand now why you kept this visit from her."

The accusation in her tone was warranted, but unnecessary. I already felt guilty about it. Not about my actions, but about the lack of honesty. I'd promised truth to her, and I intended to keep that promise. I'd share this with her, eventually. Perhaps even before I actually did anything to those arseholes who had hurt her.

For now, at least, all I was doing was gathering information.

But my sister could see my long game here as well. And, apparently, she didn't approve. "Are you sure this is necessary? Why is this so important to you?"

"These are bad men, Camilla. I'd think you, of all people, would support this."

"And I do, for the most part. But not at the expense of your relationship. If this isn't important to Celia…"

She didn't have to finish her sentence. I could guess the ending. If this wasn't important to my wife, why put so much energy behind it? Why make it such a priority? Camilla knew firsthand what my pursuit of revenge had done to my first marriage.

But Celia wasn't Marion, and this quest was *for* her, not in spite of her. "It is. It will be," I insisted. "She just hasn't realized it yet."

Camilla considered me, her skepticism evident. Her support was slipping away, and I didn't know how I'd go about getting it again if I lost her now.

"I'll do it, Edward," she said, to my surprise. "Because these are bad men, and there are other young girls who need to be protected, and I would very much like to be a part of that. Not because I need any closure where our father is concerned, but for them. Is that clear?"

"Whatever you say. And thank you." I didn't appreciate the high-handed attitude, but I had her on my side. That was all that was important.

Except, I couldn't let it lie there. "Have you truly never felt any relief from the other times I've sought justice on your behalf?"

Her expression pinched with frustration. "That's an unfair way to frame the question. Of course I've slept better knowing Mitch can't foster children anymore. And I'm much happier having our family money back in our pockets instead of in our cousins'. And how you helped with Frank...I'm always going to be grateful for that, and you know it. But am I a better person knowing that the people who have wronged me have also suffered? I can't say that I am."

"Well, I can say that I am."

"Good for you then. I hope that's really true." She held my stare for brief tense seconds. Then she released me, standing up, an obvious dismissal before she'd even spoken. "You better get out of here if you're going to get shopping done as well."

"I already picked up her present earlier this week." But I stood as well.

"Oh? What did you get her?"

Her curiosity seemed genuine, and I hated leaving on such a fraught note. I pulled my phone from my trouser pocket and flipped through my gallery until I found the picture that had been taken for insurance purposes then handed it over.

Her eyes went immediately wide as she studied the ruby drop pendant. It was a top quality Burmese stone surrounded by twenty-five diamonds and just the thought of what my wife would look like wearing it was worth the small fortune I'd spent.

"It's absolutely stunning," Camilla said, her expression telling me she finally understood why I had to do what I was doing where Celia was concerned. That she finally understood what the woman meant to me.

I expected her to say something to that effect, but instead, she asked, "Do you know how rubies are formed?"

Surely I'd known at some point. At the moment, I couldn't recall the exact chemical process, so I shook my head.

"They're from the mineral corundum, which is usually colorless, a combination of oxygen and aluminium atoms. But when the substance is exposed to intense heat and pressure, some of the aluminium atoms may be replaced by other substances and then the stone takes on other colors. Chromium is what makes the deep red of a ruby. They're rare, though, because the presence of iron or silica prevents the formation, and the earth is abundant with those minerals.

"You've had bad things happen to you, Eddie. You've survived the heat and the pressure, and, trust me, I know what that does to a person. It can destroy us, if we let it. But it can turn us into gemstones too. Beautiful and solid and undestroyable.

"But you can't reach the splendor of the ruby if you let the iron in."

It was a pretty analogy, one she was too proud of for me to feel good about tearing apart. Thankfully, Freddie ran in then, distracting us from more serious conversation.

Still, I knew the truth. I'd accepted it a long time ago. I would never be the ruby in her story. There was no fear of ruining my color. There was no possibility of letting in too much iron.

I'd survived, though, solid and undestroyable all the

same.

Because I *was* the iron.

NINE

CELIA

I gasped, my knees buckling as Edward added a third finger to the ones already thrusting in and out of me. I'd already had two orgasms and my nerves were highly sensitized. My skin felt like fire and, if he weren't holding me up at the waist, I was sure I wouldn't be able to stand.

"One more," he commanded, his thumb skimming over my clit.

"I can't." Despite my protests, my insides were clenching, preparing to go wherever he led.

"You can. You'll do it for me."

I clutched onto his stationary arm, needing more support. "I didn't realize this was supposed to be a punishment."

His chuckle was low, making his beard tickle against my cheek. "It's not. But I enjoy that you can't tell the difference."

He was savage, and my love and hatred for that aspect of him mingled until I was in miserable bliss.

"Open your eyes," he urged. "Look at us."

I did as he said, my breath hitching at the sight.

We were standing in our en-suite in front of the full-length mirror. I'd been watching, until the last wave of pleasure had forced my eyes to clamp shut, but seeing our image anew sent me spiraling higher. He'd brought me directly in here after spending the evening at the opera. Though he'd stripped me to nothing but my heels and my jewelry as soon as we'd walked in the bedroom, he was still fully clothed in his tux, his undone bow tie the only thing to suggest he was in for the night.

It was an overwhelmingly erotic sight—him fully dressed, his head resting on my shoulder as his hand snaked between my naked thighs, the brilliant ruby pendant at my neck catching the light in our reflection.

We were sinfully beautiful together.

Was this how the serpent had looked tempting Eve? Was this how he'd enticed her to eat his fruit? In moments like this, he owned me completely, and it was hard to fathom anything I wouldn't do for my ruthless devil.

My focus shifted to his face. His expression said he knew the power he had over me. It should have been frightening, but, instead, it only fueled my arousal. Only strengthened my desire to please him, and when his brutal smile appeared and he ordered me to "Come," I happily went over the edge, spiraling into the abyss of my surrender.

He continued to hold me, coaxing the last of my release from my body until I was completely spent. Then he shifted me in his arms just enough that he could take my mouth with a vicious kiss. "Happy Valentine's Day, my little bird."

"I love you," I said.

He responded with another kiss, sweeter though just as deep as the last. After he relinquished my lips, he brought his pussy-soaked fingers up to feed me instead. I sucked each one thoroughly, cleaning off every drop of my wetness.

"Now to clean *you*," he said, his eyes dilated with want. After making sure I was able to stand by myself, he moved to the oversized clawfoot tub behind us and turned on the faucet.

"We're taking a bath?" This night just got better and better.

"*You're* taking a bath," he corrected.

I frowned in disappointment. It was a large enough tub, and I was eager to make him feel as good as he'd just made me feel—repeatedly. He was yielding a pretty stiff erection, from what I'd felt poking at me as he'd made me come. Surely, he couldn't ignore that.

But he was my master, and he decided my life for me now. It was hard, but I was learning to trust his decisions more than question them. I tried not to argue unless it really mattered, and this wasn't one of those times.

I let out a breath as I gave the reins over to him, and focused on the sight of his tight backside, bent over to adjust the water temperature. A wave of euphoria spiked through me. He was so good-looking. And I was so lucky.

This was my life, this was my man, and I was in awe.

I had demons. I always would. Their hold on me diminished every day, though, thanks to therapy, diary-writing, and constant vigilance to mindfulness. And more than all that, thanks to Edward. In the two months since we'd been back in London, he'd pushed me and challenged me, ensuring I remained in the land of the feeling instead of sinking into the void of nothingness. He'd continued his sessions with me on occasion, which were tough and cathartic and helpful beyond expression.

But perhaps what had helped even more had been giving him my submission.

God, it was hard sometimes. Not to fight and buck against his control. It was my default to protest.

But it also felt natural to give in.

And when I did, when I truly gave myself over to him, I felt more alive and whole and powerful than I ever had.

Satisfied that the water was hot enough, he returned to me. His eyes scanned hungrily up my body, halting at the necklace he'd given me earlier in the evening. He raised his hand to trace the pear-shaped diamonds that enclosed around the ruby. "I don't think I can stand taking this off of you. You're too stunning wearing nothing but my jewels."

Submission be damned, I had to put my foot down. "I'm not wearing anything this valuable in the tub." I hadn't seen the price tag, but I knew luxury when I saw it.

He smirked, as though he were considering overruling. But then he moved behind me. His fingers paused at the clasp, the tips skating across my skin and making me shiver. "I feel like I've collared you."

Goosebumps skated down my arms. I liked being claimed by him, in every way that he wanted to claim me. Be it with his words or his cum or his jewels, they all expressed the same thing—that I was his.

I swerved my head toward him. "I don't need the necklace to feel the same."

Content with my response, he undid the clasp. Then he

handed it to me to hold while he took off his jacket, which he traded me for the pendent. "Hang this up, please, while I put these away."

He turned toward my vanity where I'd left the box earlier in the night when he'd presented me with the gift. I went the other direction, to the closet. I hung up his jacket and took off my shoes before returning.

When I got back, he was ready for me, sitting beside the tub on my vanity stool. He'd removed his cufflinks and rolled up the sleeves of his tuxedo shirt.

Seeing him like that, from the back, hit me solidly with its familiarity. My stomach quivered with both unease and want. The two feelings often traveled in tandem, Edward frequently inspiring both in equal doses.

He looked up, noticing I'd paused. "Come get in."

"You're really not joining me?" I asked, hoping I was wrong about where this was going.

"Just you, bird."

The unease turned into dread, my belly dropping. "I know what you're doing."

"Then get over here and let me do it." He poured a dollop of body wash onto the oversized bath sponge, the vanilla fragrance taking me back to another time, to another man sitting by a bathtub waiting for me to get in.

I'd told Edward about the baths when I'd first told him about Ron, but only recently had he dug into that in one of our sessions, getting me to give him the details. They'd occurred nightly when I visited him, and began innocently enough. I'd always enjoyed the way it felt to be rubbed down and washed, loved the feel of hands scrubbing through my hair from a very young age. As I'd gotten older, he'd added sensual bath beads that made my skin feel like silk. The bathing became more drawn out then, his touch lingering when he washed the tiny buds of flesh on my chest, his fingers more exploratory between my legs.

The first time he'd brought me to orgasm, I'd thought he must be magic. There'd been colors across my vision and the sweetest burst of elation. With that one little trick, I'd been spellbound.

All these years later, I'd told Edward, the thing I found most shameful about those baths were that they'd been my favorite part of my relationship with my uncle.

And now Edward was recreating the experience. Like he always did.

"Sometimes he joined me in the tub," I said, reluctant to spend the rest of our evening on an activity that would require a great deal of mental energy on my part.

Edward raised a skeptical brow. "Did he?"

"No."

"Come on," he said with a gesturing jerk of his head. "It will just be a bath. It will be nice, if you let it be."

If he were going to wash me, as it seemed he most certainly intended to do, then it didn't matter what else happened—it would already be more than just a bath. I'd be caught between what he was doing to me and what it reminded me of, warring internally for one to win out as more significant than the other.

That's what all his redos were, though, weren't they? And in the end, as exhausting as the mental battle was for me, he always ended up turning something bad into something nice.

I continued over to him, giving him my hand so he could help me into the tub.

"You even added the bath beads," I said sinking into the extraordinarily soft water. At least he'd made it a decent temperature. Ron had preferred that baths be more on the warm side than the hot. This one was scalding, the way I liked it.

Edward smiled slyly as he brought the sponge up to scrub along my neck. "Shh, now. Let me pamper you."

So I did.

He took his time, washing every inch of my skin with thorough deliberateness. He talked to me the whole time, as I'd told him Ron would do, but the words were all his own. He told me how attractive I was, which was perhaps generic, then told me how my attraction affected him. How he got dizzy from my scent. How his blood felt thick in his veins when he was around me. How he had to constantly remind himself that he was a civilized human and not a primitive being who was motivated only by his lust.

The very nature of the situation pulled me to the past, settling around me with eerie familiarity, but every time I thought the memories threatened to overwhelm me, Edward's soothing praise and declarations of affection would anchor me to the present.

It was nice.

And weird.

And my emotions were all over the place, but mostly it was nice.

"It might take more than one go to erase this," I said when he moved on to soap up my hair, teasing.

"Greedy girl."

God, though, his fingers kneading into my scalp did all sorts of crazy things to my insides. Melted me and built me up, all at once.

Then the conversation took a turn.

"Have you thought anymore about joining me in going after him?" Edward asked, threading his hands through my hair.

"No," I said instantly.

"Liar."

He pulled the extendable nozzle from its holder and turned it on to rinse out my hair. I tilted my head back and let the water wash out the soap, the sound of the steady spray accompanying the thoughts his last words had stirred up in my head.

I had spent a lot of time thinking about Edward's revenge on Ron. Of course I had. I still had no interest in participating, but I desperately wanted to know what he was planning, how soon it would happen, how badly it would disrupt my parents' lives.

I worried too for Edward. That his actions would go too far and get him in trouble. That he'd be caught.

That concern always led me to the worst of my fears—how far would Edward go? What was he capable of? What had he already done?

"You said you've gotten revenge on people before..." I said, as he applied conditioner to the ends of my hair. I closed my eyes, pretending I didn't want soap in my eyes but really not able to look at him while I asked my question. "Did you ever kill anyone?"

Behind the dark of my lids, the silence that followed was ominous.

"Death is far too forgiving for many people's sins," he said eventually.

I wanted to be relieved about his answer—murder was something I absolutely couldn't get behind. But did that mean he tortured them instead? Because that was intolerable as well.

But also, he hadn't denied killing anyone.

"What does that mean?" I pressed.

He sat back to let the conditioner sit and met my eyes. "There are other ways to bring people pain, bird. Generally, the punishment should fit the crime. But I do prefer ruin."

"Okay. You ruin people." I nodded. Then I shook my head because I still had no idea what that looked like. "Ruin people how?"

"Well. Mitch, the foster parent who abused Camilla, for example. No one believed her claims were strong enough to pursue in court, despite the scars she wears. So instead, I framed him for embezzlement. He spent only three years in prison when he should have spent a lifetime, but he lost his wife, custody of his children, and the ability to foster any other kids, so I called that a win."

"Oh." I let it sink in. Framing a man for a crime he hadn't committed wasn't technically a good thing, but was it really that bad when the guy deserved some sort of punishment?

I hated myself because I actually didn't think it was bad at all.

"Then the cousins who'd stolen our money," Edward said. "I drained them of every penny they had, including taking away the restaurant they'd opened up with our funds as the seed. They should have gone to jail. Instead they went bankrupt and had to live off government handouts. Seemed fitting that they experience what Camilla and

I had to, if you ask me."

Sure. I could get behind that.

"When Hagan was still a teenager, he was approached by some men who pretended to run a modeling agency. Said he had a look that would sell. He believed it, and, unbeknownst to me or his mother, he drained a good portion of his savings account to pay for bogus talent agency fees. There were other victims as well, but the men left town in a hurry and were able to dodge any attempts at prosecution.

"I had the means to track them down. My people gave them the opportunity to pay everyone back and turn themselves in. When they didn't, they beat them within an inch of their lives."

My breath caught. I'd been a terrible person with questionable ethics for a long time, but violence was a different kind of terrible altogether. It was disgusting and vile.

Then why did I feel almost proud?

And a little bit turned on?

Edward picked up the nozzle again to wash out the conditioner. As soon as he was done and the water was turned off, he had more. "There's another man I want to tell you about. A man I discovered recently who has been serving a life sentence for several accounts of rape and assault of a minor. He seemed to have a predilection for prepubescent girls. Some of the accounts were limited to just fingering and oral sex, but other girls he raped, brutally."

I shuddered, a bitter taste forming in my mouth. As awful as my assaults had been, they'd never been that. I'd been lucky in comparison.

"He was beaten severely in prison, as many child sex offenders are. Sent to the infirmary with several broken ribs and damage to his testicles. I imagine he's also been raped."

"Hopefully several times," I said, feeling more malicious than I liked. "He sounds like he deserved it."

Edward nodded. "He did, didn't he? Oh, I should also tell you his name. Charles Endcott. He spent time as a private chauffeur a couple of decades ago before going on to become a school bus driver."

Charles.

Ron's chauffeur. The man who I'd gotten off in the back of the limo at the age of ten. I felt like I wanted to throw up.

I also felt something else, something stronger than my revulsion.

I felt validated.

I felt relief.

I felt like fucking cheering.

"How do you feel hearing that?" Edward asked, his eyes studying me.

I didn't have to tell him. He could see it on my face, surely.

"But you didn't make that happen." It was almost a question. It had only been a couple of months since I'd told him about Charles, not enough time to track down the man and put him on trial. Still, it wouldn't surprise me to find Edward had a hand in his prison beatings. How had he even tracked the guy down?

"No, I didn't," he admitted. "It feels just as good when I do."

I swallowed. It was despicable how good I felt about someone being beaten and raped. Even someone who deserved it. But I really did feel a rush from it, especially knowing that he was no longer able to hurt other girls.

No one had believed me when I was young. I hadn't been able to go after him the legal way, but if I'd spent my adult years trying to go after his ass instead of playing Hudson's silly game, how much better the world would have been for it.

Once again, Edward was the serpent and I was tempted. It would have made me feel powerful to be part of something like that. I still could be now. It wasn't too late. The two of us working together, badass heroes, of a sort.

But even if the world would be better for that sort of vigilantism, would *I* be better for it?

I looked over at my husband, a devil who had promised to take care of his own. A thought occurred to me. "Did you ever seek revenge on Marion's behalf?"

He shook his head once, then said, "That doesn't matter."

"But I want to know."

"And I don't want to talk about it." He began cleaning up the bottles of body wash and shampoo to put on the side table where the items were usually kept, his actions as well as his tone shutting down the topic.

My jaw went rigid. He always closed down when I tried to talk about Marion. It infuriated me, but more than that, it hurt.

And I couldn't help but make up a slew of awful ideas about why he wouldn't talk about her. What had happened between them? Had his determination for revenge been part of it? Had he gone too far on her behalf? On her behest?

Or were his reasons simpler and more devastating to imagine. He'd told me before that she'd been the one to leave him. Was he still in love with her? Did he love her more than he loved me?

If I submitted to him as fully as she had submitted to him, would his feelings change? Could I win him over completely?

When he was done cleaning up, he sat down again and sighed. Reaching out, he traced my tense jawline with a gentle stroke. "You don't have to change your mind about Ron. He'll go down no matter what. But there are other men, men who should be dealt with. Men who are dangerous to others."

He wanted me on board, and I wanted to be his. I opened my mouth to agree to whatever he wanted from me.

Then I shut it again.

No. I couldn't try to earn a man's love. Not anymore. Not ever again.

I loved Edward, but I had to stay true to me, above all.

"You're right. They should be dealt with. And I hope they are. But it can't be by me. It's a path that leads too closely to the person I was, and I'm not going back there again."

He sat silent, his fingers moving down my neck and across my collar, tracing the bone with a delicate caress. Did he think this would persuade me to his point of view? Or had he moved onto something else?

I kind of liked the something else. A hunger was blooming at his touch, despite the three orgasms he'd given me earlier.

On the verge of giving into his seduction, I pulled myself together and turned to him, reaching my wet hand up to cup his cheek. "And not by you, either, Edward. You don't need to do this for me. I don't want you to, okay? Please don't go revenging on my behalf. Promise me you won't."

His eyes locked with mine, steady and dark. He held them there for a heavy beat.

Then his gaze moved down. To my lips. Then to my arm where his fingers now danced across my bicep. "You know, I understand why he'd bathe you," he said, his voice a rumble of need. "Touching you like this is a drug."

My stomach flipped, setting off a storm of butterflies. Somewhere in the last several minutes, he'd managed to make me forget about the baths of the past, about their predatory nature. Even talking about Ron, tonight had been about me and Edward in the present.

His words now should have been a reminder that I'd once been a sexual object to a man who should have loved me like a parent, should have made me cringe and feel the shame I'd always felt for being cast in the role. And they did, in a way, but they also made me remember I'd come out the other side. That I could be sexy and sexual and it would be appropriate. That I could be desirable and it not be indecent.

I felt very desirable in this moment. And full of desire.

As if connected to my thoughts, Edward stood with me as I stood, his mouth latching with mine. I threw my arms around his neck and, when he lifted me from the water, wrapped my legs around his waist, neither of us caring that he was still in his tux and I was dripping wet.

He carried me to the bedroom and made love to me

until I was drowning in ecstasy, until I was sated and bone-less, until the conversations of the night became flecks of pigment instead of the whole picture and I was completely lost to being his.

TEN

EDWARD

Camilla peered at me from the other side of my desk and nervously fidgeted with the cuff of her blouse. "What will my excuse be for staying at the hotel? I live in London. Why would I need someplace to stay?"

She was stalling her departure, anxious about her mission to intercept Ron Werner at the Savoy. She wasn't as good at improvising as I was, so these last minute details were important to her. I reminded myself of that, resisting the urge to rush her out.

While she was on edge, I was eager. I'd been waiting almost my entire life to bring down the man who'd ruined my father. I'd thought I'd been close to triumph when I'd married Celia, but though the taste of victory should have been on my tongue it had been bitter, knowing what I'd have to do to my wife in order to obtain it.

Thank God that hadn't worked out the way I'd planned.

Now, my enemy wasn't mine alone. My motives for taking down Ron Werner were as much for her as for me, and that made the nearness of his demise all the sweeter.

"You just purchased your new flat," I said, with more patience than I thought I had in me. "Say you're having your kitchen redone."

"You live in town too. Why wouldn't I just stay with you?"

"Because we're on the outs. The papers are still talking about it. You left your son with us for the weekend, because he missed his uncle so." I ignored her eye roll. "But you couldn't stand to stay in the house with *her.*"

"Celia, you mean." She sighed. "You really want me to play up this family feud with her?"

"I think it makes sense, yes. From what she tells me, his abuse has gone unmentioned for decades. He may not even consider she holds animosity toward him—who knows what a monster like that believes about his actions—but in case he does, it would be good that he doesn't think you have any reason to be sympathetic toward her."

"I suppose you're right," she agreed. "I just want it all to be believable. I don't want to be the reason this messes up."

"You won't be. You'll be—"

A knock on my office door interrupted my train of thought, the rap too light to be Jeremy. "Come in," I instructed, sure I knew who would enter.

"Sorry to disturb you." As I'd guessed, Celia sauntered in, a small package in her hand. She carried it directly to me. "You said to bring this up right away when it arrived. Jeremy was in the middle of changing a bulb in the reception room, so I offered to take it."

"Thank you." I took the box, my eyes reluctant to leave her. She'd begun taking on design work recently, which meant leaving the house and meeting with clients, so I'd taken to dressing her in clothing that wrapped her up completely. I was possessive by nature and preferred others saw as little of her body as possible unless I was on her arm.

Not that it made a difference. She was still delectable wearing wide-leg gold studded black trousers and a long-sleeved sweater, not an inch of skin showing below her neck. Maybe even more so.

With effort, I pulled my gaze to the package, tearing into it as I half listened to the conversation between the women.

"I really appreciate you letting Freddie stay here. I hope it's not too inconvenient."

"Not inconvenient at all. We love having him here."

"He won't be a bother with your work?"

"Of course not. Anwar's here and the staff. And it gives me an excuse not to hyperfocus on my projects."

The box opened now, I pulled out one of the matte business cards and looked it over. It was clean, simple. Only her name, email, and phone number.

"It looks good," I said, handing it over to my sister.

She took it, twisting her lips as she admired it. "It does. It should do."

Celia gestured at the card. "May I?"

Camilla passed the item over to my wife who examined it, her brows knit together as she did. She had to have plenty of questions—why it was so stark. Why it didn't say that she was the Consulting Art Director at Accelecom or, if it was for her photography hobby, why it didn't list her website.

The question she voiced, however, surprised me. "Fasbender?" she asked, referring to the fact that Camilla had chosen to drop the Dougherty.

"I've officially gone back to my maiden name," she said in explanation. "It's a new era. New home. New name. New me."

She looked better for it, too. Her eyes were less sullen, her face more filled out. I hated to admit it, but being on her own was doing wonders for her.

Or maybe it was her own thirst for vengeance that was bringing her to life. It was the first time I'd involved her. I should have considered doing so long before.

Celia gave a teasing grin. "Am I to assume this long weekend means there might be a man involved? Edward said you were staying in town."

Camilla gaped as she looked wide-eyed from my wife to me.

Celia followed her gaze, her smile disappearing when she realized she wasn't going to get an answer. "It's okay," she said, her voice tight. "You don't have to say anything. It's really none of my business."

She handed the card back toward Camilla who refused to take it. "Edward," she spit sharply, and though that was all she said, I knew what she wanted from me.

"It's not a secret from you, Celia," I said. "We'll tell you. It's just a matter of whether or not you *want* to know."

"Is this about Ron?" Celia's voice was steady, but I could see the card shaking in her hand.

I reached out to take it from her, and she immediately wiped her palms down her trousers, as though they were sweating. "He's staying at the Savoy through Sunday."

She swallowed. "I didn't realize he was in town. Do

you know why he's here?"

"He seems to be attending a party this weekend. An acquaintance. I'm not sure the relationship."

Seeming to be dissatisfied with the rate at which information was being exchanged, Camilla jumped in. "I'm going to try to meet up with him at the hotel bar. Accidentally."

"And then what?"

I studied Celia's expression, but she'd put up her mask, her emotions tightly guarded.

Either she didn't care in the least or she didn't want me to know how much she cared. Since she was still standing there, since she'd asked for more information, I had to think it was the latter.

Which meant this was the time to convince her that she should be involved in going after her uncle, not just because it would please me, but because it would be deeply satisfying to her.

"Camilla is going to try to pique his interest, that's all," I said. "Casually let him know she's aware of his interests. Give him her card. Later, she'll reach out and invite him to Exceso. He should feel safe in that environment, no matter whether he trusts the person inviting him or not. There he'll connect with plenty of the type of men he's interested in knowing. I won't even have to interfere. That's how relationships work there.

"But I do have some friends there who will be looking out for him. One is an undercover FBI agent who will be there at the same time. He'll get close to Ron and hopefully, either through Camilla or directly, he gets an invitation to whatever Ron has planned next in the States. Once we get him on his own soil, at an event he's hosting, we should be able to take him down for good."

Again I watched for a reaction and found nothing.

"Well?" I prodded.

"It's a noble plan and all. I admire the amount of thought you've put into it. But it's not going to work."

"Why is that?" Camilla asked, concern evident in her tone. "Did we miss something? What part won't work?"

"All of it, really. You're going after him as if he's a serial pedophile, trying to appeal to some attraction he has for little girls in general. There was only just me."

I *had* missed something. I'd missed *this*. It had been apparent to me from the first time she'd told me about him that Ron was a predator. Men didn't get that good at that kind of grooming without having practiced before. And when they were done with one victim, they moved on.

It had never occurred to me that Celia wouldn't realize the same thing.

"You're sure about that?" I asked gently, hoping I didn't have to be mean to make her see the truth.

She paused to consider for only half a second. "Pretty sure. He's dated many women since then. Long-term relationships. And who else would he have had access to? Who's letting their daughters stay over at his house? I was a singular situation."

"You were *special*."

"Right." But she hesitated, not as sure as before.

"You were his Lolita," I pressed. "His girlfriend. He loved you because you were you, not because you were a child, is that what you're trying to tell me?"

She scowled, her arms crossing over her chest defensively. If my sister hadn't been present, I was certain she would have pressed back.

But she was trying to be respectful, because I demanded that from her, and I took advantage of her silence to push on. "I know you aren't that naive, Celia. Are you willfully ignoring the truth here?"

"Are you willfully being an arse?" Camilla asked, not bound to the mandates of respect that my wife was bound to.

It gave Celia enough time to come up with her own response. "I'm being honest, Edward," she said firmly. "I want to get him as much as anyone."

"Do you?" It was a fair question since she'd told me before that she wanted nothing to do with my revenge schemes.

She answered with tightly pursed lips.

I changed tactics. "There have been other girls," I said softly. "It wasn't just you."

"How do you know that?" Her voice was thinner now, her guard finally coming down.

I opened a desk drawer and pulled out the file I'd been collecting. I threw it on the edge of my desk, facing her, and opened it up, spreading the items out so she could see the photos, police reports, and copies of cleared checks I'd managed to obtain through my investigators. "He has a circle of friends who are rumored to have been involved with illegal sexual activities. Some have even faced charges, nothing that has stuck. There have been several undisclosed payouts over the years, however, including two from Ron. One made to the daughter of one of those long-term girlfriends you mentioned. I'm guessing that's where he's got his access."

The color drained from Celia's cheeks. "What?"

"And he got access through his friends. He and the lot of them hold regular events. Semi-annually, it seems. The location varies, always at one of their country houses. Based on the few accounts that have made it to my sources, I believe they're parties like the one where your uncle auctioned you off at."

"He auctioned you off?" Camilla asked, horrified.

I hadn't told her the details. They hadn't been necessary. Now, though, it seemed important to remind them both why Ron Werner deserved to be destroyed.

"I think I need to sit down." Celia looked for the closest seat.

I was up out of mine before she took a step. I helped her to the chair against the wall, then knelt in front of her.

"There have really been others? Besides me?"

I reached out to stroke her cheek with the back of a single finger. "I'm afraid so, bird."

"Oh, God. I didn't know." Her tone was broken and weary, and yet it sliced through me. If I could have taken the pain from her, I would have. I would have siphoned every terrible ache, adding them to my own until I couldn't tell the difference between hers and mine. I was a blackhole, yet despite the gravity of my emotions, I couldn't draw hers to me without taking her with them.

And I was devil enough to do that. To take her along with all the poison she felt. To drag her into my schemes with me.

"I didn't want to believe it. I knew it was a possibility, but I didn't want to be responsible." She put her hands together and propped her elbows on her lap.

"You aren't. It's not your fault." I leaned up to kiss her forehead. "You tried to tell."

"I didn't try hard enough."

I tilted her chin up forcefully. "Stop. I won't hear that from you." My eyes darted between both of hers. "We're doing this now. You got that? We'll stop him now."

She nodded. Then, after thinking about it for another few seconds, she shook her head. "I just don't understand. How could he be involved in something this big for so long and not have been stopped?"

"Powerful men with lots of money," Camilla said, reminding us of her presence. "They're above the law."

If Celia realized I was included in that group, she didn't acknowledge it. "Can't your FBI friend just show up at one of Ron's events and catch him in the act? Why does it have to be the two of you?"

It had to be me because of her. How could she not realize that? I had to be the one to do this for her because it was my job. Because I was her husband. Because, when I'd said I would love and care for her, I'd made those vows with utmost sincerity.

"The parties are all kept very hush hush," I said instead. "Only people on the invite list know the time and location. Also, the authorities can't go in without a warrant, and they don't have enough reason to get one, legally. They need an undercover operation for something like this, and going after Ron Werner is not on the priority list."

"Wasn't on my father's either."

And that was why Warren Werner was still on my vengeance list as well.

But I wasn't about to get ahead of myself.

I pulled the handkerchief from my front pocket and handed it to her. "He might have someone he's paying off to keep his activities on the down low. It's possible he's just too big of an entity to even consider going after. I'm guessing they all are."

"I guess that shouldn't surprise me." She dabbed at her eyes, then, with one last sniffle, pulled herself together. "Can I see those pictures?" She nodded to the open file on my desk.

I grabbed the few on top and handed them to her.

"This man," she said pointing to one in a group shot. "And this one. And this one. Those men were there that night. They were...they..."

They'd been the men who'd "bought" her. She didn't have to say it. I knew. There had been five of them in total. I'd been hoping that I'd found at least a few of them.

I'd hoped I'd found them all.

"I'll get them too," I promised, leaning against the edge of the desk.

"Me too." Camilla reached out to take Celia's hand. "I want to get them too."

Celia smiled faintly, and my chest tightened. I hadn't realized how much I wanted them to like each other until that moment. It had been silly to think otherwise, to believe I could keep my world compartmentalized, especially when I so wanted Celia to be a part of all of it.

It hadn't been that way with Marion. But then Marion had wanted to be kept separate.

"What can I do to help?" Celia asked, drawing me from my thoughts.

Camilla responded before I could. "You don't need to

do anything."

I didn't quite agree with her answer. "You can help me try to identify the other two who were there that night. To make sure I have them on my radar."

"Okay. I will." Celia grew serious, her eyes piercing. "What about with Ron? What can I do to help get Ron?"

The exhilaration that rushed through me was nearly blinding. I'd done it. I'd brought her to my side, and, hell if we weren't going to be formidable together.

"Can you feed a little gossip to your parents?" I asked. "I think it would help if Madge Werner thinks you and your sister-in-law are not friendly."

"Yes. I'll call now," she said, rising from her chair.

It wasn't far to the door, but I hurried to walk her there. "Are you all right?" I asked quietly, when we were at the threshold. Camilla was still close enough that she could likely hear our whispered conversation, but I didn't care about that. I cared about my wife.

"I'm fine," she insisted. "I should have gotten involved sooner."

I cupped her face with my hands."There was no need. I told you I'd take care of you, of this, and that's what I'm doing."

"I know, and I appreciate it. But you were right—I need to do this." She brushed her lips against mine in a soft kiss. "You were right about something else, too, you know."

"What?"

"When we get him? It's going to feel real, real good."

ELEVEN
CELIA

"The sofa goes there. The chair goes there."

Freddie moved the furniture pieces on my model, adjusting them the way a three-and-a-half-year-old boy thought they should go rather than what was functional. It was fortunate I even had the thing. These days, most designers rendered their designs on computer. I was one of those people, though, who had a better vision when I saw the thing in 3D. Real 3D, not a flat-screen version.

I handed him the fireplace, giving up on my work. "And where should this go?"

He thought about it for a minute then moved the piece to be in front of the windows.

"That's an unusual place for a fireplace," Edward said as he came into the space I'd once used as a bedroom. It had been completely transformed to be a cozy work area, and while I was glad for the space and for the work, I couldn't help but think it might be better suited as a nursery.

It wasn't a thought I had too often, but Freddie's visit over the last couple of days had settled the idea more firmly in my mind. I hadn't had a lot of experience with children before him and had always assumed I would be terrible with miniature humans. Turned out I actually had a knack.

At least I had a knack for Freddie.

"I don't know," I said, defending the kid's choice in fireplace placement. "The smoke can go right out the window now. No need for a chimney. Quite convenient."

Freddie's eyes suddenly went wide with panic. "Father Christmas comes down the chimney!"

"He has a point, Celia. There has to be a chimney for Father Christmas."

I laughed. "I'll work on adding that to the design then."

"You do that. Meanwhile, it's time for this one to get to bed." Edward swooped Freddie from his chair and flew him like an airplane to Anwar who was waiting in the doorway. Once the boy had been deposited in his caretaker's arms, Edward ruffled his hair. "Sleep well, you monster."

"I'm not a monster," Freddie said.

Edward feigned surprise. "You're not? What are you then?"

"I'm a little boy!"

"Maybe you'll be more recognizable after your bath. Now get to it. No more delays. Blow your auntie a kiss first."

Freddie kissed his hand and opened it with what was supposed to be a blow of air but came out more like spitting. I pretended to catch the kiss and placed my palm to my cheek. "Got it," I said.

Edward walked the pair out the door and as far as the

stairs, then returned to stand in my doorway, his hands thrust in his pockets.

"You're good with him. I bet you were an amazing father." I focused on rearranging the model pieces instead of looking at him. So he wouldn't think the statement was significant. Because it wasn't. Not really. I knew where he stood on having more children.

"I wasn't," he said, surprising me into looking up. "I was much too young. Too impatient. Too preoccupied. I never had time to play with them like I should have."

Part of me longed to know what had preoccupied him, if it had been his relationship with his wife or simply the details of building a wildly successful business.

But another part of me—a stupid, hopeful, optimistic part of me—wanted to grab onto the thread he'd so casually thrown out. "Maybe you should try again, then. Now that you're older and more settled."

His expression became stony. "No."

That was it, nothing more. One syllable, and the subject was officially closed.

I sighed, wondering if this was a battle I wanted to try to wage. I'd gone into our marriage knowing his thoughts on the matter, I'd stayed when our relationship became real knowing he hadn't changed his mind. I hadn't wanted them, so it hadn't been an issue, except that maybe that had been a lie. Maybe I had wanted them. Maybe I'd always wanted them. Maybe that want had just been one more of the feelings I'd buried deep in numbness.

But did I want a child more than I wanted Edward?

I didn't. So there was no battle to wage.

"Besides," Edward said, as though sensing where my

head was. "I'd much rather play with you." As easily as he'd scooped up Freddie, he bent and swept me up from my chair. "Work is done now. Let's play."

I tilted my head wondering what he was up to. Then when he set me down in front of the white side of the chess board he'd given me for Christmas, it was evident.

"This wasn't exactly what I hoped you had in mind." But I moved my pawn.

He sat across from me and pushed his pawn out to meet mine. "I'm sure I have more in mind than this. Just, this first."

That was promising. I moved a knight. He moved a bishop. I moved my other knight. He moved one of his.

The rhythm of our game should have focused me entirely, but my head was elsewhere, had been since I'd interrupted his conversation with his sister a couple of days prior. It had been a heavy revelation, realizing that Ron had other girls. I was disgusted, of course. And sad—sad that I hadn't done more to stop him. Sad that he had other victims.

The worst part, though, was that I also felt jealous.

It was stupid that I could feel that way and gross and shameful. It showed how deeply he still affected me. Ron had groomed me to care that I was special, and even after everything, after the auction and therapy and finding real love, I still was programmed to care.

That had shocked me.

But Edward had known. He'd understood that there was closure needed where my uncle was concerned, and he'd been certain that vengeance was the road to achieving it, even when I'd insisted that it wasn't. That I was fine.

I hadn't been fine. Not if Ron still had the power to make me feel those kinds of things. I could see that now, could see what Edward had seen all along, and except for encouraging me to journal and schedule an impromptu session with my doctor, he hadn't pushed the topic since I'd left his office. He'd given me space, and I was grateful.

But now I was ready to talk.

"Have you heard from Camilla? Was she able to meet with Ron?" That was an easy place to start. I moved a pawn.

Edward's other knight came out. "Yes."

I picked up a pawn and stared at him, dying for more. "And...?"

"Make your play."

I set the piece on the board, not even looking to see how wise of a move it had been. "Did it go as planned?"

He moved a knight before he responded. "It went as expected. He played dumb, but he took her card. He did ask who had told her he might have knowledge on the subject."

I played my bishop, knowing no questions would be answered until I did. "What did she say?"

His knight took mine. "You aren't paying attention."

I scowled and tried to focus on the board. I took his knight with my queen. "I'm not?"

"Not the wisest move."

I wasn't exposed. I'd taken one of his pieces. I couldn't see any flaw in the thought process. He was just trying to rile me. "Keep your commentary to yourself, please. And tell me about Camilla."

With a sly smile, he castled. "She didn't exactly an-swer. Just said that she'd recently become a sort of rela-tive, by marriage. Left him with that."

My stomach felt queasy. It felt dangerous knowing that Camilla had interacted with him, that she'd referenced me in any way. *This will always be just between us*, Ron had said to me, over and over and over. It was cruel how I could still worry he'd be mad.

It made *me* mad.

I moved my other bishop. "I want you to get him," I said as he moved his own bishop in response. "I want you to get all his friends." I took his bishop with mine.

Then, seeing my opportunity, I made a move of an-other sort. "And I want to talk about who else you think deserves my wrath."

He paused, his fingers on his rook, his eyes on me. He studied me for a beat before sliding it to the next space. "Who says I think anything?"

I glared at him. "Don't even pretend you don't have thoughts. You've been hinting that there are others you think I should go after, and I know you meant those five arseholes, but I think you have more people in mind than that. I haven't wanted to discuss it, but I'm giving you a chance now. Talk."

He gestured at the board.

"Goddammit." I castled. "Now talk."

He slid a pawn out with a chuckle. "How about we both talk?"

I moved a pawn. "Fine. Let me state for the record that we are just talking. You won't do anything based on this conversation. You hear me?"

He chuckled. "Giving me orders, are you?"

"I'm serious, Edward."

His face grew somber. "We're just talking," he agreed.

"Good. Now you."

Another black pawn came out. "Your father."

My breath lodged in my chest. That was why we needed to have this conversation. Not because I thought he might be right and that I should seek justice from other people who had wronged me, but because he thought I should, and the unspeaking of it was like a silent wedge between us. If it wasn't addressed, it would eventually drive us apart.

With great determination, I moved my piece and found my voice. "My father didn't have anything to do with ruining your father's company. I told you. Ron had autonomy."

He played a pawn. "We aren't talking about your father wronging me. We're talking about how he's wronged you."

I looked at the board, but all I could see was my father's face the day I'd told him what his little brother had done to me. "You think I should get back at him for not listening to me about Ron." I made my move absentmindedly.

Miraculously, I didn't lose any pieces with Edward's next play. "I think he deserves to pay for that. Yes."

I moved my queen. "He made a mistake. I was a little girl."

"You were his little girl, and he should have protected you. That's a father's job." He slid his bishop diagonally across the board. "Not only did he not protect you, but he used you to protect himself, putting his shares in your name to evade taxes. Those are not acts of a good father. You yourself said that your relationship with him is strained."

"Which is why I should probably do as my therapist suggests and talk to him." I had no plans to at the moment, but the idea made more sense than whatever Edward thought I should do.

"Talking doesn't pay back what you're owed."

"I don't know that he owes me anything. Besides an apology. He didn't make me go back to Ron's after that, at least." I wondered what his reaction would be when Ron was finally arrested, if he'd apologize then or pretend I'd never said anything. "Anyway, he's going to get blowback when all of this goes down with my uncle. That will make me feel better."

"But it won't make *me* feel better."

I stared at my husband, dumbfounded. Was this still somehow about what Werner Media did to his family or was Edward that upset for me? I'd explained that my father wasn't responsible for Ron's actions, so it shouldn't be that. But the other option was more unbelievable.

Did he really love me that much?

"Take your turn," he said, not giving me any insight.

I made a thoughtless move and lost a pawn on his next turn. After I played again, I opened my mouth to ask about his motives with my father, but he spoke first. "There are others besides your father. John. The man who took your virginity. That was statutory rape."

"Technically, yes, but I asked for it."

"It doesn't matter. It was illegal. He should pay."

"Like you should pay for all of your illegal activities?"

He took my bishop. "We aren't talking about me."

Right. Because he was the devil. He doled out the punishments, he didn't ever pay for his own.

We made our next several moves in silence, mostly because I was beginning to think there was no reasoning with my husband, and worrying what that meant for our marriage.

It meant that I had to try harder, was what it meant. I wasn't accepting any other option.

"Who else?" I asked after he took another of my pieces from the board.

"I have mixed feelings about the boy who tricked you into dumping your boyfriend for him. He broke your heart, and he did it maliciously, but you paid him back already by sleeping with his father, didn't you? And he did step up when you got pregnant by claiming to be the father. That seems like retribution in its own right."

I took one of his pawns. "I agree. He should be off the hook. You would have a hard time taking Hudson Pierce down anyway."

His fingers froze on his queen. "That was Hudson Pierce?"

Shit. I'd forgotten I'd kept that from him.

Maybe it was good to come clean about this, though. "Yep. That was Hudson."

"So the father you seduced was Jack Pierce."

I shrugged, guiltily. "It wasn't one of my finer moments."

Edward blinked several times, and pride jolted through me. It was rare that I surprised the man. It made me feel like a worthy opponent when I did.

Even though he did take two of my pieces with each of his next two moves.

"So when Hudson bought out the majority in your father's company, it wasn't just because he didn't want you interfering with his relationship. It was more like the end-game in a long chess match."

"Actually, it was exactly like that. He won, obviously. And I have no desire for a rematch."

Edward's eyes narrowed, calculating, and I had a feeling that it wasn't the current game he was assessing.

"I mean it, Edward. I'm not going after Hudson for anything. He and I are done. If he hadn't won, it's very unlikely I would be with you here now. And don't forget, he has those shares. He could hurt us if we tried to hurt him. Which I do not want to do." I was bordering on pleading, but this was important. Not only had I accepted the status of my relationship with Hudson, but also I'd played the man before. I'd seen what he could do, how devious he could be. I did not want to be on the other side of that again.

"Fine," Edward said, his accompanying exhale proving his sincerity.

I relaxed, letting out tension I hadn't realized I'd been holding. Then his bishop took mine.

I swiped his bishop with my king in response, which wasn't that brag-worthy considering the state of the board, but it made me feel good all the same. "Is that all? Are we done?"

"With this game? Practically." He moved his queen down the length of the board. "Check."

"No way. I still have a fighting chance." I didn't. I'd only ever beaten him twice, and we played quite regularly. For now, though, I could move my king out of play. "But I meant with your list."

He moved his queen again. "Just one more person to

add—the man who introduced you to your games."

My stomach dropped. *Checkmate.*

And not because of anything on the board.

The man who introduced me to The Game was also Hudson, another fact I'd refrained from telling my husband. And thank God I had, because if Hudson had that stacked against him, there was no way Edward would let him off without some sort of recompense.

Except, this was only a conversation. This was *my* list we were discussing. Edward wasn't doing anything to anyone. We were only talking about possibilities, and there was none where Hudson was concerned. Period.

"No," I said. Now to see if my one-word decrees were as effective as Edward's.

"No? I think very much yes. He was the reason you were such a cold-hearted bitch when we met."

"Dragon," I corrected, moving my castle. "Cold-hearted *dragon.*"

He moved his queen, and again I was in check. "You can't say he doesn't have sins to pay for."

"He has to pay for his own sins just like I have to pay for mine. Personally, I'm not holding anything against him." I scrutinized the board for long seconds, trying to get the shaking of my hands under control. What if he found out it was Hudson? Would that make him retreat or double down? It could go either way. I didn't like the lie, and I wanted to tell him the truth, but I wasn't sure how far my husband would go in his search for justice.

One thing was certain—I could not let him take on Hudson Pierce.

I could feel him studying me the way I studied the

board. "What happened between you?" he asked, in the cold detached voice he used in our sessions.

No. This would not become a session. I would not pour out my heart over this. "I've already told you all that matters," I lied, moving my king to safety once again. "He knew how to be cut off from the world, emotionally, and I begged him to teach me how he did it. Like with John, I was the one who asked for it."

It took him a bit to find his next move. "Like with John, your wishes were irrelevant. He taught you how to hurt people. He made you a weapon. That's wrong whether you asked for it or not."

"You're exaggerating. He didn't make me a weapon. He helped me become mean, but I wasn't dangerous." I brought my queen nearer to my king, hoping it would be enough protection.

"What you planned to do to me wasn't dangerous? I beg to differ."

Edward's tone had grown sharp, bringing my gaze up to his.

His expression was serious. Deadly serious. "Maybe it's you who want revenge on him because of what I set out to do to you. Maybe this has nothing to do with him at all."

"Possibly." His eyes took on that mischievous gleam that was present throughout our earliest meetings.

A chill traveled down my spine. Or a thrill. It was hard to tell the difference between the two where Edward was concerned.

"I'm pretty sure you and I are even, darling, considering what *you* planned to do to *me*."

He smiled, and if I hadn't won the round, I'd at least

gotten a point.

The game resumed. He moved his knight. I took it with my bishop. He took my bishop with his queen. I moved my king. He moved his.

"You called him A," Edward said, breaking the silence. "In your journals. Was that his initial?"

The hard, heavy dread returned to my stomach. I'd thought the subject had been dropped. Silly me.

"I'm not answering that," I said firmly. And I was in check again.

"Why won't you tell me about him?" The sharp edge had returned, demanding I give answers.

It wasn't fair. He pushed and pushed and pushed and expected me to always capitulate. And yet he never once yielded to me. Was that always to be our roles?

No. I could submit, but there had to be a limit. He had to give back. "Why won't you tell me about Marion?" I challenged.

His eye twitched but he otherwise ignored the question, the same way he was now ignoring the board. "Did you love A?"

A beat passed. "No."

"You paused."

"I wanted to be sure of my answer. And I'm sure the answer is no." I hadn't always been sure. There'd been a time when I'd thought I loved him, but if I admitted that, would he figure out he was also the boy who tricked me into falling for him? Had he already figured it out? Was that why he was asking?

But I was wrong about his angle entirely. "Then Marion and I are different."

"That makes no sense. You should be telling me about Marion *because* you loved her. She was a significant part of your life. Why won't you share that with me?" I was frustrated, and it showed.

"You want to know about Marion because you want to compare yourself to her." With only a glance at the board, he took my rook with his. "I'm not feeding your tendency to try to be something other than who you are."

I winced. "That wasn't very nice."

"Was it untrue?"

God, he could be cruel. So brutally cruel.

Brutally cruel and honest. "No, it wasn't." I was insanely jealous of Marion, mostly because I knew nothing about her except that she'd once owned Edward's heart. It was possible she still did, and that hurt.

If Edward thought the man who taught me The Game owned my heart, would he be jealous too?

"I didn't love him, but, if you must know, he did break my heart." I could be cruel too, in case he'd forgotten.

His nostrils seemed to flare, but beyond that, he remained stoic. "Even more reason why you owe him this. You'll never get over him otherwise."

Oh, for fuck's sake. "How will *you* ever get over *Marion*?" I threw back, wondering if we'd crossed from discussion to argument.

"Stop worrying about Marion."

"Stop worrying about A!"

He held my gaze, his fists curled on the sides of the chessboard, his lip curled downward.

Then suddenly, with one dramatic sweep of his arms,

he brushed the chess pieces off the board, scattering them all over the floor.

I stared, taken aback. As angry as the move had been, he seemed calmer now, as though he'd only needed to let out his temper and then he'd be fine.

Still, I asked, "I guess this is a fight now?"

His mouth quirked up into a half-grin. "How about we skip the rest of the arguing and get straight to the punishment for disagreeing with me?"

I felt the impulse to argue more for half a second.

And then I recognized it for what it was—an attempt at conciliation, and I was all for that. Being "punished" by Edward was better than fighting any day.

"Yes, sir," I said, for once not bothered by the term of address.

His pupils darkened as he began undoing his belt. "Crawl over the table and put your head in my lap. If you're such a dragon, prove it to my cock."

I did as he said, climbing across the board then, with my legs still on the table, bracing my arms on his thighs so I could take his fat, steel rod into my mouth. Sometime between the first spurt of pre-cum on my tongue and the moment when he released down the back of my throat, his hips bucking with wild abandon, his hands wrapped firmly in my hair, I let our quibble go, dismissing it as a simple lover's spat.

But deep down, in the place inside me that I used to bury my feelings, I knew the truth—this conversation was far from over.

TWELVE
THEN: EDWARD

"Hold this, will you?"

Before I'd answered, Roman thrust his whiskey tumbler into my hand so he could pull a lighter and cigar out of his inside jacket pocket.

"Is that a good idea?" I asked, as he bit off the end. It was his house and his party, so he knew I wasn't asking because I questioned if it were the right environment.

"I'm already dying, Edward. Smoking a cigar seems like a splendid idea." He winked as though it wasn't macabre to speak of his approaching death so casually.

Stage four colon cancer, spread to the liver and stomach. And he'd chosen not to pursue treatment. There wasn't any point, he'd said.

Instead, he was throwing a party.

"You're making it hard to not enjoy this," I said, because I knew it was what he'd want to hear, but I most certainly was not having a good time. I didn't have many friends, mostly because I didn't like the bother of relationships. Roman had become more than that, though. He was family. Practically a father, and I'd already lost one of those. I wasn't ready to go through the pain of that loss again. No amount of drinking or celebrating would ease the storm of gloom gathering inside.

"It's a phenomenal evening," Marion said, her French accent faded from so many years in the UK. "It's a beautiful way to honor this season of your life. Much better to have the festivities now instead of later."

Instead of after his funeral, she meant. She was more tactful than I, though, always able to be charming, no matter the circumstances.

"That's exactly what I was going for." Roman took his tumbler from my hand and clinked it against my own filled with cognac. "May we never go to hell but always be on our way."

I grimaced and chuckled at the same time.

Then he turned to Marion to clink her wine glass. "Sante, my dear."

"Somehow it seems gauche to say it in return." Her smile was lovely, both demure and reassuring at once.

"Cheers will do just fine," he said, his gaze warm.

"Cheers then, Roman."

When the older man's focus moved again to me, he had the expression of a stern mentor. "Your wife knows how to play along. Take a cue from her, my boy."

I forced my lips upward, or at least less down. "Here's to friends and family who know us well but love us all the same."

"That's better. Not great, but better." He tipped his drink back, finishing it off before setting it down on the tray of a passing waiter.

I sipped my drink more slowly, taking the burn in measured doses, wishing I could do the same with the news of Roman's health. It was too fast, all of it. He was too young, and I needed him. A selfish reason to want him to live, but wasn't all affection selfish?

"Camilla has a new boyfriend, I see."

I shook myself from my thoughts and followed Roman's gaze across the ballroom. Camilla was there on the arm of her latest beau—Frank Dougherty. She'd been through a string of men over the past several years, none of them any good for her. Most of them had disappeared before I'd been able to discern just how not good for her they were. Frank was the first in a long time to stick around.

"What do you think of him?" Roman asked.

Like the others, he didn't deserve her, that was certain. He was bred well enough, but he was entitled and impulsive. He had no job, and, with the way he splurged, he was sure to reach the end of his trust fund before he turned thirty.

But money didn't buy happiness, as well I knew, and if Camilla was happy with the lazy prick, then I could support the relationship.

I just wasn't yet sure she actually was happy.

Once upon a time I would have discussed my concerns with Roman in full. Now, it seemed unkind to burden him with such trivial affairs. "I don't know yet," I said, trying to be honest without going into it.

"Edward's worried he's a brute," Marion said, wrapping her free arm around mine. It was subtle, but I read the subtext of the gesture clearly. She was goading me, challenging me publicly. Not that it was much of a challenge.

She liked to get in trouble, knew that I liked catching her in it, but she was submissive through and through. She liked to please way more than she liked to get in trouble for defying.

Roman studied me. "That's fine criticism, coming from him."

"He's a different breed of brute," I said with a defensive scowl. "He's pushy and controlling and indulgent. With Camilla, specifically. I'm not sure he knows when to rein it in."

Roman stared at me, his gaze so pointed it was impossible to miss the meaning.

Fuck, he had a point. I might as well be describing myself and my relationship with Marion.

But Marion was into what I offered her. I hated to think about what Camilla might want in a sexual relationship, but I was worldly enough to know she might be into it as well.

"I'm sure you'll step in when needed," Roman said, seeming to understand my concerns.

"Yes, I will."

At my side, Marion let out a sigh, small but noticeable. If she had more to say about my methods of interference, she should say it. Not now, but later, when it was just the two of us.

She wouldn't, though. She never did.

"How are the kids?" Roman asked. "Hagan's...what? Seven now?"

Marion brightened at the turn of conversation. "Nine. Genevieve is seven."

"That's right. What are they up to now?"

I rolled my eyes. This was as bad as pretending to enjoy his death party, only this time he was the one acting disingenuously. "Don't answer that, Marion. He doesn't care for anything to do with kids."

"I don't," he agreed. "I was being polite."

"Excuse me, may I steal you momentarily?" A man I was only somewhat acquainted with ushered Roman away to introduce him to his companion. As though he had any reason to want to meet new people now.

God, I was an arse.

Marion shifted next to me, the kind of movement that said she'd likely been uncomfortable for some time and had been holding it in. Only now that we were alone could she let her poise go.

I smiled, realizing I was the source of her discomfort. Pulling her into me, I positioned my mouth near her ear. "Are you feeling the reminder of yesterday's punishment?"

"Yes, sir."

She'd asked for it, essentially, when she stayed in my bed after we'd fucked the night before. Separate bedrooms had been her decision, a space she said she needed due to the intense nature of our relationship. Choosing to not sleep there was one of the not-so-subtle ways she used to indicate she wanted some physical discipline.

The irony was that I would have preferred for her to sleep at my side. Every night.

I resented her for that, if I was being honest. It was that resentment that I'd clung to when I'd doled out her punishment. "Perhaps I was a little vicious with the belt."

"That's not what's feeling sore."

I pulled back to look at her and saw the color rise in

her cheeks.

I had been vicious with more than the belt. After leaving her with red welts along her backside, I'd taken her ass. And I hadn't been gentle.

Still feeling cross today, probably more because of the event we had to attend than because of anything that had to do with us, I'd found a way to torture her further.

"I suppose you've been a good girl today. You can remove the plug." I reached in my pocket and took out the drawstring bag the toy was kept in. I exchanged it for her wine. "Bring that back to me immediately. I'll hold your drink while you're gone. Oh, and Marion," I grabbed her arm, drawing her back so that she could hear me when I whispered. "I'll know if you touched yourself."

"Yes, sir."

I watched her walk away, admiring the tight fit of the white gown I'd selected for her to wear. It was a style she wasn't comfortable in, one that showed her curves and didn't allow much room for movement, but when I'd set it out for her, she'd put it on without batting an eye.

I loved that about her, that she would bend and yield to my every command.

But sometimes it wasn't enough. Sometimes I longed for the struggle, and though she'd give me that too, when I asked for it, it was never real. It was a game we played with very specific moves. She'd go against me on something with no meaning. I'd pretend to be angry. She'd pretend to beg for my forgiveness. I'd punish her. Then she'd go back to submitting to my every wish.

It had been satisfying for a while.

Lately, I yearned for it to be more authentic.

"Ten years and two kids, and she's still a perfect little doll. You lucked out with that one, didn't you?"

I looked over to see Roman had returned, another whiskey in his hand, still puffing his cigar.

"Yes, I suppose I did." No marriage was perfect, after all. No one person could ever be exactly what another needed. I should be satisfied with what I had.

And I was.

Mostly.

"You have the rings back now, I assume. Will you give them to your wife?"

I'd spent much of our friendship hunting down my parents' wedding rings. My cousin had kept them, claiming they'd been lost. After I'd bankrupted her and her husband, she'd pawned them. Then they'd been sold, even though I'd had a description of the items sent out to every pawn shop within a hundred miles. It had taken me years to track them down and had only just recently acquired them.

The relief I felt at having them in my possession was impossible to describe. It was akin to the way I used to feel when I was little, when my parents would stay out late, and I'd wait with the silly worries of a small child, afraid they wouldn't return and then finally my mother would slip into my room to place a kiss on my forehead, and the world would suddenly feel right again.

"I haven't decided yet. They would need to be resized."

"What does she want?"

"Marion doesn't seem to have a preference." *Whatever you think is best,* she'd said. "She's fine with what she's currently wearing. I'll likely save my parents' set for Hagan."

"Did you have to pay too high a price for them in the end?"

The new owners had been very reluctant to sell. They'd used them for their own marriage, so, of course, the rings had sentimental value.

I'd had to pay out more than I'd paid for Marion's three-carat princess cut. "It wasn't above my limits, though I shouldn't have had to pay at all."

"I didn't realize you had limits." Roman's smile was teasing, but his tone said differently.

I turned to face him straight on, but I couldn't think of a comeback. He had every right to suggest that I acted without restraint. I'd never shown him otherwise.

The question was out there now, though—*did* I have limits?

I wasn't sure that I did.

And that was terrifying.

"What about the pawn shop owner?" he asked.

I'd wanted to destroy him. I'd wanted to take his entire business down, wanted to ruin his reputation, wanted to make it impossible to work another day in his life. He'd ignored the requests I'd sent asking dealers to be on the lookout for the items. I'd promised a reward in exchange.

This particular owner must have thought one in the hand was worth more than two in the bush. He'd sold them for less than what I would have offered.

Roman had been the one to talk me down. He was just trying to make his living, he'd said. He hadn't intended malice on you directly.

"I didn't touch him." It had been hard, but I'd staved off the desire. For Roman.

He grinned, the smile reaching his eyes this time. "Ah, you *can* listen to reason. Good thing I was around."

But he wouldn't be for much longer. The truth sat heavy on me, a suffocating boulder on my chest.

And the other words unspoken between us: Who would reason with me when he was gone?

Roman was pulled away once again, a weepy niece this time with fond memories she insisted on sharing.

I was grateful she'd chosen to share them with him alone. I was already feeling overwhelmed with emotions, and the storm that had been brewing inside me was threatening to become a hurricane.

"Here you go." Marion returned to my side and discreetly slipped the drawstring bag with the butt plug into my pocket before taking her wine from my hand.

"Feeling better?"

"Feeling empty," she said, probably trying to soothe my obvious bad mood with the promise of dalliances to come. "Maybe we can—"

Whatever she'd come up with to distract me from my melancholy went unheard, when someone hurrying through the room bumped into her, sending her wine spilling.

She gasped, her eyes wide with horror as the red stained the front of her white Oscar de la Renta gown.

"What the hell?" I looked around for the offender and saw it was a waiter, rushing toward the kitchen. He hadn't even stopped.

I ran after him, irate. "Excuse me!"

"Edward, it's fine," Marion said, at my heels. "I'm sure it was an accident."

I stopped to level a glare at her. "Even if it was an accident he should have apologized."

It would have been a simple thing for her to stand her ground, to say it didn't really matter all that much, that it was just a dress and accidents happen.

That opinion was clearly written all over the lines of her face.

But when she opened her mouth to speak, she said, "Yes, sir. He should have."

Her refusal to push only fueled my indignation.

I spun in the direction of the kitchen and found the waiter as he was exiting, a tray of desserts on his shoulder.

"Excuse me," I said with gritted teeth. "Yes, you."

He was genuinely surprised at my aggressive tone. He truly was unaware of his careless behavior.

Well, I was here to enlighten him.

"You bulldozed your way through here moments ago and bumped into my wife, making her spill merlot all down her dress." I gestured toward Marion who still carried the empty glass, her skin and dress sticky with the wine.

The kid—he couldn't have been older than twenty-one—went nearly as red as the stain my wife wore. "I...I didn't realize. I'm so very sorry, sir."

"It's not me you should be apologizing to, it's my wife."

He shifted toward her, his posture bent with the full tray still on his shoulder. "I'm so sorry, ma'am. I guess I wasn't paying attention. Please give me the drycleaning bill. I'll take care of it."

"Marion?" I looked to her, giving her an opportunity

once again to let the boy off the hook.

Without giving him a second glance, she met my eyes. "Thank you, sir."

Jesus. Even now? Even in this moment she was still at it? Still playing the faithful sub?

"I'm not sure that will be enough," I said, flatly.

"Sir?" The color now drained from the waiter's face.

"I don't believe your apology is enough to mollify my wife. She may require more."

"Is there a problem over here?" Roman asked.

I hadn't noticed his approach. If I had, I might have backed down sooner, because I already knew he would step in when needed. He would reason and rein.

But would she?

It wasn't what she'd signed up for. She'd promised to stand by me, to honor and obey. She'd never promised to save me from myself.

He was here now, though, and I'd already started this, so might as well finish. "Yes, there's a problem. This irresponsible young man here plowed into Marion, spilling her wine all over her outfit, then ran off without even so much as an acknowledgment. He's offered to pay the drycleaning bill, but only after I tracked him down. And clearly this is stained. I highly doubt it can be removed and this is a designer gown."

Roman regarded us, taking in the ruined outfit, the boy's frightened expression, and my obvious rage. "I can have the amount for the dress taken from his wages."

"I doubt his wages could cover it." I stared directly at my wife as I spoke. "I think he should be fired."

Roman's eyes narrowed, but, perhaps realizing I had some point to prove, he didn't argue. "If you insist."

I didn't insist. I didn't *care*. It was a fucking dress, it was a fucking accident.

But the hurricane inside me had taken hold. My friend was dying, my sister was preoccupied, and I was out of control. My wife was the only one left, the only possible hope of bringing me back to a place of calm.

"Marion?" I asked, knowing it wasn't fair. Knowing no matter how she answered, she'd fail.

She didn't even glance at Roman. Didn't even pause to consider. "Whatever you think is best, sir," she said, surrendering to my wishes as beautifully as ever.

I pulled her in, kissing her more aggressively than was appropriate in front of company.

"Yes," I said when I broke away. "I insist. Fire him."

I could have kept going. I could have fired the entire crew, and still my rage would have barrelled on. Still, no one would have intervened. Roman was right—I had no limits. And Marion, the woman who counted on me to be her master, would stand by my side no matter what.

It was a frighteningly powerful realization—with my ambitious aims for revenge and ruin, there was no one to stop me but myself.

THIRTEEN
NOW: CELIA

I sat down at my vanity and switched my phone to speaker so that I could do something productive while my mother spilled her gossip.

Until I'd moved to London, I'd lived my whole life in close vicinity to her. We saw each other so often, the only thing to talk about was the goings-on of others. I'd thought with an ocean between us we'd share more of our own lives, that she'd tell me about herself. That she'd ask about what was happening with me.

Turned out that wasn't the case.

"You should have seen it, Ceeley. She had the tackiest hairpins, in the shape of bumble bees. She might have well been one of the children at the event instead of the organizer. It was so embarrassing. I refused to even let the paper take my picture with her."

"Good call," I said, setting the phone on the counter. I had no idea who she was talking about. I'd only been half listening, and as long as I made a comment or a sound every now and then, my mother wasn't any wiser.

As she started into another story, I opened the jar of my moisturizer and applied it over my face and neck. There was a reason why calling home first thing in the morning was a bad idea—it made for an awfully late start to my day. At least I hadn't planned to do any design work. Genevieve was graduating from university the next day, though, and we had a party planned afterward at the country house, a party I was completely in charge of.

Thank goodness for a competent staff. It meant I didn't have to do most of the heavy lifting. I wasn't even planning to go out to the house until the morning, but there were still a lot of details to oversee.

"Who else is there to tell you about? I know I'm missing something."

"Hmm," I said, as though I were trying to be helpful. I didn't care about anyone in her social circle. Not a one. The only person she could tell me about that interested me was Uncle Ron, and there was no way I was going to be the one to bring him up.

It had been three months since Camilla had met up with him at the Savoy, and while it hadn't been expected that he would reach out to her, there was always a hope that he might. The next step to the long game wasn't supposed to take place for another couple of months, when Camilla planned to invite him to Exceso. I'd wanted it to be sooner—now that I was part of the scheme, I was eager to get it going—but Edward felt we'd have a better chance at earning his trust if the "right" people were on the island when Ron was there. Apparently some men with questionable sexual interests would be visiting in the fall, so the invitation would be extended at the end of summer.

Still, I wished there was something that could be done now. Was he currently planning his own event? Would he be attending one soon? Those were the things I wished my mother might tell me. If we could find out about one of his soirees, we could skip the island all together and inform Edward's FBI friend of the gathering.

But my mother never had anything to say about my uncle at all. She didn't know much about what was happening in Ron's world, or she didn't find it interesting to share. Either way, he never came up, and it would be too suspicious for me to ask.

All I could do was continue to press my supposed animosity with Camilla and hope that she'd tell Ron, in case her relationship with me was an obstacle to trusting her.

"While you're thinking," I said, flipping the cap of my foundation open, "can I just vent for a minute? I've managed to avoid having to see Edward's sister for the last several months, but with Genny's graduation, I'm going to have to see her."

She picked up on the cue perfectly. "You're in charge of the seating at the dinner, correct? Make sure she's assigned a place far from you. And be sure to tell that husband of yours not to invite her to drive with you to the ceremony."

"Oh, good thought about separate cars." My mother was experienced with snubbing people. It was nice to know she was helpful in something. "Seating isn't going to matter. It's all stand-up buffet so people can mingle. That means she's easier to ignore, but also easier for her to infect others with her hateful ideas about my relationship with Edward. If I can keep her near me, however, she'll be a pain, but at least we can control the drama."

None of it was true, of course, and perhaps the drama was a little more than necessary, but since there might be photos released to the media, I wanted there to be an ex-

180 | LAURELIN PAIGE

planation of why Camilla was included front and center.

"That's really a shame. Circumstances are what they are, though. You'll have to play nice. It will be hard, but I raised you for just this kind of thing."

No shit, she had.

"Oh! I just remembered a bit of interesting news!" She spouted into some new scandal, and I went back to my face.

I finished applying my foundation and had picked up my bronzer brush, having tuned out, when something she said caught my attention. "Wait a second...say that again?"

"You know the Holcombs," she said, in a way that suggested she wasn't actually telling me what she'd said before but inferring what it was she thought I'd missed from her original story. "They've owned those stables near the country club for forever. John owns them now, or I guess he did own them. Malachi passed them on to him when he died. You might remember John. He's been working there in one form or another since you were a teenager."

Yes, I very much remembered John. He'd been in his late twenties, and I'd given my virginity to him when I'd still been underage.

The hair at the back of my neck stood up, my insides tightening with a knowing kind of dread. "What did you say happened to the stables, Mom?"

"They were repossessed by the bank. I'd thought the Holcombs owned them outright, but apparently they'd gotten another mortgage, and I don't know. They had some financial difficulties a few years back and must have gotten behind. I didn't realize they were still struggling."

I put down my makeup brush and picked up the phone, turning the speaker off. "You're saying that they lost the stables? That the bank foreclosed?" I had to be sure I had this right.

"Outrageous, isn't it? It seems they were in default and the bank was working with them, but then the title got sold to an investment company and they foreclosed. John and his family were living on the site. They had to move in with his little brother. Not sure what he's going to do now for work. Such a shame to no longer have those stables available. They were so close for families in the city. They're for sale now. Hopefully someone else will buy them and open them up for business again."

Yeah, that was the shame of the situation. That privileged rich folk no longer had a convenient place to keep their expensive thoroughbreds.

God, this was terrible.

Terrible because the situation was terrible, but also terrible because I had a deep-sinking feeling that Edward was involved. It couldn't be a coincidence, could it? He'd said he thought John deserved to be punished for having sex with a minor.

But I'd told him not to do anything. And he'd agreed.

Fuck.

Maybe I was wrong.

"Mom," I said, interrupting whatever she'd been saying. "Something's come up. I'm going to have to let you go. Talk soon."

I hung up without waiting for her to say goodbye.

Tying my robe around me as I stood up, I left our suite and went to my office space. It took a minute to find where I'd last put my laptop, but once I found it, I booted it up and did a search for stables for sale in that area of New York. It was easy enough to find the Holcombs'. There were only two other properties available, and the Holcombs' was the only one listed as having been foreclosed.

And right there, in the foreclosure information, the current owner was listed as EMF Enterprises.

EMF. Edward Michael Fasbender.

I wasn't familiar with the company, but there couldn't be any question about who owned them.

I printed the page and slammed my laptop shut. Party preparations be damned. My day's agenda had just changed.

I'd been to Edward's office on numerous occasions, but since the first time when I weaseled my way past security, none of those visits had been unannounced. Usually, when I was asked to present my pass, I was able to give my name and the security guard could check the list that had all of the day's approved visitors and see I was on it.

Today, Edward hadn't known I was coming, so I wasn't sure what would happen, if the guard would let me up or have to call for permission. Fortunately, it turned out I'd been put on the permanently approved list, which would have been satisfying to discover if I hadn't been so mad.

But I *was* mad. Fuming mad. Which was why I hadn't called ahead. I was the kind of mad that couldn't be put off or dealt with over the phone. I needed to see my husband in person.

Before the elevator doors opened on his floor, I took a

centering breath and threw my shoulders back. Edward's secretary wasn't fond of me, and I didn't have the patience for a battle with her today. Besides, I was saving all my energy for Edward.

Charlotte spotted me as soon as I got off the elevator, her eyebrows furrowed in confusion. She clicked a few keys on her computer as I approached her, likely checking to see if she'd missed my name on Edward's schedule.

I took advantage of her momentary distraction to plow right on past her. "I'm going in," I called over my shoulder. His door was open, which meant he wasn't with anyone, thankfully. I took care to slam it shut behind me before marching toward his desk.

He was on the phone and was undoubtedly surprised at my arrival, but he had practiced skill at containing his emotion, and he managed to keep a solemn face and steady tone as I approached him.

I slapped the printed paper from the real estate site on his desk in front of him. "You promised," I said, not caring that he was otherwise engaged or that my voice could likely be heard on the other end of his call.

He hadn't shown respect for me in this matter. Why should I show any for him?

Edward only had to glance at the paper to know what it was, a final confirmation that he was indeed behind the bank repossession of the stables. "I'm going to have to call you back," he said into the receiver then immediately hung up.

Before he could launch into denials or excuses, I attacked again. "You promised not to interfere, and then you went ahead and did this!" I pointed my finger forcefully at the proof.

He sat back in his chair, cool as a cucumber except for the darkness in his eyes. "I didn't promise."

"You did! You said…" I trailed off, trying to remember exactly what had transpired in our conversations. The last time we'd talked about it, we'd argued. The time before that, when we'd bathed, I'd asked him to promise not to strike out on my behalf…

And he'd changed the subject.

He read my realization in my features. "See? Never promised."

His juvenile behavior only fueled my anger. "Fuck you, Edward. This is bullshit. That man has a family! John Holcomb didn't do anything except succumb to the wiles of a horny young girl. He doesn't deserve to be punished."

He shrugged dismissively. "That's where we disagree."

God, his nonchalance was maddening.

And I was all anger and rage. I wanted to pound my fists against him. Wanted to bring out my claws.

I braced both of my hands against his desk so I wouldn't strike. "How is this justice? He doesn't even know what he's being punished for!"

"He committed a crime."

"And how many crimes have you committed?" I leaned toward him, daring him to name them, to recognize his hypocrisy.

He sat forward, his gaze piercing. "It's a dog eat dog world, Celia. I'm on top for a reason."

He didn't care. He knew he was a hypocrite, and he didn't even care.

"You are narcissistic and self-righteous," I seethed. A

devastatingly attractive devil who cared first and foremost for himself. Was his heart even attainable? I was insane to ever believe it might be mine.

"Narcissistic and self-righteous? To want to stand up for my wife?" His tone had an edge now, his composure slipping.

Somehow that felt like progress.

"I didn't ask you to. In fact, I expressly asked you not to." I searched his features to see if I'd gotten through to him at all. But the expression etched there was as determined and unyielding as ever.

I shook my head, mystified, and stepped away from his desk, suddenly feeling like I needed the space between us, as though my bewilderment needed room. "You know what I don't understand, Edward, is why. Why did this insignificant stablehand mean anything to you? Was it jealousy?"

"You can't seriously need me to explain this to you."

I studied his smug expression, trying to figure out what I wasn't getting, and finding nothing but this answer. Why else did he care enough to invest the energy to go after a nobody in the suburbs of New York? "That's the only reason I can come up with. You're so possessive and entitled that you can't stand that another man was the first to fuck me, is that it?"

God, if that was really what this was about...

A horrifying thought occurred to me. "Was that why you recreated that whole 'pretend-you're-a-virgin' night?"

Edward shot up from his chair and leveled a stern glare in my direction. "You're trying me now, Celia."

He'd reacted too quickly, too defensively. Had I hit the

nail on the head?

It hurt, but I explored the idea further. "It had nothing to do with making my memories better for me. It was all about you claiming a part of me that didn't belong to you."

He stepped out from behind his desk, and, automatically, I took a step back.

He stopped and pinned me in place instead with his gaze. "That wasn't the reason I did that, and you fucking know it."

"Do I?" I searched my feelings, and yes, in my gut, I did know that. He'd done what he'd done because he'd wanted to erase the bad and replace it with his good. He may have had personal reasons for doing it—he did enjoy breaking people down, after all—but he could have left me like that, broken and ruined, and he hadn't.

He took advantage of my pause, traveling several steps in my direction before I noticed. When I did, I put my hand up, as if to stop him. "If not that, then *why*? Why are you obsessed with being a vigilante with people in my past? It's over and done. I've moved on. You forced me to move on."

"And this is the next step in your healing process." With confident caution, as though he were a lion trying to coax his scared prey, he took another step toward me so that my palm was almost touching his chest.

He was magnificent like that, when he was a predator. When he was single-minded and primitive. When it felt like he could devour me with a single bite.

Even angry, I was strongly aware of my heartbeat. It quickened when he was like this. Tripped over itself with anticipation.

"How the hell is this healing?" I asked, dropping my

hand and shaking my head of the wanton thoughts. "It's unproductive. It's petty."

His jaw set firmly. "It isn't unproductive at all. Nor is it petty. Taking out your anger on someone who deserves it is a very useful coping method."

"This isn't coping. *You* aren't coping. You're just as fucked up as I ever was." I threw up my hands, frustration agitating me so completely I couldn't stay still.

"Because I still have not got the vengeance I need to move on." He leaned forward as he prowled toward me.

I hadn't realized I'd backed up with him until my legs hit the couch, bending me over the backside. Immediately, I straightened, determined not to bow in his wind. "Oh, is that how it works? Anytime you're mad, anytime you feel slighted, you have to strike back in order to get past it?"

"Why not?" He was feral, his eyes dilated, his lip curled.

Ugh, he was so attractive. And so arrogant. And such an asshole.

What kind of world did he think we lived in? How would anyone be civilized if they were constantly lashing out at every insult? Was that how he expected me to be with everyone? With *him*?

"How about this?" I asked, my breaths coming out hard and shallow. "I'm angry at you right now."

I hadn't meant it as a challenge, or maybe I had. Either way, that's how he took it, and one beat later, his arms were around me, his face angled above me. "Good," he said, his lips whispering over my lips. "Then it won't just be me who's taking out my wrath on you."

His mouth crashed against mine, and he kissed me

with a forceful and tempestuous kiss. He was greedy and aggressive, his tongue possessing my mouth, the length of him pressing tightly against me so that every inch of my body met with firm, hard Edward Fasbender. It was difficult to think when he invaded me like that. Difficult to remember that I was anything besides blood and lust and hormones, that I was a person who could think for myself rather than just bend and submit.

Difficult, but not impossible.

I wrestled my mouth free and leaned away.

He raised a brow, as though daring me to defy him, and so I did. I raised my palm to push him away, but he grabbed my arm and wrenched it behind my back, which for some stupid reason made my pussy throb.

I brought my free hand up, not even sure what I meant to do with it, but he caught it in midair.

"No?" he asked, his eyes dark, the blue rims like thin rings around a planet of black.

No, of course no.

But my body said differently. My back arched toward him, my skin flushed, my skin broke out in goosebumps.

And when he shifted to grip my wrists with just one hand and the other ventured under my skirt to rub against the crotch panel of my panties, he found them wet.

"Tell me to stop, and I'll stop," he said, his fingers working beneath my material.

I gasped as his skin made contact with mine, and though I hadn't yet decided that I wanted this, my legs widened to give him room.

"You don't want me to stop, do you?" He traced along my wet seam. "You want to want to, but you don't actually."

"If you're talking about the shit you pulled on John, you're wrong. I do want you to stop."

"I'm talking about ruling you. You wish that you didn't love it. You wish that you didn't need it."

I wanted to argue, but just then, he shoved two long fingers inside me, and even if his thrusts hadn't taken my voice away, I wouldn't have told him to stop.

Because he was right. I did love it. I did need it.

I tilted my chin up, my mouth reaching for his.

Again, our lips collided. This kiss was bold and ruthless, his fingers mirroring the fervor as they fucked in and out of me with shameless strokes, until I was writhing, until I was a rush of heat and euphoria, until he'd swallowed every last one of my whimpers of pleasure.

Then we were a flurry of movement, both of us desperate to be connected, to remove anything that stood in the way. My panties were pulled off and tossed to the floor, his jacket joined soon after. His pants were unbuckled and undone and pushed down just far enough to get his cock out. My skirt was pushed up and when I threw my arms around his neck, he lifted me, setting me down on the back of the sofa.

As he lined himself up at my entrance, I silently congratulated myself for having chosen a low-back couch when I'd redesigned his office before we'd gotten married, and then he was there, inside me, pushing so deeply into my body that I felt more than penetrated. I felt conquered. I felt owned.

I let my dangling shoe fall off, then bent my knee and brought my foot up to rest on the back beside me, opening myself wider to him, giving him more access. With one arm wrapped firmly around my waist to hold me up, he rammed into me, over and over at a dizzying speed. His pelvis hit against my clit, sending delightful shocks through my body that had me gasping in rhythm to his jabs.

I was already halfway to an orgasm, already too blissed out to form words when he started talking.

"You want to know why?" His voice was strained, but he could still speak coherently.

I could barely remember my name, let alone form an answer, especially not to a question that I didn't fully understand.

Thankfully, he clarified. "You want to know why this man? Why righting this wrong was important to me?"

He didn't expect me to respond. It was obvious when he cupped his hand around my neck, his thumb stretching across my pulse point, pressing just enough to make speech difficult.

No, he didn't need me to say anything.

He needed me to listen.

"Because I love you, bird," he said, his thrusts somehow reaching even deeper. "I fucking love you so much that I can't separate myself from you anymore. Your pains are my pains. I feel them as if they happened to me, and I can't let them go unpunished, not because I care about how much these sins hurt me, but because I understand how much they hurt you."

Exhilaration shuddered through me, and my pussy tightened around him. He lowered his arm from my waist to my hips, drawing me closer, refusing to let my body push him out.

He pressed his forehead against mine. "You are mine to care for and protect and fight for. You gave that honor to me. Let me own that. Let me love you right."

I was overtaken with rapture, rapture that exploded from my center, up through my belly and my chest until it was everywhere in my body, until I was shaking and sobbing and moaning out Edward's name. Until I was shattered by the euphoria. Until I was nothing but blissful radiating energy.

And then immediately, as the spots before my eyes disappeared, while he was still plunging into me, chasing his own release, my thoughts cleared and awareness seeped in.

This had been a valid argument, a subject that we clearly needed to resolve, and instead of fighting it to the end, I'd let him distract me with sex.

Again.

If this was how every disagreement was going to end up, I was literally fucked.

Which meant I had to find another way to fight.

But how could I fight him on this? When he truly believed that he was right. When he wouldn't listen to reason.

When he was this obsessed with his end goal.

My husband was like an addict, addicted to the rush of dispensing retribution. He said he sought justice, but his motives were wrong. Justice was best doled out with impartiality. There shouldn't be emotions involved, and he was completely wrapped up in his feelings. That made him dangerous. How far had he gone? How far would he go?

How far would I let him go?

A voice of reason chirped in the back of my head, warning me to walk away. Take what he'd given me, the new person that I was, and leave. Find a better way in the world without him.

But I fucking loved him too.

And I was selfish with that love. With *his* love. I wanted to be cared for and protected and fought for. No one had taken that role before. Hudson had come the closest, teaching me how to be what I'd thought I needed to be to survive. Edward had been and done so much more, and I didn't know how to give it up.

If he *was* addicted to vengeance, I was addicted to him. Walking away was not an option I could choose easily. I had to stay. I wanted to stay.

But that didn't mean I had to give in.

He wanted my submission, and I could give him that to an extent. I could still push back when I needed to. I could stand up for what I believed was right. I could fight for my own wants.

Yes, that's what I'd do.

If this marriage had any chance at all, it was time I made my own demands.

FOURTEEN

EDWARD

I tucked myself inside my pants and glanced over at my wife as she straightened her skirt. "Nice outfit. I'd rather it was the dress I picked out, but this one proved easy to work around."

Honestly, I didn't care what she was wearing at the moment. She was ruffled and flushed from fucking, and, as far as I was concerned, she'd never been more beautiful.

She bent to retrieve her underwear. "I was making a statement."

Her voice was terse. Apparently the physical activity had done little to alleviate her rancor. It had sure helped relieve mine.

Not that her ire wasn't justified. I would have expected her to be angry about my actions with the Holcomb estate. I just had never expected her to find out.

There was nothing to do now but tread lightly. "Message received," I said, an attempt to smooth her feathers.

She paused, her pants halfway up one leg. "Was it?"

This wasn't going to be as easy as I'd hoped. Dealing with her was certainly different than dealing with Marion. When she protested to something I'd done, she most often didn't voice it, and on the rare occasion that she did, she was generally soothed with domination and a round of rough sex.

My old tactics weren't going to work, and I had yet to figure out what would.

I sighed, sitting on the arm of one of the chairs she'd chosen for my office. "I am who I am, Celia. You might not have known who that was when you married me, but you certainly have learned since then. You chose to stay."

Her rigid stance eased. She finished dressing then came around the couch to face me. "You're right. I did. I didn't expect that you'd change, but I also didn't expect you'd be completely unreasonable. Marriage is supposed to be about compromise."

"You've been married before, then?" It was a knee-jerk reaction. Definitely a dick statement.

"I've never been divorced," she countered.

I couldn't hold back a smile at that. "Touché."

Perhaps neither of us were an expert in marriage, but I had both success and experience in business and negotiation. She and I had negotiated our partnership. We had our roles.

I stood to retrieve my jacket that had ended up on the floor in our earlier haste. "It certainly would be easier to navigate this relationship if you would just submit to my authority, like you agreed that you would."

"You knew who I was when you married me. You chose to stay." She was infuriatingly smug, having thrown my own words back at me.

"I thought I'd broken you down after that."

"I agreed to elements of submission. I never said I'd be docile." Her brow creased, and her voice softened. "Is that really what you want from me?"

I already knew the answer, but I thought about it for a moment anyway, remembering what life had been like with Marion, how unfulfilling her obedience became over time.

"No," I said, as I buttoned my jacket. "I much prefer you like this." Challenging, perhaps, but never boring.

She crossed to me. "This isn't fair either, though," she said, straightening my tie. "You like me to fight you because it turns you on, or whatever, but you still expect to always win. I'm only supposed to think I have a chance at getting what I want. Eventually, I'm going to realize it's futile, and I'll…" Her palm smoothed down my chest, pausing above my heart, which pounded against my rib cage, anxious about where her train of thought had been headed.

"You'll…what? You'll leave?"

She shook her head and smiled. "I was going to say I'd stop fighting. Because what would be the point?"

I wasn't sure that would be any better than her leaving.

"I don't always expect to win," I said, taking her hands in mine.

"Really? Tell me one time that you haven't." I hadn't gone after her mystery partner in crime, but I wasn't writing that off as a battle lost yet. When I couldn't come up with any other response, she pulled away. "One time, Edward."

This was ridiculous. Of course I didn't always win. Because I couldn't think of any instance that I hadn't didn't mean that it had never happened. It simply meant I wasn't holding a grudge about it.

I circled around behind my desk and looked at her, still staring at me waiting for an answer. "You're wearing the wrong dress," I said, suddenly. "And I haven't even hinted at a punishment."

"That's not going to cut it. I need to be given wins about things that matter."

"You're working now." I unbuttoned my jacket and sat down, relieved that I'd been able to come up with something meaningful.

Except, once again she shook her head. "Not because I asked to. *You* decided I'd work. You oversee my clientele and how much time I put into it."

"I haven't gone after your father."

"You're going after his brother. I'm not sure that isn't the same thing."

I ran my fingers over my forehead, feeling the beginnings of a headache. "Fine. You want to win sometimes. I hear you. I'll make an effort in the future to be more conscientious of not dominating every aspect of our lives."

"Nope. That's not enough. I want some things now. I deserve some things now, especially after the bullshit you pulled, going behind my back like this with John."

"I should have known you already had something in mind. Go ahead. Let me hear it."

I gestured for her to take a seat, but instead of sitting in the chair in front of me, she came around to my side and perched on the corner of my desk.

I swiveled my chair to better face her. I wasn't sure I

liked her there, sitting over me like that. It felt like the balance of power had shifted, and that made me uneasy.

"First," she began, and I definitely didn't like that there was a "first," suggesting that a list was about to follow. "I want you to pull the sale of the stables and offer them back to John. He was behind on his mortgage, I know. Go back and work out something he can manage."

"I can't do that."

"You can't? Or you won't?"

I considered. "To be honest, a bit of both."

"I understand that you have some deep need to do these things you do, Edward, that seeking vengeance fulfills something in you that nothing else can. Well, you got your vengeance in this situation. Vengeance that I consider to be completely out of line, but it's done. Now you can move on. Which means you shouldn't have any lingering emotional attachment to getting the stables back to John."

It wasn't that simple. As though I could trick my brain into not realizing that a settled matter was being unsettled.

But there was merit to her argument. I'd played it out. I should feel satisfied. It should be enough to be able to move past it.

If it wasn't enough, what would be? Would I still be unfulfilled after Ron?

I ignored that thought and concentrated on the practicalities. "Look, business doesn't work like that. I bought out the Holcombs' existing bank note, but I never planned to continue to carry it. That hasn't been budgeted for."

"Then I'll pay you what he's behind. I have money."

"It's a good chunk of money."

"Then I'll sell some of my Werner shares. They are in

my name now."

My jaw tightened. "You definitely won't do that."

"You'll get John back his stables, or I will do that." She folded her arms across her chest with stubborn determination.

It ignited something primal in me. Something that made me want to roar and take her down. Make her surrender. Make her yield.

She was right—I did always have to win.

Old tactics aren't going to work.

She had me. Much as it hurt to do so, I had to give her this. *Zugzwang* was the term for it in chess, when a player was forced to make a move that put him at a disadvantage. I was extremely good at putting others in that position. I didn't like it so much being on the other side.

I leaned back in my chair and lifted my ankle to rest on my opposite knee. "Look at you, getting better at chess all the time. I'll speak to my loan officer and work out something by the end of the week."

"Thank you."

The satisfied gleam in her eyes made my chest warm. Losing didn't have to be so bad, I supposed. "Feel better?"

"Yes, but that wasn't really a victory. That was righting a wrong. Even though everything will work out for John in the end, I'm sure you caused him a lot of stress in the meantime. Not to mention public scandal."

So that was how she'd caught on. Her mother must have included his woes in her latest round of gossip.

"It still feels like a loss to me."

She shrugged and stood. "That's the recipe for a perfect

compromise. Neither party walks away feeling satisfied."

"If that's what marriage is supposed to be, I'm glad I've been doing it wrong."

"I'm sure you are. Not so fun when you have to be a team player, is it?" Finally, she circled around and sat in the chair in front of me.

"What else? I know you have something more." I had a feeling this wasn't going to be as easy of a loss to take.

"I do." She straightened her back, as if gathering courage. "I want a baby."

"Absolutely not." There were other ways she could win. I'd give her the moon. I'd give her a million different things. This would not be one of them.

She didn't cower, though, as she usually did when the subject was broached, and I cut it off. "No, you don't get to decide, and that's it. This isn't a dictatorship. You have set the foundations for every part of this relationship, and, in the end, I have bent to your will, each and every time, whether I wanted to or not. Now I'm putting my foot down. I'm telling you what I need, and what I need is a baby."

It was strange how her request pulled at something in me, deep and buried. Some lizard part of my brain that was programmed to spread his seed, ignited. Wanted to stand on the desk and pound my chest and ravage her again with the intent to impregnate her right that minute.

Fortunately, I was a civilized man, and the more civilized parts of my brain could overrule the caveman with saner rationale. I'd already had my children. I'd been a mediocre father at best. There was no wisdom in putting another child through that, and frankly, I had no desire to battle with the constant pressure associated with parenting.

The answer had to be no.

"I *don't* need a baby, Celia. In fact, I very much need to *not* have a baby. I understand your desire to have a win, but it can't be at the cost of my needs."

Her lips turned downward. "That's funny. You don't seem to consider my needs when you make any of your decisions."

I put my leg down and leaned forward. "That's practically all I consider anymore. All the time. What's best for you in every situation. You still may not see it, but going after John Holcomb was for *you*."

I'd never been like this with Marion. Everything was always about me. I was the self-centered star of the universe. With Celia, even my need to ruin the man who had destroyed my father was outweighed by the need to destroy the man who had destroyed *her*. She might not have expected me to change when she married me, but I had, maybe not for the better, but for her.

And she didn't see it. "I know you think it was for me, that you've convinced yourself it was, but when you outright ignore my wishes, you are not actually acting in my best interest. I am a fully capable human being. I may like being pampered and cared for, and I may kind of love it when you make decisions for me, but I am not incompetent. When I feel strongly enough to make a stand, that should matter."

She was passionate, but the anger from earlier had dissipated. It made it easier to listen, and, because I knew she was really making an effort, I tried harder to hear her.

"I am well aware of your capabilities," I said, recognizing she needed me to acknowledge her competence. "You are very intelligent and quick-witted and resourceful, as well as independent. I don't desire to take care of you because I don't think you can't take care of yourself. It's because I long to take that burden from you."

"And I love that about you."

"Capable as you are, however, sometimes your scope of vision is limited."

"And, sometimes, so is yours!" she exclaimed, with evident frustration. "You know what a loss I felt when I had my miscarriage. You know how it was devastating enough to send me to dark places, how it made me do bad things. It seems fairly obvious that having a baby would do the exact opposite. It would bring me to good places and good things. You say that you love me and that you want to care and provide for me above all else. If giving me this one thing that I truly want isn't part of that, then it's kind of hard to believe that you really feel the way you say you do."

"You know how I feel." My tone was as raw as my insides. "You *know*."

"And now you know how I feel."

We sat in silence for several heavy seconds, our gazes locked. I wasn't a man who gave in. I wasn't a man who resigned. I wasn't a man who didn't win.

And that's who she claimed she needed me to be now. Someone who I wasn't.

I took in a deep breath and let it out. "Is this going to be a deal-breaker if I refuse?"

I could hear my heart thumping in my chest, could feel the milliseconds crawl in her pause as if they were hours.

"It might be," she said after what felt like an eternity.

My chest tightened, like it were being squeezed together with a vice-grip. I'd never understood the saying about losing a battle to win the war in quite the way I did at this moment. Fucking zugzwang.

"Come here." I opened my arms, needing them to no longer be empty. Needing them filled with her.

She sank into my lap and clutched onto me as though she felt the same.

I buried my head in her hair, inhaling the scent of her shampoo before kissing her temple. "I don't want to lose you, bird."

"Then don't."

Anxiety about the prospect of her leaving morphed into concern about the thing she needed in order to stay. "I can't be the father I was before. I was distracted and unavailable."

"You won't be."

Fuck, was I really considering this? Was I really agreeing?

Concern rose to borderline panic. My mind fought to order it, to give the crazy idea structure.

I pulled back so I could see her. "I need to make sure that I'm able to focus this time. I need to wrap up these... outstanding debts, so to say. Ron, specifically. It may be another year or so. Can you wait that long?"

She searched my face, bringing her hand to cup my cheek. "Are you saying yes, then?"

It was hard to get a deep breath, but I tried. "If you can wait."

"I want you to be able to focus on us, too, and I know how important finishing up these plans are to you. You've been working toward this for a long time, and I wouldn't dream of interfering with that. So, yes. I can wait. Not forever, but a year or so isn't that bad. Gives us more time to be ready."

"All right." It still felt hard to breathe. "All right," I said again. For her. I could do this for her.

I kissed her, sealing the deal.

But as sweet as her lips were, my mind couldn't stop spinning. A hundred possible addendums fought for my attention. Only one made its way through the fog.

"One more thing," I said, breaking away suddenly. This was important. "Besides Ron, I need to go after A."

Her body went stiff as she pulled back. "No. I said no, Edward, and I meant it. I still mean it."

"He deserves to pay retribution even more than John Holcomb. You can't let that go."

"Actually, I can."

"*I* can't," I said, more firmly. "You said you understood my need to do this."

"I said I understand that you have the need, not that I understand the need itself. And I will support you as best as I can with it, but this man has nothing to do with you. He has nothing to do with *us*. And there has to be a limit somewhere, Edward. I will support you, but I won't enable you, and going after A is going too far."

How long had I yearned for someone to give me these boundaries? It had seemed like forever since Roman had died. Since someone cared enough, was strong enough to insist that I needed to stop.

But I was like a heroin addict who needed one last fix before going to rehab. "*He* would be the limit. *That* would be the end. Ron, the men associated with him, and A." She moved as though she wanted out of my arms, but I only tightened my grip. "And then you get your baby, bird."

204 | LAURELIN PAIGE

Her expression remained steadfast. She opened her mouth, but before she could speak, Charlotte's voice came through the intercom.

"Mr. Fasbender, sorry to interrupt you, but you have yet another unannounced visitor."

She enunciated the "unannounced visitor," an obvious jab at Celia's surprise visit.

As disruptive as her arrival had been, I didn't appreciate Charlotte having an opinion about when Celia showed up. "Tell whoever it is to make an appointment, like everyone who isn't my wife is supposed to do."

"That's just it, sir," she said, and already dread was filling in my stomach. "She isn't everyone else. It's Marion."

FIFTEEN
CELIA

My mouth went dry, and even though I was still sitting securely in Edward's arms, the room started to sway. I'd expected to meet Marion the next day, at Genny's graduation. I hadn't expected to come face to face with her here, in Edward's office, without the formalities of the event to hide behind.

And, especially, after the conversation we'd just had and the tense way it had ended, I wasn't ready for this.

I wasn't ready for this at all.

Edward looked just as taken aback, but his surprise was only momentary. Then his features smoothed, and his expression turned stoic. "Give us a few minutes," he told Charlotte, before clicking off the intercom.

He stood, taking me with him, then set me aside as though I were something inanimate that had been on his lap rather than his wife. He turned to glance in the mirror behind his desk, and adjusted his dress shirt and tie before running his hand over his mouth and beard, removing the bit of gloss I'd left on his lips.

"Edward..." There were so many things I wanted to say, wanted to ask. *What is she doing here? Were you ex-pecting her? Why are you primping for your ex-wife?*

The most pressing issue at the moment, however, was my own appearance. We'd fucked and we'd fought, and I was doubtful I looked anything what I'd like to look like when meeting the woman who my husband might very well still be in love with.

"I can't..." I searched the room, as if somehow a secret escape door would pop up.

His forehead pinched, and he stared at me, stared *through* me, as though he'd forgotten I was there. Then he shook his head, and his eyes cleared. "You can clean up in my en-suite."

It was what I needed, but it wasn't reassuring. Reassuring would have been, *You look perfect, just the way you are.* Reassuring would have been, *I'll get rid of her.* Reassuring would have been, *You're the one I want, only you.*

Instead, he'd sent me on my way, then instantly turned his attention from me to his phone. He picked up the receiver and dialed three numbers, obviously an inter-office call. "I need you to do something," he said to whoever was on the other line. "Come to my office and interrupt me in ten minutes. Remind me that someone's waiting for me in the conference room."

He didn't want to spend time with her any more than I did.

That, at least, made me feel better enough to grab my purse and make my way across to the bathroom that was tucked into a nook at the opposite end of the office. Once inside, I shut the door and pressed my back to it, trying to catch my breath.

This wasn't a big deal, I told myself.

They'd been divorced for ten years. Even if Edward had still had feelings for her when she'd left, he had to have gotten over her by now. There was no way he could have been harboring a broken heart all that time.

Right?

Whatever the answer, it didn't change the situation. Forcing myself to focus, I went to the sink and fixed my face and hair as best I could in the mirror there. I applied my lipstick then threw it in my bag, my eyes pausing on the stack of washcloths on the counter. I'd just been fucked and should probably clean between my legs.

But I was jealous and petty and the notion that Marion might be able to smell sex on me was pretty damn satisfying. So I skipped that bit of freshening, took a deep breath, then put on my best fake smile.

Showtime.

I opened the door and immediately froze when I heard voices. I'd expected Edward to wait for me to invite Marion in, for some reason, but he hadn't.

"...thought we might do best to see each other privately before tomorrow," Marion said, her slight French accent giving her away.

"I'm not sure why you thought that was necessary."

"We've seen each other so few times since the divorce." Her voice was tentative and demure. "And after the last time…"

"That was a mistake," Edward said sharply, and my stomach dropped.

What had happened? *What* was a mistake?

"Which is exactly why I thought we should talk. I'm

sorry if I assumed incorrectly, sir."

I had to brace my hand against the wall to steady myself. I'd known she was submissive, that she'd been submissive to Edward, but he'd told me so little about their relationship and I hadn't been able to picture what it must have been like.

Now, I could envision more than I wanted to. Enough to make me sick with envy. I hadn't even officially met her yet, and I already knew she was so much better for him than I ever could be.

Tears threatened at the corners of my eyes.

It felt like forever before Edward responded. When he did, his words were warm but firm. "I am not your sir, Marion. Not anymore."

That felt as good of a cue as any. Blinking back the urge to cry, I came around the corner of the nook with gusto.

Both Edward and Marion turned toward me at my entrance. They stood several feet apart from each other, and while I was glad for that, I was disappointed that I couldn't look at both of them at once.

I chose to focus on her. She was notably surprised they weren't alone, but she covered quickly, and when she did, it was impossible not to stare. She was beguiling with her dark hair, her olive skin, her bright eyes. Much more beau-tiful than I'd gleaned from her pictures. They hadn't been able to capture her presence, which was breathtaking in its unpretentiousness.

It was terrible how strong the urge was to claw her eyes out.

Maybe I hadn't changed as a person after all.

"Marion, this is Celia," Edward said. "My wife." My

jaw tightened at the way he'd amended my title, as though it were an afterthought. "Celia, this is Marion."

I crossed the room to stand next to him, hoping he'd put an arm around me or take my hand. Something to claim me as his.

But his hands remained at his sides.

"Yes, I'd heard you'd remarried." Her eyes darted from Edward toward me, then back to him, as though she were seeking his permission to look somewhere other than at him.

Only then did he put his hand at the small of my back, automatically almost, as though sensing what she needed from him.

"It's a pleasure to meet you," she said, her gaze firmly on mine now. "I have heard good things of you from my children."

I wondered exactly what they'd said. I'd become a little closer to them over the past six months, but before that, I'd spent the entire first year of my marriage to their father on an island in the Caribbean. I could only imagine the awful impression it had given them, let alone their mother.

"Likewise," I said. I could feel an old familiar mask falling into place. One that I hadn't worn in a while but had once been second nature. "I must say, though, they never told me how beautiful you are. I see where Genny gets it."

She flushed, seemingly thrown by my compliment, which had been the intention. She was gorgeous, but she was also a decade older than I was. There was likely some insecurity about her ex having married younger, whether she admitted it to herself or not.

"Merci beaucoup," she said, flustered. "But I can say the same for you. Edward has chosen well for himself."

Edward's hand fell from my back, and with it, Marion's gaze fell from mine.

"I must admit," she continued, looking at him. "I'm surprised to find he married a Werner."

My stomach clenched. Of course she would have known about his having it out for my father. It hadn't occurred to me until just then. She might even think our marriage was part of his revenge schemes. Which, it had been, but not now. I couldn't stand the idea of her thinking we weren't real. But how the hell could I correct it?

I glanced toward Edward, hoping he'd step in.

"Well...yes," he said returning her gaze. "That's a complicated story, actually. Too long to get into at the moment."

Was it really? I was sure it could have been simplified if he tried.

"Ah, well. Another time, then." Marion's smile was small but sweet. I would have pushed him for more info right then. I was too curious about shit like that to let it slide.

Her eyes said she might be curious as well, but she didn't press. She was so serene. So demure.

And he'd loved her.

Why the hell had he ever stayed married to me?

An awkward beat past, long enough to make me too unsettled to stay silent or behaved. "So Marion," I said, threading my arm around Edward's. "What brings you by the office today? I thought you'd be staying closer to Genevieve. I didn't expect to see you in London."

She went pale, her mouth falling slack.

"Marion was in town to see friends. She stopped by to see if there was anything last minute she could help with before she headed up to Cambridge." He patted my hand. "I assured her you had everything taken care of."

I wanted to kick him for stepping in for her. Then I wanted to kick myself for being so bothered by it.

"Exactly that," she confirmed, obviously grateful for the excuse. "I didn't feel comfortable just stopping by your house since you and I had never met. And I was in the neighborhood, so I thought why not. Thankfully, my name was still on the security list here, and I was able to come up."

Dizziness swept through me again, making me glad that I had Edward to clutch onto. Her name was still on the security list. Sure, it could have been an oversight, but after ten fucking years? Edward wasn't the type of man to overlook those things, and I highly doubted he tolerated employees who did either.

If her name was on there, it was because he wanted it to be. Because he wanted her to stop by. Because he hoped.

I couldn't decide if I were more jealous or hurt. The emotions felt too similar, and both felt like shit.

I smooshed the feelings down, way down inside and put the mask back on. "That was so nice of you to offer. Everything's handled, though. Since I have a job as well as a house to run, I made sure to delegate those tasks early on. I find it's the only way to balance it all."

Edward stiffened beside me.

Sure, it was catty. Marion had only ever been a house-wife, a job that I admitted was incredibly difficult, but she had also had a full staff to assist her, and I was desperate to make myself feel better, *seem* better, in whatever way I could.

"That's very wise. It was especially hard when the

children were little. Nothing got done around the house without delegation."

Unlike when I'd spoken, there was no spitefulness in Marion's tone. She was just being honest, and that hurt somehow more than if she'd been malicious. She was the mother of Edward's children, and that was something I was not. While he'd agreed to having one with me, his last addendum was a no-go for me. I wouldn't give him Hudson's name. Not for a baby. Not for anything.

And since I'd yet to find something Edward truly yielded to, there was a chance I'd never have his child.

Standing in front of Marion, it was an even more bitter pill to swallow.

Thankfully, the office door swung open, and Camilla peeked in. "Eddie, Barry is waiting for you in conference room three."

"Thank you, Camilla. I'd lost track of time." Edward stepped away from me, moving around his desk and straightening it as I'm sure he always did before he left his office.

Camilla's brows lifted in surprise when she saw who else was in the room. "Marion! I didn't know you'd arrived yet. How are you?"

Of course Camilla and Marion would have had a good relationship. Fuck me with a side of ranch. Could this situation get any more mortifying?

I tuned out their reunion and focused on Edward. He was as unreadable as ever, his jaw hard, his expression guarded.

I wished I could get inside his head. Even more, I wished he was inside mine, wished that he saw how I was hurting. Wished he would say what I needed to hear to make it better. I didn't know what that was, but he should know. He usually did.

But he wasn't aware of me at all. He busied himself with his desk, then, once satisfied, he nodded toward the door, silently ushering all of us out.

I lingered and ended up being the last one out, following even him, which meant I had a bird's-eye view of his hand resting at Marion's back as he escorted her out. It was probably automatic. He likely didn't even realize he'd done it.

That didn't lessen the sting.

"Sorry to cut this short," he said to her. "There's even more to do today than usual since I'm taking tomorrow off."

"An empire doesn't run itself," Marion said in a tone that suggested she was merely repeating something that he'd said to her before.

"No, it never has." He glanced down at his hand on her back then quickly dropped it, as though he'd only then realized it was there. "See you tomorrow."

Then he went down the hallway leading away from the elevators toward the conference room. He walked three steps then, just when I was convinced he'd forgotten me altogether, he turned around.

"Oh, Charlotte. Can you please call for Celia's car?"

Maybe I should have been glad he was taking care of me, the way he said he always would.

It wasn't close to being enough.

But then he turned to me. "Celia," he said, his voice summoning.

I was in his arms instantly, relief flooding over me as

214 | LAURELIN PAIGE

his warmth surrounded me. I was overthinking all of this. I was over-*feeling* it. As usual. He'd probably call me out on it later, when we were alone. He'd remind me that I was the one he loved then, when it was just the two of us. When it mattered.

He kissed me chastely on the cheek then tilted up my chin so he could look at me. "I know what that was back there," he said softly. "You're past catty behavior, and I most certainly won't tolerate it in my wife."

Adrenaline rushed through my body, a combination of rage and heartbreak.

To anyone else, it would look like he was simply telling me goodbye, not reprimanding me like I was a child. Like I was his doormat. Like I was Marion.

I had a feeling that was how he'd behaved with her all the time when they'd been married. She'd probably liked it.

I, however, did not.

Especially when what I needed was reassurance of his love. Not reassurance of his ownership.

But we were on display, and I had as much reason as he did, if not more, to want Marion to believe we were as happy in our relationship as they'd ever been.

So I cupped his cheek and made sure to smile when I whispered my reply. "Then perhaps you should exchange your current wife for an older model."

More loudly I said, "See you tonight." To remind Marion that I was the one he was going home to. Because *I* was his wife, and I *was* that catty.

Before he could say anything else, I pulled away and crossed to the women, leaving him to go to his pretend meeting. I didn't know if he lingered in the hall. I didn't look back.

The elevator had arrived by the time I reached the others.

"Marion and I are going to grab some coffee and catch up in the downstairs cafe, if you'd like to join us," Camilla said as we walked into the elevator.

"No, thank you. I have to be getting back." There was no way I could stomach sitting with the two of them feeling like a third wheel.

Though, if Marion was staying in the building, there was a chance she might see Edward again. He'd clearly been the one to get out of visiting with her, which meant I shouldn't worry, but maybe that had been because he hadn't wanted to be with her *and me.*

I almost told her I'd changed my mind.

But if Edward wanted to see Marion alone, he'd see her alone eventually. Me hanging around trying to prevent it wasn't going to change anything.

Camilla and Marion continued to chat as we rode down. I pulled out my phone, just to have something to busy myself with so I wouldn't have to talk with them.

"I was sorry to hear about Frank," Marion said, somberly.

"Were you really? I know how you and my brother felt about my marriage."

I couldn't help looking up. I hadn't had any idea that Edward hadn't approved of his sister's relationship with her dead husband.

"It was a terrible situation, nonetheless." Marion paused. "I saw Edward around then, and I wondered if he…" She broke off, her gaze fleeing to me, as though she'd forgotten for a moment that I was there.

"Wondered if he…what?" I asked.

But then we'd arrived at the lobby, and the elevator doors opened, and the security guard was waiting for me with a message to meet my car down the block.

"See you tomorrow, Celia," Camilla said, then she and Marion headed to the cafe without a second glance.

I cycled through several emotions as we made the drive home, replaying the entire office visit in my head. By the time I shifted myself through the hurt and confusion, I found I was angry.

Fuming.

Because he'd never told me anything about him and Marion. Because he was a closed book most of the time no matter how open I'd been with him. Because he demanded I share every last secret, including Hudson, when he'd shared so little with me. Because of the asshole thing he'd said when I was leaving.

If he hadn't been such a major prick, maybe I wouldn't have had to act catty. Did he think of that?

Well, I had no qualms about telling him. In fact, when he got home that night, he and I were going to be talking about a lot of things, whether he wanted to or not.

I spent most of the afternoon working on the finishing details for Genevieve's graduation party. Then I arranged with the cook for dinner to be light so Edward and I could have plenty of time for the arguing that was very likely to follow. And, after a late afternoon swim, I changed into the dress he'd laid out for me, to show that I could be what he wanted, even when I was so very often not.

And when Jeremy came to me with the message that something had come up and Edward wouldn't be home for the night, that he'd meet me at the graduation tomorrow, my rage disappeared inside the pain of betrayal. I somehow managed to keep my tears in until I had reached my bedroom and was alone.

Sixteen

Edward

I parked the car on the pavement at the side of the house and used my key to go in the side door. It was immediately apparent that preparations for Genny's party had already begun. The mudroom was stuffed with odds and ends, knickknacks and such that usually adorned furniture but had been moved to accommodate trays of food and glasses for wine.

The kitchen, on the other hand, was immaculate, every surface having been cleared so that the caterers could unload their goods in the morning. If it weren't for the smell of pasta baking in the oven, I'd have wondered if I'd mistaken the invitation for dinner.

I pulled out my mobile to check my earlier texts and saw three missed calls from Celia. I'd had it on silent as I'd driven to Bluntisham, which had taken me nearly two hours. I was debating about calling her back when the house manager of the country estate appeared.

"Good evening, Edward. You're looking well," she said, her voice cheery despite the late hour.

"Thank you, Iba. The same to you. The little one keeping you young?"

She beamed at the mention of her newest grandchild. "Keeping me busy, anyway."

"Good busy, I hope." When she nodded, I changed gears. "I was supposed to meet—"

She cut me off, our relationship informal enough to disregard the strictest rules of polite conversation. "Already outside waiting for you. I pushed her to start without you. Told her you wouldn't mind."

I put my phone back in my pocket. "Of course not. Thank you for looking out for her."

"No worries. Get on out there, and I'll follow with a plate for you shortly."

I made my way through the kitchen door to the solarium. Before continuing out onto the patio, I paused to gaze at the woman sitting outside while she didn't know she was being watched. Her profile was to me, her mobile in one hand, her fork in another. She seemed older than I usually thought of her—something about her posture or her facial expressions as she swiped the screen of her device. And she was breathtaking. More so than ever.

As if she could feel my eyes on her, she looked up, her face breaking into a grin when she saw me.

I took the cue to push open the door and join her outside.

She set down her phone and stood as I approached her. "You're late."

"I am. I didn't get out of the office until seven, and traffic was horrendous." I embraced her, placing a kiss on her temple.

"I suppose I'm lucky I got you here at all. Frankly, I'm surprised you said you'd come. Especially on such short notice."

Genny's casual tone didn't match the implications of her statement. How many times over her lifetime had I been too busy for her, too involved with business or schemes to give her the attention she desired?

The reality sat like a hard lump of coal in the pit of my stomach. Especially, when the truth was, if I hadn't already been feeling guilty about my relationship with my children when she'd texted, I would likely have blown her off this time as well.

I forced a smile. "I'm glad I could make it work, princess."

"Me too. Thank you." She gestured for me to sit. "I'm sorry. I've already started, as you can see. I'll get Iba—"

On cue, the sprite older woman appeared with a plate of food and an uncorked bottle of wine. "Pinot, good?"

"Is that what you're drinking?" I asked my daughter as I took the wine bottle and examined it. It was a decent choice paired with the tomato-based pasta. I wondered if she'd selected it herself. It was funny to realize that I didn't know her preferences for alcohol or whether she drank much at all.

"I was a bit overwhelmed with the wine cellar," Genny admitted. "Hope I didn't choose poorly."

"You didn't." She glowed when I praised her, and for the millionth time in my life, I told myself I needed to do it more often. What was it about me that made it so hard to love my children openly? Was it because I'd lost my own parents when I was still young? Was it because my father hadn't been that affectionate when he'd been alive? Was it because expressing emotion made me feel vulnerable?

Most likely it was all of those combined. It set me up to be a mediocre parent at best.

And Celia wanted me to go through all of it again.

I poured the wine and took a long swallow. The day had been one that deserved something harder than this at its end. For now, this would have to do.

"The house looks nice," Genny said after Iba had left us to dine alone. "The garden's already set up, and the menu looks lovely. Celia has done an amazing job."

"I'll let her know you appreciate it."

"I wasn't sure about the two of you at first. I'd wanted to see you dating for years, but you sprang that marriage on us out of nowhere, and you have to understand that I wondered a bit if you'd gone off your rocker. I can see now why you chose her. She's very good for you."

"She is." I took a bite of my pasta, hoping it would loosen the tightness at the back of my throat that accompanied the subject of my wife. It had been a tumultuous afternoon, mostly revolving around her. It bothered me that Celia believed I could never let her win, that I could never choose something that was both right for her and wrong for me.

It scared me more that she might be right. Was having a child with her really the only way I could prove otherwise?

And then there'd been Marion...

"Have you seen your mother yet?" I asked, wondering if Genevieve could provide some clue as to why Marion had stopped by the office.

"No." She swallowed her food with a sip of wine. "Talked to her, though. She's coming in tomorrow morn-

222 | LAURELIN PAIGE

ing from London and flying out again the same night. I'm gutted she didn't bring Enzo or Sante with her. I haven't seen either of them since they were in nappies."

I had to fight not to scowl. I didn't like to show judgment in front of my children where Marion was concerned, but it was hard not to express obvious distaste when it came to her parenting skills. I had been subpar at the job myself, but at least I hadn't deserted them. When Marion had left, Genevieve had only been twelve, Hagan only two years older, and I could count on both hands the number of times she'd seen them since.

Then, on top of denying them her presence, she kept her youngest sons from them as well.

The only thing stopping me from saying something nasty was the awareness that much of her behavior was due to me. If I'd been better to Marion, if I had been what she'd needed, if I hadn't compartmentalized her place in my life, she wouldn't have left, and she could have been there for her children. It was my fault, in the end.

Always my fault.

"Sante and Enzo are still young. They'd easily bore at commencement ceremonies, and your mother would have to constantly find ways to entertain them. Perhaps she didn't want to draw attention away from you."

"Perhaps." Her pursed lips said she didn't buy it for a second.

She had understandable resentment for her mother. Was that why she'd wanted to meet tonight? Her text hadn't ex-actly sounded urgent, but the fact that she'd reached out at all was unusual enough to garner concern.

I studied her for several seconds, noting the tense furrow in her brow and the way she kept tracing the collar of her shirt with her fingers. She was nervous. Marion couldn't be the reason I was here. Her mother didn't make her nervous.

"As much as I enjoy a random dinner with my daughter—soon-to-be-graduated, top-of-her-class daugher—I feel fairly certain you have something you want to discuss."

"I do." She wiped her mouth with her napkin then draped it over her plate. Then she rolled her shoulders back, preparing herself to dive in. "There will be a lot of people asking tomorrow what I plan to do next."

"Yes, that is the way with graduations."

"I didn't want to tell anyone else before discussing it with you."

But we *had* discussed this. She planned to move back to London and take her time finding a position that utilized her skills. She didn't need a job right away. I was more than happy to provide for her. "Go on."

"I'm declining the flat you offered to pay for."

I had meant it to be a graduation present. I raised a brow. "Have you found somewhere else you prefer to live? Get me in contact with the flat owner, and I'll sign the lease. Or would you prefer we purchase something outright?"

"Actually, I have found somewhere else. In Lambeth. And I've already signed the lease."

I sat back. A flat in Lambeth was definitely not where I wanted my daughter living. Too Bohemian. Too cheap. "You already signed? Without my approval?"

"I don't need your approval because I'm paying for it on my own."

"I see." And this was why she'd been nervous. She knew how I felt about her dipping into her trust fund. I'd thought she felt the same.

"Not with my inheritance," she clarified, as though reading my mind. "I got a place I can afford on my salary."

"Salary?" Now I was nervous as well.

She swallowed. "Yes. Uh, I've accepted a position with Mills and Varga on their content development team."

I knew what the right thing to say was. Even behind her anxiousness, her excitement was evident. The right thing would be to acknowledge that. To congratulate her. To support her in her decisions.

Except that her decision was wrong, and I couldn't temper myself to pretending otherwise. "M&V?" The disgust was evident in my tone. "The cable network? Why on God's green earth would you do a thing like that?"

"I know they're bottom of the barrel, as far as you're concerned. I know I said I'd wait to accept any offers until I was sure. But they're media, and that's where I want to be working, and it's a job I not only got without you, I got it in spite of you." She spoke rapidly, reminding me of similar speeches when she was still a teen, ones where she begged to go on weekend trips with friends or to take a break from playing cello. It had been difficult to let her make her own choices then, when the outcomes of her decisions weren't so critical.

Now her future depended on her choices, and even though she was an adult, I very much wanted to pull the father card and put my foot down and say no.

I forced myself to count to five before speaking. "What happened to pursuing PR work? You've always wanted to work in public relations. With your class rank, there are plenty of good jobs available in that area."

She rolled her eyes, making her momentarily look like the little girl she'd been. "I've never wanted to work in PR. *You* wanted me to work in PR because you thought it was a field more suited for a girl. Your words, not mine."

I winced at the reminder of the sexist remark. "Yes, I might have said that."

"I can't believe you still have such traditional values," she huffed. "Women are as capable as men, you know. They've proven it. Even more so, in some cases."

"Definitely in your case. I have no doubt you are more capable than every last man in your class." There. I *could* be supportive. It wasn't even a lie.

"But…?" She left space for me to fill in the rest.

"There is no but."

She threw her forearms down dramatically on the table, her palms up. "Then why have you encouraged Hagan to follow in your footsteps and not me? Why haven't you once suggested that I come on board at Accelecom? You have to know it's the field I'm interested in. I've said so numerous times."

I put my fork down, my appetite gone.

She was right—I had known. She'd said as much for several years, even before university. There were several good positions at the company she was already qualified for. I could offer her one. Start her Monday morning.

But I wouldn't.

Because, as much as Accelecom would benefit from her being on the team, I couldn't have her working there. The company I'd built was a media empire, but the truth was, the only reason it had been built was so I could eventually take down Warren Werner.

And even though Ron was now the man I wanted to ruin, I wasn't done with Warren's company. He was on the eve of retiring, and the stocks were in my wife's name. While I didn't plan on talking to her about it anytime soon, there were opportunities there that I refused to overlook.

It took a certain kind of man to have that vision. A man that was ruthless and relentless. A man that would behave cruelly and without ethics.

I didn't want my daughter to know that man.

Maybe it *was* sexist to want to exclude her and not my son, but Hagan was a different sort of breed than Genevieve, having nothing to do with his gender. He was detached. He was ignorant. Even working at my side, he didn't see the truth about who I was, and if he ever did, it wouldn't faze him.

Genny was too smart to miss anything, too earnest to not have serious objections to my questionable morals, and too ambitious to expect that I could hide my truth from her by placing her in a remote role of the company. It wasn't only that I feared what she'd think of me, which was an honest concern, it was also that I feared what it might make her become.

I refused to be a father who put her down that path.

And if she had to believe that I thought less of her because of her gender in order to keep her from following in my footsteps, then so be it.

"You aren't suited for Accelecom, princess." The words sounded as cruel and patronizing out of my mouth as they had in my head.

Good.

It was what she needed to stay away.

Hurt flashed across her features, but she quickly recovered. She'd learned that well from me, how to pretend to be unfeeling. How to turn to stone.

"That's what I thought." Her tone was even and sure. "Hence the reason I took the job at M&V. It's better this way. No one can accuse me of nepotism."

Yes, it was better this way. Outside my arena. Safe.

But that left Mills and Varga.

I groaned. Did she really have to choose to work at a company so beneath her? A network that I could easily buy out if it were decent enough to add to my portfolio. "You're so much better than M&V. There has to be someplace with a better offer."

"Not in media."

"What about Winton Globe? I could talk to Sheldon—"

"I don't want to work in print. That's so archaic, Dad. And I really don't want your help. I want to do this on my own. So don't think about giving me a big check for a graduation present, because I won't be cashing it." She'd started our conversation with more maturity than I'd ever seen from her.

Now though, she was bordering on a temper tantrum.

In turn, I slipped deeper into the father role. "It's my job as a parent to look after you. You should be grateful that you come from a family who is able to provide for you at this level. Most of your fellow graduates would be envious of your options."

"I *am* grateful. Of course I am. *But I do not want to be Mom.* I do not want to be a woman who relies on her husband to guide her in life or give her an identity or pay for her living, and if I rely on you for those things now, I'm only teaching myself to be reliant on someone else forever. I can't go down that path. It won't make me happy."

I suddenly understood so much about my daughter I never had, about what my relationship with her mother must have looked like. About all the ways my marriage had been a fucked-up model for my children.

Even leaving sex aside, Marion had clung to the submissive life. It had consumed her. How could I explain her need for dominance? Or my need to dominate her? How could Genny see it as anything other than misogynistic? How could she ever understand that about her parents?

This wasn't something a father could tell a daughter, and Genny, being as intelligent and independent as she was, had already figured out she needed to navigate this area on her own.

God, she would be such a firecracker to work with. She could help me take Accelecom to the next level. I could see it clearly. I could even find a way to let her remain independent, since she seemed to so badly want that.

For a moment, I second-guessed my decision not to invite her to come on board.

Then I remembered who I was, and what I didn't want her to be, and that was more important than giving her an opportunity she dreamed of.

Celia was right. I did always have to win.

"It's a good thing I'm not offering you a job at Accelecom then," I said, doubling down on my stance, "since according to your own guidelines, you couldn't accept it."

Her mouth opened and closed, her eyes blinking as she forced herself not to make an exception. She pulled herself together, though, like the champ she was. "Then we're on the same page."

"We're not, but I don't think there's anything I can do but respect your decisions, is there?" I swore under my breath. "M&V? Really? Do not even think of giving me one of those silly sweaters with their logo. I will not wear it, no matter how proud of you I am."

She chuckled at that. "You guessed your birthday present. I had thought about throwing in the socks as well, but they wouldn't be so noticeably embarrassing when you wore them."

That earned her a smile. "Well. This dinner has been delightful. Is there any other bomb you'd like to drop on me this evening, Genny, before I retire for the night?"

"Only one more—I'd like to be called Genevieve from now on. It's more professional. Genny is so girlish."

She was trying to kill me. She really was.

This, at least, I could give without debate. "I always did like the name Genevieve."

"Go figure." She stood, and I with her. "I should probably get back to my flat. Long day tomorrow. You're staying the night?"

I nodded. "It doesn't make sense to drive the two hours back only to turn around and come here again in the morning. You could stay here as well. I'm sure Iba wouldn't mind preparing your room." It was only half an hour to Cambridge, but, as always, I worried.

She shook her head. "I didn't bring my cap or gown and that would be an added hassle in the morning."

I nodded then reached out to hug her good night.

"Thank you for listening," she said. "And for trying to understand."

My throat burned, so I didn't speak. I just squeezed her a little harder. Then, as difficult as it was, I let her go.

Upstairs in the estate's master bedroom, I took off my jacket and sat down on the bed with a sigh. I'd brought a glass of brandy up with me, and though I'd already drunk half of it, I still felt just as restless as I had before my first swallow.

It had been an endless day.

A day revolved around the most important women in my life. They each fought for individual attention in my mind. Would Genevieve be better for pushing her away? I'd tried that tactic with Camilla, and years of additional scars and therapy later I wasn't sure I wasn't to blame for a good portion of her pain.

And Celia trusted me enough to bring another human into my universe.

Did she not understand what sort of mistake that would be? Was there any way to keep her without paying that cost?

And then there was Marion.

I'd have to deal with her tomorrow. I couldn't think about her now. Not in the state I was in.

I took another long swallow then looked at my cell phone, the missed call notification still at the top of my screen. It was well after ten. Celia should be asleep, considering she had to be up early the next day.

I cleared the notification then plugged my phone into the charger we kept beside the bed. Even if she was still awake, I wasn't sure I could find the words she'd need from me. The explanations she would surely expect. The promises she'd want me to make. Not tonight.

It was probably better that we not talk until I could.

SEVENTEEN

CELIA

I made it to Bluntisham a little after nine in the morning. Thank goodness that I had a driver so I could spend most of the ride with an ice pack over my swollen eyes. Then, the last fifteen minutes, I did my makeup, hoping the heavy layer of foundation would hide the dark bags. It was an important day for Genny, which made it an important day for Edward, and even though I was still stewing and fretting about his absence and what it meant, I intended to give them the event she deserved.

Though, the thought of seeing Marion again, of having to watch her and Edward interact amongst friends who probably knew her better than me, made me nauseated.

It was time to bring out the old Celia, the one who could fake her way through anything.

The façade fell immediately when I walked into the kitchen of the country house and found Edward standing at the island, a mug in his hand, the local newspaper spread out in front of him, a half-eaten omelet at its side. He was already in his trousers and white dress shirt. His tie was still open at his neck, but his suspenders were on, and damn did that man look good eating breakfast. It was insane how good.

"You're here," I said, stunned. I'd expected I wouldn't see him until I was surrounded by others. If I'd known I would have had a chance to talk to him alone before that, I would have prepared my anger. Instead, all I could do was blink at him in surprise.

He looked up, a smile lighting his face at the sight of me. "Of course I'm here. Where else would I be?"

All casual like. As if he hadn't just up and disappeared the evening before.

Not sure where the staff was, having come in through the side door, I paused a beat before I spoke so that I wouldn't make a scene. Still, my words came out terse. "You didn't come home last night. I had no idea where else you might be."

He set down his mug and stuck his hands in his pockets. "I didn't come home because I was already here. It seemed a waste of a drive."

That was all the explanation he planned to give? He was maddening.

"Why were you already here? Was I supposed to know you were here? Why didn't you answer my calls? Were you alone?"

He smirked as he came around the island and walked toward me. I was too angry for whatever he had in mind, but I couldn't seem to move, his eyes pinning me in place.

"You're cute when you're suspicious," he said, wrapping his arms around me.

I tried to squirm free with no luck against his firm grip.

234 | LAURELIN PAIGE

"You're an asshole when..." The ways I could finish that sentence were endless. "Well, most of the time, actually."

Refusing to look at him, I stared at his neck, at the skin that would be covered up when he buttoned his collar. It was astounding how hypnotic a man's throat could be.

He brought his hand up to my chin and tipped it until I was forced to look up and my gaze crashed into baby blues. "Yes, I was alone," he said. "When I slept, anyway, since that's what you're really asking. I was not alone before that."

My mouth fell open, but before I could react further, he went on.

"Genevieve was here. She asked me spur of the moment to have dinner with her."

"Oh," I said, processing. And then when I'd processed, I said it again, this time in relief. "Ohhh."

His daughter. That's what would take him away so urgently. Not Marion. Everything was fine.

Unless, Genny wasn't fine. "Anything wrong?" I asked, suddenly concerned.

"Nope. She just wanted to talk to me before the big day."

She'd needed him, and he'd been there for her. Came running at the drop of a hat, even. And he thought he wasn't a good father.

A different kind of jealousy pinged in my chest.

"Anything important?" I buttoned his collar and began working on his tie.

"She got a job. I'll leave her to tell you the details. Well beneath her, but she's happy about it."

I tightened the knot and patted it down. "So you will be too."

"I'm trying to be." He grimaced. "And she'd prefer we call her Genevieve from now on."

"Got it." I completely understood the girl, remembering exactly what it felt like to be that age, wanting to be taken seriously.

Still it had to be hard on Edward to realize his daughter was a grown-up. I rubbed my hand against the stubble at his jaw.

He gave a small smile that quickly turned right back into a frown. "You've been crying. Your eyes are puffy."

"Oh, God. Do I look terrible?" I pulled away and scanned for something I might be able to see my reflection in.

But he pulled me instantly back into his arms. "You look stunning, bird. I would have said so first thing if you hadn't directed the conversation elsewhere. I promise that no one will notice your eyes unless they looked hard and long at you every day, and I better be the only person who does that. So, tell me, why were you crying?"

Remnants of my fury returned. "My husband didn't come home after discussing a subject that was very important to me. Why do you think I was crying?"

His reasons for not coming home may have been warranted, but the way he had treated me was unacceptable. Marion might have let that kind of behavior slide. There was no way his current wife would.

He let out a sigh and pressed his forehead to mine. "You're right. I'm an arsehole."

"I'm glad you agree. Unfortunately, I doubt that acknowledgment alone will change how you behave."

"You're probably right there too." His candor was both charming and irritating.

I stretched my arms around his neck, allowing myself to hold him for the first time that morning. "You could try though, maybe? To be a little more considerate to what I might be thinking in situations like that? To show me the respect you expect me to show you?"

He considered. "Yes. I can try."

Well. That had gone better than expected.

He sealed the agreement with a kiss that wasn't at all chaste. He tasted like coffee and, faintly, like toothpaste, and if it hadn't been for the long list of items on my to-do list, I would have been happy to stay right there and continue kissing him for much longer.

"I better..." I said, pushing away.

This time he let me go.

I started out of the kitchen, the knot in my stomach considerably looser than when I'd awoken. The day was still young, and there were still a lot of things to be anxious about, but at least where Edward had spent the night wasn't one of them.

Or was I being too trusting?

I stopped at the doorway and looked back toward him. "You really only came out to see Genny. Er, Genevieve? There's nothing else I should know?"

"I really only came for Genevieve." He sounded genuine, and I was sure it was the truth. It would be easy enough to prove otherwise. He wasn't the type to tell disputable lies.

Still, not everything was settled between us. Whether

it was just the conversation from the day before that remained unfinished or something else stirring in the air, I didn't know. Either way, I was going to have to try to ignore it for now.

The rest of the morning flew by with preparations for the party. Camilla arrived soon after I did, Freddie's sitter in tow, so she could help out, which I hadn't thought I'd need but was grateful for in the end. Edward hid away in his office during most of the hubbub, but he came out near the end and helped with the finishing details. Then we all drove together to Cambridge for the graduation.

Marion arrived with Hagan who had brought a date, putting one more person between where she sat and where Edward sat, which was definitely a plus in my book. At least she was out of my eyesight, and while I could still feel her presence most of the time, I managed to forget about her for long stretches of time during the commencement ceremony.

Afterward was a different story.

Though Camilla was an excellent photographer, Edward had hired a professional as well so that she didn't have to work a family event. That meant lots of pictures—several of which had the star of the day posing between her beaming parents. Pictures that I was mostly not a part of since I had to head back right away to greet early guests.

The arrangement made sense—me going early with Camilla, and Edward, Marion, Hagan, and Genevieve following later—but that didn't mean I had to like it. I lingered after the last big group shot before leaving, my chest tight with envy as I watched them take a few immediate family shots.

They looked good like that, the four of them. Hagan tall and chiseled like his father. Genevieve a perfect blend of both her parents. Edward dominating each setup without even trying. Marion always posed just a little too close.

"They won't be too long after us," Camilla said, misreading my hesitation. "And if we hurry, we can have a glass of champagne before anyone else arrives."

That was all I needed to prod me away. "Count me in."

Everything after that moved in a whirlwind. Guests began arriving almost as soon as we got to the house, people I didn't know and had only heard of when filling out the guest lists with Edward and Genevieve. Fortunately, Camilla knew most of them and was able to play hostess while I took deep breaths, smiled a bunch, and tried not to hyperventilate.

When Edward showed up, I felt much calmer, even though his presence meant Marion's as well. She quickly found some friends from the past that occupied her, though, which was a relief. By that time, most of my party-planning assignment was completed. Iba managed the caterers and took care of any hiccups that occurred while Edward paraded me around the party introducing me to more people than I'd possibly be able to remember. It was busy and I constantly had to be "on," but being at my husband's side made it sort of fun. I liked the attention he gave me, the way his voice intoned when he said my name, with similar pride that he bestowed on Genny.

It was more than an hour into the event when Edward finally let me slip away while he talked boring financials with someone from the company. I still hadn't had a chance to congratulate his daughter, and it felt like the perfect opening.

She was gathered with a small group of women, but she didn't seem to be that engaged with the current conversation, so I tapped her on the shoulder to get her attention.

"You did it!" I exclaimed, embracing her when she turned around. "I can't imagine the kind of hard work it took to get top honors. Your father is proud of you. I am, too, for that matter."

She was beaming when we separated. "Thank you. And thank you so much for the party. It's exactly what I wanted. High class but laid back. It's very..." She searched for the word to describe it.

"Mature," I said, helping her out.

"Yes. Exactly," she laughed.

"I'm glad to be a part of it. It's all my pleasure." It was an honest statement. Edward was traditional and bossy with my time, but being in charge of the party planning had been my idea. The project felt similar to design work. There was an esthetic and a mood that Genevieve had wanted to capture, and I approached it in the same way I would have if she'd asked me to redo her apartment.

Plus, she was Edward's daughter, and I'd had very little opportunity to get to know her since she had been at school, and that bothered me for selfish reasons. She was a part of my husband's life that I wasn't a part of, a part of his life that I envied. Right now she and Hagan were as close as I had to having a child of my own.

"Well, good on you then," she said. "I wouldn't know where to begin to do something like this, let alone want to. Believe me when I say that your skills are much appreciated."

"I second that," came a voice from the group behind her. "Thank you for this."

My stomach dropped, recognizing who it was. Genevieve stepped to the side inviting me into the circle of women, and exposing the one particular one I'd missed. "Marion, I didn't see you there. Sorry to steal your daughter away like that."

Something flashed across her eyes making me reexamine what I'd just said. Realizing the statement had been an unintended threat to her motherhood, I didn't feel any regrets. If she had insecurities about her parenting skills, that wasn't my problem. No, my problem was my own insecurities, both about parenting and wifing.

She got me back with a jab of her own, whether she realized it or not. "No problem. We were only talking about her as a baby. Difficult pregnancy. Very easy birth."

People had spoken about their pregnancies in front of me numerous times, and it had never bothered me in the slightest. Hearing about it from Edward's ex-wife was a different story. She'd owned his heart. I was certain of that, even though he'd never said as much. He loved me too, but I didn't know if I owned his heart.

On top of owning his heart, she'd mothered his children. He'd *wanted* her to mother his children. I was equally certain about that fact. Edward didn't let even insignificant details occur in his life without his direction. There was no way he hadn't been one hundred percent on board with her getting pregnant.

And I wanted to be pregnant with his child. And I wanted to own his heart. And suddenly in that moment, despite all the evidence to the contrary, I was convinced I would never have either.

I was soaking in envy, and it was hard to pretend otherwise.

There was nothing to do but lean into it. "Was that why you stopped at two? Because of the difficult pregnancy?"

She shook her head. "The pregnancy was hard because she was a girl. I'm convinced." She laughed, making light of the superstition. "And because Genny was stubborn, even in the womb."

Her daughter winced. Apparently Marion hadn't gotten the memo about the name change.

"But it was a fluke," she continued. "I didn't have problems before or after with my boys. No, it wasn't for the pregnancy. Edward would have had more, I believe, but two was a good number to have. Easy to manage when they're small. It worked out well, I think." She gave a loving yet distant smile to Genevieve.

And I tried not to hyperfocus on the five words that stung like a million bee stings at once. *Edward would have had more.*

More with Marion, not with me. Not unless I gave up every last shred of my control. Not unless I gave up Hudson.

I was well aware that his thoughts on more children could have changed over the twenty plus years since Genny was born, but I was overwhelmingly vulnerable when it came to this woman. I was ridiculous and insecure.

I was so wrapped up in my inner misery, I almost missed Marion's question, only the sound of my name caught my attention.

"...Celia? Do you want children?"

I could feel the color drain from my face. The rest of

the women—wives of businessmen, ladies I'd only been introduced to as a second thought, socialites and trophies like my mother had been—looked eagerly at me, waiting for an answer. This was exactly the kind of gossip Madge Werner's type lived for. Even if I had a solid answer, I wouldn't want to share it with them.

Yet, I really wanted to share it with Marion. Wanted to be on her level, if only for a moment. Wanted to lie to get it if I had to.

"Oh, wow," Genevieve said while I debated how to respond. "I hadn't thought of father having more children. Are you going to?"

My mouth felt like cotton. "Uh. I…"

Surprise of all surprises, Marion was the one who came to my rescue. "I'm sorry," she said. "That was very rude of me to ask."

I looked across the garden to Edward who caught my eye and winked. The lie wouldn't come. "No. It's fine. We haven't quite decided."

"Edward's probably against it," one of the others said quietly. Did she think I couldn't hear her?

"Yes, probably," Marion agreed.

"No," I protested. "We just haven't quite figured it out yet is all. I have a job and all that." *Take that, Marion, Mrs. Stay-At-Home-Perfect-Wife.*

"You're young still. You have time." Whatever her goal had been, it felt patronizing.

"Well, not a *lot* of time," another woman pointed out.

Just what I needed to hear.

I forced a smile. "If you ladies would please excuse me, I see another bottle of red needs to be opened."

Restraining myself so that I didn't break into a run, I crossed the garden and slipped into the solarium. The room was practically made of glass, but even with the unobstructed view, being inside versus outside made it feel like I was hidden.

I turned around to stare at the group I'd just left. They were laughing together, probably at a joke told at my expense, none of them looking in my direction.

I don't care about your opinion, I told her in my head. *You don't mean anything to me. You're not a threat. I can have a baby whenever I want to, Edward on board or not. It's not like he controls my birth control.*

He'd probably controlled hers.

That made me smile, as though I'd won some imaginary battle when in reality her submission likely earned her more devotion than he'd ever give me.

"Is it hard having her here?"

I glanced at Camilla who'd sidled up beside me. She must have followed my gaze. For half a second, I considered pretending otherwise, then the impulse was gone. "If I'm being polite? Yes."

"And if you aren't being polite?"

"Fuck yes." I laughed with her, feeling better now that this tension had somewhere to go. "She's just..." There were so many things I wanted to say about Marion, most of which were completely unfounded. "So accommodating, which shouldn't be irritating, but somehow it is, especially because of how accommodating she is to Edward. And have you noticed how she looks to him all the time? When someone asks her a question or she wants to fill up her wine glass or, Jesus, when she wants to go to the bathroom. She always looks to him as though she's asking for permission."

Even now as I watched, she was looking at him. He'd come to join them, seeming to have something to say to Genevieve, and there was Marion, gazing at him like he ruled the roost.

I mean, I probably did too, but it was our roost, not hers.

Camilla let out a sigh. "They were always like that."

"But she's married now to somebody else. She can be like that with her own husband. Leave mine alone." I glanced at my sister-in-law, gauging her reaction. "Petty, isn't it?"

"Not at all."

Taking that as permission to vent, I continued. "Like... it feels like she's still with him. Or like she still wants to be with him. And if that's the case, then why did she leave him?" Suddenly I wondered if I had my facts wrong. "She *did* leave him, right?"

"Yes," she said hesitantly. "Edward hasn't told you about it?"

The question brushed up against one of my vulnerable spots, making me flinch internally as though she'd smashed against a bruise. He hadn't told me. No matter how many times I'd asked.

And that hurt. And felt suspicious. And was too embarrassing to admit.

"Is there something to tell besides Marion left him for another man?" If I couldn't hear it from Edward, maybe I could get it from her.

She gave a half shrug. "Aren't those stories always more complicated than they seem on the surface?"

If "those stories" referred to any type of relationship breakup then the answer was yes. I hadn't had many of my own, but the ones that I'd been involved with—Dirk, Hudson, the ones I'd made happen for other people—all of them had been complex.

Camilla nudged me with her shoulder. "Ask him. I could tell you some, but there are missing pieces in my version. He should be the one to tell you."

Right. Like it was that easy.

As though reading my thoughts she added, "And if he doesn't want to, *make* him tell you. That's something a wife should know."

I nodded in agreement, wondering exactly how I could make Edward do anything.

I had to figure it out, though. Immediately. Not only because it was destroying me to be left in the dark, but also because he'd just walked off into the private hedged gardens with Marion. Alone.

And I'd be damned if he didn't plan on telling me what the fuck that was all about.

EIGHTEEN
EDWARD

It was my idea to explore the garden. Marion needed time alone with me, I could see it in her gaze, constantly tugging at me throughout the day. Old habits being what they were between us, she would never bring herself to ask. I had to be the one to care for her. As always.

I hated that I could still know how. A decade since our divorce, and I could still govern her with very little effort. It was like riding a bicycle. My body did it naturally, such as when my hand pressed at the small of her back to guide her out of my office the day before. There was no thought behind these movements. It was in my bones.

I'd said I was no longer her sir, and I wasn't, but I also was and always would be.

Which meant I could have denied her the private conversation, and we would go on with our lives, the words that needed to be said between us remaining unspoken. It was my call. She'd made as big of an effort as she would, stopping by Accelecom like she did. Everything that happened next was up to me.

It was tempting to let it go and move on. For Celia more than anyone else.

But to move on, I needed there not to be anything between us anymore.

And so I suggested a walk through the garden.

"This reminds me of the hedge garden at Brayhill," she said as we entered through the arch. The garden here wasn't very big, a little more than fifty square meters enclosed with hedges that reached eight meters high. More hedges divided the space into rows, but it wasn't a maze. There were a couple of resting spots with benches, a fountain along the back stretch, and an array of florals, most of which I couldn't identify if I wanted to.

The garden she referred to at Brayhill, the country home I'd owned when we'd been married, had been much larger, a thousand square meters in size or more, and it had very much been a labyrinth. The kind that made old English country houses charming but also a lot of work to maintain.

I supposed this garden was similar since both were enclosed by hedges, but their functions were completely different. "You can't get lost here."

"That's a plus, if you ask me. Do you know how much time I spent chasing after Hagan there?"

Her statement felt pointed. I *didn't* know how much she'd chased Hagan there, mainly because I'd rarely gone on family weekends to Brayhill, and, when I had, I'd spent most of the time in my office. I missed out on a lot, too busy with my work.

But Marion wasn't the kind to make passive-aggressive remarks. Or aggressive remarks, for that matter. If she judged me for that, she'd keep it to herself.

"I'm pretty sure he would have made you chase him with or without the garden. But I see how it would be harder to find him in the maze. I liked it for that very reason. It was a good spot to wander." Particularly in the early morning, when the house was still asleep and the fog settled on the land. More than a handful of problems were sorted on those walks.

She looked up from the plant she'd been admiring, one *she* could likely name. "Why did you sell?"

"After Frank…" I trailed off, not sure what I'd meant to say. It wasn't necessary, anyway. She knew where that sentence went, that his death would have been etched into the environment of that house as firmly as the initials the kids had drawn into the cement at the end of the driveway. "Camilla would never have visited again. Honestly, I'm not sure I could have either."

She moved on along the path. "It seems fitting that it's gone."

"Yes. Selling it marked the end of…" Again I found myself at a loss for words. I let out a breath. "A lot of things." It had been the end of Marion and me, too, in many ways. Except for the island, which had always been more my place than ours, the sale of Brayhill had removed the last property that we'd made memories in together from my life. There was a melancholiness about that.

But it had also been the end of Camilla and Frank. And the feeling surrounding that was much different.

Marion pursed her lips and nodded, understanding more than almost anyone else could.

We came to an opening in the hedges, a sort of window where the plants had been trimmed back. There was one on each side of the garden. This one had a view of the back of the house.

She paused there to look out over the party. I followed her gaze and landed on Genevieve who was still in the spot we'd left her in.

"We did well with that one," Marion said. "Somehow. Despite everything. *You* did well with her."

I appreciated that she recognized her absence from our children's lives. But she was wrong to give me any credit. Marion hadn't left until Genevieve was twelve. I'd been aloof long before that. Neither of us had been there as we should have been. "She did it all on her own, I think."

Marion made a sound of disagreement, a two-syllable rumble in the back of her throat. "She's you, Edward. You should be proud."

"Oh, I am. Whether I deserve to be or not." My stare glided from my daughter to Celia, who had joined the circle along with Camilla sometime after we'd left. It was odd to think that my wife was as close to Genny's age as she was to mine, and I wondered if that was why she'd leaned into a more friendly role with my children than parental. Or maybe that was simply because they'd already been grown and out of the house by the time she'd moved in.

What kind of mother would she be? Attentive and regimented like Marion had been before she'd disappeared, or something else altogether?

It startled me to realize that I wanted to know.

"Is it real?" Marion asked, seeing who I was focused on.

"Yes. It wasn't at first, but that changed." It had to be confusing for her to see me with a Werner when Warren had been my enemy the entire time I'd known her. It didn't make me feel the need to disclose any more than that, though. It wasn't her business, and Celia was mine. I didn't want to share her with anyone, especially with Marion.

"It seemed as much." Marion turned away from the window to continue along the path. "The way you look at her. The way she defers to you."

I laughed. "She's not really very submissive."

"She is. I see it. But she makes you work for it."

"She does." There was something quite satisfying about my ex realizing that I loved someone other than her. That another woman fit my preferences in a way she never could. I supposed it was like that for most people who had once been part of a couple, but it was particularly delicious in my case, after the way that Marion had left. It was karma. Or, at least, things had come full circle.

And if things had come full circle...did that mean we were finally done with each other?

It was almost too much to believe. The chains binding me to her had been there so long, I'd become used to their weight. What would it feel like to have them gone?

I spun toward her, suddenly needing answers. "Why did you come to the office yesterday?"

Her cheeks flushed, her eyes cast down. "I don't know."

"Were you hoping something would happen?"

Her shoulders rose and fell with her breath.

"Look at me, Marion." I used the tone she'd never been able to ignore, and, as I predicted, she looked up. "What were you hoping would happen between us?"

"I didn't think that far ahead, uh, Edward. I was anxious about how it would be with you, and I wanted it dealt with before all this." She swallowed. "I love Renato. You know that."

I took a step back, needing distance. The fact that she needed to clarify her feelings meant she'd considered the possibilities.

It made me unreasonably angry. I wouldn't have touched her, I wouldn't have wanted to, but she had to stop this. She had to stop being available for me. She had to take responsibility for her actions instead of always leaving them to someone else's whim.

She loves Renato.

Bullshit if she thought that meant anything. "Your feelings didn't stop you last time."

"That's not fair. You needed me, and I don't know how not to respond to that."

"I took advantage."

"I don't blame you."

"You *should*." I fisted a hand at my hip and walked in a circle, memories of the night four years ago unwittingly filling my mind. I'd been a wreck, holding it together as best as I could for my sister's sake. Then Marion had called to check on Camilla, but I'd been the one to answer, and instead of passing on the phone, I'd latched onto the familiar source of comfort.

"I need you," I'd said.

And she'd come.

She shouldn't have. She had a husband and a family, and she shouldn't have come running, but that was what Marion did, and I knew better. I was the one who should never have asked.

That had always been our problem, though, hadn't it? I never knew the limits, and she never made me find them.

"The circumstances around Frank's death were diffi-

252 | LAURELIN PAIGE

cult," she said, stupidly defending me. "You needed someone to take that out on. Who else could you have turned
to?"

No one. There had been no one who knew the truth
about Frank except for Camilla, and she certainly wasn't
someone I could have leaned on.

It didn't change the fact that I'd made a mistake. My
weakness didn't excuse anything.

"I told Renato after the fact," she added after a beat.

That shouldn't have been surprising. "And he was
okay with it?"

"He wasn't exactly. But we sorted it out."

I could imagine just how they sorted it out. She likely
hadn't been able to sit comfortably for a week.

That wouldn't have been enough for me. If my wife
had cheated...

I was such an idiot. "I was about to say I wouldn't have
been so understanding, but I suppose we both know that's
not true."

She and I and Renato...it was a fucked-up situation all
around.

And it wasn't my problem anymore. *She* wasn't my
problem anymore. She was his. And that was exactly how
it should be.

With that realization, my anger dissipated. "Anyway. I
was grateful. But it won't happen again."

"I know. You have her now, and you've always been
faithful, at least as far as women go."

Then it was settled. We were over, and she understood.

I shoved my hands in my pockets and started leading

us back toward the exit, thinking about her last words as we walked. She was right that I would always be faithful to my wife. But, even if I didn't have Celia, I wanted to say that I wouldn't let Marion and me happen again. The truth was, I didn't know that for sure. Because I couldn't imagine myself without Celia anymore. Whoever I'd be without her would be too unrecognizable for me to attach certainties to.

Celia. My little bird.

There were things I should tell her, things about Marion and Frank, things I wanted her to know. But how could I let her know those parts of me and still expect her to stay?

Marion hadn't stayed.

That was a piss-ant excuse, and I knew it. The reason Marion had left had nothing to do with who I was and very much to do with who I wasn't.

It was time I faced that once and for all.

I stopped abruptly and faced my ex. "When you left, I never asked why."

"Are you asking me now?" She straightened her spine, girding herself for an uncomfortable exchange.

"I'm not. I know why. I didn't want to admit it for a very long time, but I know."

"Thank you for telling me," she said, and even if there was some chance I was wrong and my reason differed from hers, it didn't matter. The point was that I'd accepted it, and that she knew.

I thought that would be the end of it, but just as I started to walk on, she asked, "Will things change with that understanding?"

"Between us?"

"Between you and her."

That was a question I didn't have an answer for. On the one hand, Celia wasn't Marion. Our problems would never look like the problems that had broken up my first marriage. On the other hand, I understood the things that might come up between us, I understood the traits of my personality that were divisive, and I understood that understanding did not necessarily equate change.

"Do you care?" I asked, finding deflection easier.

"I want you to be happy," she said, and the rawness of her voice as she said it made me believe it was true.

It occurred to me that I wanted that for her too. I'd wished misery on her for a long time after she left. I didn't know when that had changed.

"Are *you* happy?" I asked now.

"I am. There are things I regret losing—Hagan and Genevieve, to be specific."

"You could still win them back if you decided to try."

"Maybe." She focused somewhere in the distance and sighed. "Or maybe things are best as they are. Because I *am* happy."

I was surprised to realize I envied that.

Not that I wasn't happy—I was, for the most part. But I was well aware that the rage that drove my desires for vengeance were toxic. They were iron, according to Camilla. It tainted every other emotion I had. It shaped all my relationships. It prevented the ruby from forming.

I understood that.

Understanding didn't mean I could change.

It was better with Celia, though. The fury inside me

was reshaping, and, for the first time in my life, here with Marion, I felt closure without having to first destroy her.

And so when Celia's incensed gaze pinned me coming out of the garden with Marion, I smiled. She was jealous, and I'd have to do some explaining, but she loved me, and it was the closest to pure happiness I'd ever felt.

Nineteen
Celia

After the party had ended and everyone, including the caterers and the clean-up crew, had finally left, I filled two glasses with cognac and took them with me to the solarium.

Edward had offered to help Iba to her car, her arms full of leftover food that would go to waste at the house since we were leaving the next day. I hadn't told him where I would be waiting when he got back, but I was confident he'd find me.

Inside the windowed room, I set one of the glasses on a table next to the loveseat then dimmed the overhead before taking the other glass to the armchair across from it. The string of lights that had been put up outside for the party were still lit, creating a romantic mood. Not exactly what I was going for, but it would do. In my experience, the darker setting made confessions easier.

I stretched my neck, easing the knots there as I looked out over the yard. The day had been busy and full, and the party had been, by all accounts, successful, but I'd spent the entire time preoccupied with Edward. Even when en-tertaining strangers or running around trying to find Iba to tell her we were out of toilet paper, I'd been aware of my husband. He was a magnetic force, always pulling my thoughts and my body in his direction. Like gravity hold-ing me in his orbit.

I'd never felt that way about anyone before. Not just that in love but also that attached. I was still reeling from the newness of it, eighteen months after we'd wed.

I was also still adjusting to the way he affected me. How he'd brought me peace yet could stir up levels of jeal-ousy within me that I'd never thought possible. His trip to the garden with Marion was innocent—it had to be consid-ering the way he grinned at me when he'd returned. The devil himself wouldn't flaunt his discretions so openly.

Would he?

No. I couldn't believe he would. But innocent as his visit with her may have been, there was still a divide be-tween us where his ex-wife was concerned. As near as he drew me, as forceful as his pull was, I could never close that final gap, and I was sure it was because of her. They were over, their relationship was done, but whatever had happened between them still mattered. She'd left him feel-ing so defenseless that he seemed to think he had to protect himself, had to shut part of himself off. Had she broken him so severely that he couldn't bear to love that hard again?

Or had he withheld those parts of his heart because they couldn't belong to me when they still belonged to her?

"I'd expected you'd already have gone up to bed."

My head jerked up to find him standing in the doorway. "I thought we'd sit a while first." I nodded toward the love-seat. "I got you a drink."

His smile was bright but suspicious as he sat down where I'd indicated. "How attentive, and after everything you've already done today." He took a swallow of his brandy and stared at me, his gaze hot and inviting. "Might be nicer if you weren't so far away."

It would have been a lie to say I wasn't tempted. We'd only spent one evening apart, but it felt like weeks since I'd been in his arms. Been underneath him.

But it was past time for this to be addressed. "I had something else in mind, actually."

"Oh? Do tell."

I cleared my throat. "This is how this will work," I said, trying my best to mimic the words he'd once told me. "We will sit here, and, when you're ready, you will tell me about Marion, why she left you. It won't be pleasant, as I'm sure it affected you deeply. You will tell me everything relevant surrounding your breakup. I may ask questions. I'll expect answers. And all of it, every single word, will be true."

"Are you trying to lead a session?" He tried to glower at me, but I could tell he was fighting off a laugh.

"I *am* leading a session."

This time he did laugh. "You're cute when you think you can play my part."

"You're charming when you're patronizing. It won't work. I'm committed."

He narrowed his eyes and sat back against the cushion, considering. Calculating. "What if I'm not interested in participating?"

"I wasn't interested either when these began, and look at us now."

"I didn't leave you much choice. You had to comply."

"Believe me when I say I'm not leaving you much choice either." I wasn't exactly sure what my threat was, because there *had* to be a threat if the statement was to hold any weight. If he asked I'd have to be ready to say the worst. Ready to *do* the worst. And, as important as this was to me, I wasn't sure that I was ready to go that far.

Thankfully, just the hint was enough.

"Ballsy," he said, swirling the contents of his glass.

"I learned from the best."

He brought the glass up to his lips and took a decent sized swallow. "I suppose it is time we discuss this. For the record, after the last couple of days, I have realized we should. I just hadn't expected to dive into it tonight."

The tightness in my chest loosened ever so slightly.

He took another swallow of his drink then settled in, crossing one leg over the other, ankle on the knee. "But you must be exhausted, bird. Are you sure you're up for this?"

"You're stalling."

"Since you're playing me, it's only fair that I play you. You went down this road kicking and screaming, if you'll recall."

"You fought back with patience. I can be patient."

"Yes, you can be. You have been." Acknowledging how long I'd waited for him to open up was already significant progress. An eager anticipation fluttered inside me. Was this what these sessions had been like for him?

God, if so, that man could handle his angst like a statue. As for me, I had to cross my ankles to keep my foot from wanting to bounce.

"All right," he said, earnestly. "Let me decide where this should begin."

"If you aren't honest, I'll know," I teased. Though I wasn't sure that was true.

"It will be authentic, bird. You might not like what you hear, but it will be authentic." His reassurance was typical Edward—soothing but not soothing enough to get comfortable.

Typical Edward, though, was something I was quite used to. So in *my* typical fashion, I challenged him right back. "I'm sure I can handle it. If you can."

He smirked.

Then he grew solemn. "Marion was quite submissive, as I've told you. As you've seen now. It wasn't just a bedroom game for her. It was a lifestyle choice. It wasn't just about being subservient. In every area of her life, she wanted to be molded and instructed and commanded and dominated."

"And you liked that." It was impossible to keep the bite out of my tone.

"I...did," he admitted. "And then I didn't."

"You didn't like being in charge? I call bullshit." Apparently, reading him was easier than I'd expected.

"Oh, I did like that. I'll never grow tired of that." He didn't wink, but it felt like he had. "I didn't even really mind the time and energy it required to live like that, though, at the time, I thought I did. I had things that were more important that needed my focus."

"Your business," I guessed.

"Yes. And other things."

Other things. Like planning a takedown of my father.

His revenging certainly had a life of its own. With our different opinions on the subject, I thought it best to avoid that topic. "You were busy. I got it. Making a schedule for her and setting out her clothes got tedious."

"We are not making this about you," he said, correctly assuming my subtext. "If I thought it were *tedious* to do those things for you, I wouldn't have insisted that you let me."

"What's the difference? How can you be so sure you won't resent it for me when you did for her? I'm sure she didn't even argue with you about it like I did."

"That was exactly it."

"She liked it, and *that's* what irritated you?"

He let out a rather hefty sigh. "The problem wasn't that she accepted those things. It was that she accepted *everything*. She didn't ever argue, except when she wanted to bait me into a punishment. She didn't stand up to me. She didn't speak her mind. She wanted me to decide all of it, and so I did."

"How boring."

He pierced me with an unapproving glare. "You're being catty, but yes. It was boring after a while. And not always very safe."

"You mean sex? Did she not have boundaries or something? Did you go too far?" I wasn't just being catty—I was being petty. I felt like my mother, greedy for the triflest of gossip because, if Marion and Edward had problems in the bedroom, I was going to feel a thousand times more secure in our marriage since our sex was fanfuckingtastic.

"The sex was just fine, thank you." Ouch. "Brilliant, to be truthful." Double ouch. "I do appreciate being the boss in that arena."

"Really? I couldn't tell." Add snide to my list of faults. *Way to be an adult, Celia.*

Fortunately, Edward was grown-up enough for the both of us in the moment. "The problem wasn't her boundaries. I knew them—better than she did even—and I respected them. The problem was that with no one to challenge me, *I* was the one with no boundaries."

My breath lodged in my chest. "I'm surprised to hear you admit that."

"You're starting to see why this story isn't a favorite of mine." He slid his ankle farther down the supporting leg, fully crossing them now. With his brows knit, he spent silent seconds smoothing away an invisible wrinkle, seemingly lost in a self-analysis.

Then, after a dismissive shake of his head, he went on. "Anyway, believing that you are unstoppable is fun for a while, but it gets lonely. Especially when the other aspects of our life were added in. She didn't want to share a bed to maintain the separation of master and servant. She didn't help with family decisions except to praise whatever I'd decided. I rarely knew what she was really thinking about anything. I had a sub, not a wife, and for that reason, I began to resent those parts of our marriage specifically. I no longer enjoyed picking out her clothes, and deciding what she was going to do with her day was, as you said, tedious, and I stopped putting as much effort into it as I should. It put a strain on our relationship, naturally. Those things were important to her. She needed them to be happy. And I wasn't there for her."

Something began to shift within me as he spoke, and I stopped listening for things to boost my esteem and started hearing him. Started hearing the story of two complicated people who began down a path together. Started to understand how it must have hurt when those pathways diverged.

"Did she complain?" I asked, quietly.

"No. But I knew. It was my job to know, and I knew. It didn't change my behavior, but it weighed on me. It was a vicious cycle. The guilt was another distraction that took my time away from focusing on her."

"Yeah. That guilt shit can be a mighty energy sucker."

"Yes. You understand." His smile was brief, lost behind another tip of his glass to his lips. "We'd been married about twelve years, three of them particularly tense, when I decided something needed to be done about it. Actually, that's not true. I had decided that several times before then, each time promising to myself and to her that I'd do better, I'd *be* better. I just was never able to follow through for whatever reason. Different reasons. All poor excuses, but I clung to them and went out of my way to validate them. Which didn't help things. So twelve years in, our marriage on the rocks and knowing she needed to be dominated, believing I couldn't be the one to do it sufficiently, I took her to Exceso for a week. And I introduced her to a dominant I knew there, Renato Fernandez."

My eyes widened. "You introduced her to the man she ran away with?"

"Yes."

"Did you...?" I tried to picture it. *Hi, here's my wife, I can't fulfill her needs so she's all yours.*

That wasn't how marriages worked. No matter how subservient she was, she wasn't property. That couldn't be how it happened. "I don't understand. You *wanted* her to leave you?"

"That hadn't been my intention, no. That was just how it turned out in the end."

So if he hadn't *given* her away...

Comprehension clicked in. "You *shared* her."

"Yes."

I blinked at him, my mouth gaping. "And she just went along?"

He shrugged. "She didn't say one way or another. She never did. She trusted me to make those decisions for her and when I did she simply said, 'Yes, sir,' and complied."

"I don't know what to say." I didn't know what to *feel*. I couldn't decide if it was sick or wrong. Was it even consensual? If she didn't speak up to stop it, then...yes?

But if I had been in her place, if I had been Marion...

Edward uncrossed his legs and sat sharply forward. "These were different circumstances, Celia. She was a different woman, with different needs. I would never—*never*—share you with anyone."

"Let's not make this about me, remember." But that was exactly the lens I was looking at this through. If he ever told me to go to one of his buddies willingly, we'd be over. Immediately.

"I need you to understand that before I go on." His gaze was heavy and insistent. Pleading.

I swallowed down the bad taste in my mouth and tried to focus on what he said. I was not Marion. "I would never go for it, and you know it. You wouldn't even try."

"No, you wouldn't go for it, but that night you and I were on Exceso, you wouldn't have had much choice. If I had really meant to give you to one of those men, you better believe they wouldn't have cared if you consented. It's vital to me that you trust that I would never have gone through with it. You are mine, and no one else's, is that clear?"

"Yes." It came out clipped and tight.

"I need you to say that you understand definitively. That you know I would not do that to you."

He'd told me this that night too, and since, and I did believe him. He hadn't shared me then, and, like he'd said, he could have. For that matter, except for when we were wrapped up in hating each other before we'd married, everything he'd ever said and done backed up what he was saying now. In fact, he was almost overly possessive of me.

Well, not *overly* possessive. Since I liked it.

"I believe you, Edward. I'm yours and no one else's."

"You are," he confirmed. Satisfied, he sat back. "Besides, with Marion, sharing wasn't about sex. Or, it wasn't just about sex. There was that too, which I was part of when it was happening. At least, in the beginning."

"Wait, wait, wait." I pressed my palms together and brought my fingertips to my lips. I was still trying to process that the Edward I knew and loved was not the Edward that Marion had known and loved. "You had a threesome?"

That was it. There was no way I was ever going to compare with her in the bedroom.

He shook his head. "I didn't participate. I watched."

"Oh." Still processing. "Was it hot?"

He chuckled. "Some of it was very hot. When I could get past the seething jealousy."

"Fuck. Why is that just as hard to hear?"

"Because you believe my jealousy says something about how I must have felt about her. It doesn't say any more than the fact that I let it happen in the first place. She was my wife. I loved her. I didn't want her in another man's bed, but I was willing to allow it because I knew it was the only thing that might help me keep her."

"Quit topping from the bottom." This was supposed to be *his* session, not mine, and yet *he* was still analyzing *me*. And still saying things that made it impossible to stop thinking about *us*. "So you're saying that you wouldn't share *me* with anyone, even if it was the only way to keep *me*?"

"Bloody hell, Celia, you're impossible." He growled with frustration. "That would never be the way to keep you, so it's a moot point. It seems you may have other similarly arduous demands, though, so if you want my love for you tested, I'm willing to bet you'll have your way soon enough."

Because I wanted a baby, and he didn't.

I wasn't ready for that conversation again. Not yet. "Okay. You did what you needed to do to keep her. What happened then?"

"It helped, actually," he said. "Renato helped our marriage, I mean. Not because of what occurred that week on the island, but because afterward I urged them to continue their relationship online, and he overtook the tasks I'd grown to resent. He managed her day. He gave her assignments. He gave her what she needed.

"And, I thought, that would be enough for her. She was happier, and I felt...well, free. We made it through two more years together that way. Then, one day—it seemed like it was out of the blue at the time, but in retrospect, I see that it was little by little that she fell for him. That he became more of her master than I was. That she was less and less mine. She wasn't even the one who announced that she was leaving. Renato flew in from Turin and told me with her at his side. He helped her pack her bags, told her what to bring, and she left."

"And you just let her?"

"I was barely in command of her anymore at that point. I should have seen it coming. I wondered for a long time after what would have happened if I'd told her to stay. For the kids, maybe I should have. But asking her to stay would have meant offering to be someone I wasn't, and I couldn't bring myself to say the words."

"Oh, Edward." I slumped in my chair, the reality of what he'd been through finally hitting me. I ached for him, for the man who had loved and tried. For the man who had been forced to fix his marriage on his own. For the weight he must have felt with that burden, and the greater weight he must have felt for having to make a painful choice, one that ended up only bringing him more pain in the end. One that had repercussions on his children.

His guilt had to be endless.

"It's not your fault," I said, realizing that was the reason he'd kept this from me. I leaned forward, my body reaching toward him even as I stayed seated. I wanted to go to him, but also wanted to respect his space. "You couldn't have known. You did your best. You can't blame yourself."

"I know," he said, softly.

"Do you?"

We'd had this conversation in reverse, him assuring me my role in blame, me saying I understood, but not really. It had been horrendous sitting where he was now.

He studied me, as though checking my expression for wounds, as if I were the one who had been confessing my heartache, because he knew what it felt like listening to a loved one's pain.

Then, he came to me. Kneeling in front of me, he wrapped his arms around my calves and kissed the inside of my knee. "She didn't break me, Celia. I know you think she did, but she didn't."

"It's okay if she did. I'll understand."

"I know you will, but she didn't." His hands slid up, over my knees and glided over the skirt of my dress. "I was devastated when she left, not because of her—not because I missed her more than I should, but because I had failed. I had failed at being the husband she wanted me to be."

I ran my hands through his hair, wanting to give him reassurance.

"That stayed with me a long time. I was convinced I didn't know how to do this—this love thing. This commitment thing. Because I hadn't been what Marion needed." He looked up at me, his blue eyes bright. "It wasn't until I met you that I was able to see that she wasn't who I needed her to be either."

My eyes pricked. I spread my thighs wider, inviting him closer.

He came, stopping only when he hit the chair. Reaching up, he brushed his knuckles against my cheek. "I don't want to win all the time, Celia. I don't want to always be the one who decides. I don't want to be alone in this marriage. I want you to challenge me. I want you to step up and stand in my way. I want to boss you around and dominate you, but that can't be everything there is between us. I need you to be with me too. *Beside* me."

Tears spilled out over my cheeks. "I am with you, Edward. Beside you all the way."

He didn't let me say more. His mouth captured mine,

tugging me forward. I slid down to my knees in front of him, pushing the chair back with my body as I did. His kiss grew savage. He devoured me like a hungry man, like he had been too long without affection, without understanding, without love, and now he was starving for it.

Fuck, I was starving too, ravenous for what only he could give me. Together, our hands worked fast, removing clothes at lightning speeds until we were both naked and sprawled out on the floor.

He paused as he perched above me, the head of his cock notched at my pussy, while he traced my swollen lips with a single finger.

"Don't tease," I begged. "Fuck me, Edward. Fuck me hard."

He pushed inside me then, slowly, ignoring my pleas for speed. Even after he was deeply seated, he didn't move faster. He took his time, making sure I felt every inch of his cock on each one of his strokes. It was maddening how it prolonged the build of my orgasm, stretching it out like the anticipation of a dawdling sneeze. Coupled with the way he gazed at me, his eyes spearing me with equal intensity, I felt more filled by him than I ever had.

He spoke to me as he fucked me without ever using words, whispering kisses along my jawline, murmuring his hands along my skin, articulating his love through each thrust of his cock, until I was overcome by his discourse, my entire being shivering and trembling with sensation.

I love you, I said without uttering a single syllable, as I arched up, my back bent with the atomic force of pleasure ripping through me. My pussy clamped around him, and he stilled, rooting firmly inside me until my climax had finished. Then, when he resumed his thrusts, he relaxed his tempo further, threatening to drive me even more insane as he leisurely drew another orgasm from my body.

Minutes might have passed. Or hours. I lost all sense of time and space, my focus anchored only on him and the infinite joy that existed in that singular moment. I'd meant what I'd said to him—I was one hundred percent committed to be with him through this marriage, to be by his side, but right now I was perfectly content being underneath.

Later, when we were in our bed, my cheek pressed against his chest, I began to remember the issues that existed beyond the here and now. We'd entered a new phase of our relationship. We'd leveled up, and I didn't want to ruin the mood when I felt so deeply connected to him, but there was no real progress in our new position if we didn't face it all.

"What about the other stuff, Edward? The things we talked about yesterday." The baby I wanted, the revenge he wanted. I was grateful for the dark and that I couldn't see his expression from where I lay in his arms.

"Well," he said, his arms tightening around me. "First, we deal with Ron."

"Okay."

He placed a kiss on the top of my head. "Then, when that's done, we'll fight. And one of us will win. But we have a while before we have to think about that, so let's leave that for the future."

And, for once, I didn't challenge him. I didn't push him or make a stink. I simply agreed and clung onto the truth that we'd both acknowledged now—that I wasn't Marion, that he didn't want me to be—and hoped that meant he understood I wouldn't fight fair.

TWENTY

EDWARD

I studied the prospective report in front of me, zeroing in on required labor. The last report on this subject hadn't been as favorable. That had been a year ago, shortly before Genevieve graduated.

"We need someone else on the development team," I said to Hagan, who sat on the other side of my desk. "Do you have someone who's capable?"

"I have some possibilities."

When he didn't say more right away, I sensed he was reluctant to air his suggestion. I looked up from the report to him. "Whoever it is, tell me."

"Just...are you sure you don't want to move Genevieve over? She's really got a unique viewpoint and could be an incredible asset."

I had to force myself not to growl. When I'd broken down and hired her before the holidays, I'd made sure Hagan understood that she wouldn't work anywhere near my department. I'd drilled it into him. "We've been over this."

"We have, but we haven't. I don't get why you hired her if you don't want to actually use her skills."

I set the report down and folded my hands together on my desk so that I wouldn't be tempted to punch it. "I hired her because she wouldn't accept a handout any other way. And because that pathetic excuse for a network made a poor line on her resume."

When she continued to reject all my attempts to give her assistance, I'd reluctantly offered her a position in out-reach, a department I rarely worked with, and given her an annual salary that provided her a comfortable cushion. After a couple of years, she could move on to something worthwhile. Accelecom would look good under her belt. There was no one in the industry who could deny her with that experience.

She'd only accepted because she was eager for good work in the field. Once she did, I felt a mammoth relief, despite knowing I was bringing her to the fringes of my world. It was the right thing to do, in the end, though I was still irked that she refused to move from the miserable dump of a neighborhood that she'd selected.

Maybe I could negotiate that in exchange for bringing her to the development team…

No. That was too close to me. Too close to her discovering the person I didn't want her to realize I was.

Without any warning, my office door flung open.

"My father is retiring," Celia declared as she strode in. It had been nearly a year since the last time she burst past my assistant, the day she'd yelled at me for acting on her behalf behind her back before asking for a baby. I was grateful that she didn't use the tactic often, but my wife did indeed know how to make an entrance.

On the heels of her announcement, Charlotte's voice rang over the intercom. "Your wife is here."

"Thank you, Charlotte. I'm well aware." A second glance at Celia's expression inspired me to add an addendum before I released the button on the intercom. "Please make sure we aren't disturbed."

"Will do."

Hagan spun around in his chair to face Celia. "Warren is stepping down from Werner Media? Who is he naming as his replacement?"

He'd beat me to the burning question. I looked back to her, eager for her response.

"He hasn't named anyone yet. He isn't planning to make a formal announcement for several weeks. My mother told me this morning that he's only just definitively decided." Her voice tightened, and, only then, I realized she was on the verge of tears. "He's going to find out. He's going to name someone, and if Hudson doesn't vote in his favor, he's going to find out he doesn't own the majority shares anymore."

Technically, Warren already knew he didn't own the majority shares because he gave all of his to his daughter. But even if Celia hadn't signed over her voting power to him, she would never vote against his wishes.

None of that was the point.

I stood up from my desk and came around to embrace her. "Shh. No need to worry down that route. You have no idea how this will play out."

She pulled out of my arms. "I know that Hudson wants to have the upper hand, and without my father at the helm, he doesn't have that anymore. He loses his ace. Trust me when I say he's not going to just hand that over."

My head was at least five steps ahead of her, my pulse racing from the possibilities that this change in situation might bring.

I forced myself to slow down until I'd brought her up to speed. "If Pierce still believes he needs to put pressure on you after all this time—"

"He will," she insisted. "Trust me on this. He will."

I wasn't so sure. Few people had the doggedness to intimidate a foe for long periods of time. If Hudson Pierce truly was one with such tenacity, well, then he was a man after my own heart. One to be admired.

Either way, it was best to plan for the worst. "Then he'll want to keep that card as long as possible. He'll let the position go to the person your father chooses so that he can remind you that he's only allowing it as long as you behave."

That was how I would play it, anyway. His threat over Celia only worked as long as his ownership of the shares remained secret. Once that was out, he had no more leverage.

She frowned as she considered my logic.

"I feel like this is an appropriate time to ask what you're talking about. Are you saying Hudson Pierce owns more shares of Werner than your father?" Hagan had no issues inserting himself into conversations that might not concern him. It made him a good businessman. It also made him an annoying son.

I opened my mouth to tell him to get out of my office, but Celia spoke first. "It's a long, complicated story, but the short answer is yes. Hudson secretly owns more shares and has promised to let my father continue running the company as though he's in charge as long as I…" She sighed. "As long as I leave him alone, really."

"Ah." His expression said he understood clearly. "Dad's usually on the other side of those arrangements. Listen to him on this one."

I grimaced, not sure I liked how well my son knew me. It shouldn't have come as a surprise, really, considering how long we'd been working together. He was a bright fellow after all.

But Hagan's knowledge of my less ethical dealings wasn't where my focus needed to be at the moment. "Think it through," I said to Celia. "Like you said, there is no advantage to Pierce letting the upper hand go."

She nudged a tear away from the corner of her eye with her knuckle. "Hudson will want to have a say in who my father chooses, though. He has a lot of money wrapped up in Werner. He won't just care about keeping a thumb on me. It's also in his best interest if the company succeeds."

Now she was thinking logically. "He's trusted Warren so far. There's no reason Pierce won't trust him to pick his replacement." I thrust my hand in my pocket so she wouldn't see it twitching from my anxiousness to get to the next part of this scenario.

She brought her hands together and rested them against her lips. "You're right," she said with a nod. "You're right. I don't need to worry about this. It's not a problem."

"Precisely." I gave it a single beat before I launched her in a new direction. "There is an opportunity here, though. Do you see it?"

Her nose wrinkled in confusion.

"You could take his spot," Hagan said, excitedly. "Accelecom and Werner could merge, and you could run them both."

He really was my son. With, perhaps, a little less tact.

Celia chortled. "That wasn't what you were going to suggest, was it? Because if it was, you've clearly gone mad."

"I don't think it's all that insane of an idea," I protested. "We've done that joint deal in India recently. Your father keeps pushing me to do more joint ventures. He already likes the idea of our companies working together." The only reason I'd refrained from doing more was out of spite. Warren Werner might not have been the person who brought down my father's company, but he'd been the man who hadn't believed his daughter when she'd told him about her uncle's assaults. It was a subtle form of punishment. One I could dole out without Celia's wrath.

But merging after Warren stepped down? Me at the helm? That was even better than vengeance. That was providence.

Hagan jumped up from his chair. "I think it's absolutely brilliant."

This time I turned to glare at my son. Helpful as he thought he was being, he was not.

"I'm already leaving. Don't worry." He picked his briefcase off the floor and hustled out of the room.

As soon as the door shut behind him, I turned back to my wife who was staring at me in disbelief, all signs of amusement wiped from her face. "How can you possibly think that would be a good idea? Even if you can win my father over to it, there is no way Hudson will stand for it."

I shrugged. "Why not? You said yourself that you believe he wants the company to succeed."

"He wants power over me, Edward. If he let control of Werner go to my husband, he'd be giving me power, not holding it over me."

"Not true. It wouldn't be any different than when your father had control. Pierce would still have the upper hand. He could still overrule any one of my decisions."

She continued to gape. "You wouldn't ever really be in charge. Why would you even want that?"

Because I wanted Werner Media. I had for a long time. While my initial reasons for wanting it were no longer valid, the desire was still there, a bad habit I couldn't kick.

And now, it was possible I didn't have to.

"I would be in charge," I said. "As much in charge as your father has been for the past handful of years, and, as everyone in the world besides you, me, and Hudson Pierce—including your father—believe that Warren is running the company, I think it's fair to say he *is* running the company."

"I don't believe this." She turned away from me to pace. "I've spent the last couple of years trying to rid my-self of the hold Hudson had on me, and you want to take me right back to where I was. This is my chance to extri-cate myself from that completely."

I was about to give her another reason that this idea was, as Hagan said, indeed brilliant, but her latest state-ment tripped me up. "What do you mean by that? You'd played a game on Hudson, and he bought into Werner to prevent you from doing that again. Was there more to the situation? Why did he have more hold on you than any of the other people you played?"

She stopped mid-stride, her back to me. Then she shook her head and turned to face me. "He didn't. I meant that I've been trying to distance myself from everything from that time."

There was something off about her excuse, something not quite the truth. But I was pretty sure I could figure it out without her admission. Likely, the reason Pierce bothered her more than the others was because he was, as far as I knew, the one person who had played her back. I had a feeling she rarely had anyone pull one over on her. Before me, anyway.

I took a conciliatory step toward her. "That's understandable. I know you aren't the person you once were, and I'm sure it's hard to accept that there are others who will never realize that. But I assure you, the situation won't be any different from what it is now. In fact, if he's as smart as I think he is, Pierce should prefer that the person who takes over for your father be one that is close to you. His ace has higher value then."

Her mouth twisted as she thought it over, obviously torn. "What if Hudson doesn't see it your way? He might want to be done with me as much as I want to be done with him. He might not agree with your reasoning."

"Then we convince him." It was the wrong thing to say, and I knew it even before her shoulders went rigid and her brow tensed.

I reached out for her hand and tugged her into my arms. "*I'll* convince him," I corrected. I kissed her temple. "You won't have to have any part of it. I'm fairly confident I can point out the wisdom of having me in the position on both a business and personal level. And I'm *absolutely* confident that I can persuade your father to name me as his successor. He'll never know the decision wasn't his."

Celia remained stiff, yet she didn't pull away. She clearly wasn't convinced, but I had a feeling she wouldn't stand in my way if I pursued this plan. And I *would* pursue this plan.

But I wanted more than reluctant acquiescence. I'd spent the last year trying to live up to my word, encouraging her to be my partner. I wanted her on my side on this.

And, for the life of me, I couldn't understand why she was against it.

I massaged the small of her back with the flat of my hand. "Don't you want to see Werner stay in your family? Don't you want to pass it on down the line?"

I wasn't playing nice, baiting her like this. We hadn't spoken again about a possible child in the last eleven months, but it was always there between us, the thing we both knew she wanted.

Soon, we'd discuss it again. Camilla had made significant progress with Ron. He'd initially accepted her invitation to Exceso last September, but then pushed off actually going until January.

The delay had made me more anxious. I needed to feel more in control of the setup. So, despite the worries that my marriage to Celia might make it hard for Ron to trust me, I went to the island in January as well, just to be sure the introduction to Leroy Jones, my FBI contact, happened as it should.

Once we were all there, the pieces fell into place. Though I didn't much interact with Ron personally while I was there, he saw the unorthodox sexual acts that took place on the island, realized I was more than open to the majority of them, and any doubt he might have had about me was seemingly erased.

Camilla was the linchpin of it all. She introduced Ron to Leroy who did his part by sharing child pornography with Ron that he'd borrowed from the bureau and talking up the young girls he'd supposedly taken advantage of, all in the hopes of gaining Ron's trust. They hadn't shared contact info when they parted—Leroy insisted it was too suspicious, that these men kept private details to themselves as much as possible—but Ron did promise to contact Camilla when he next had an "event" so that she could forward the invitation.

That had been five months ago with no word since. Still, I was sure that he'd reach out soon. That he'd be arrested and put away. That I'd finally be free of the burden of revenge, and Celia and I could move on to figuring out the rest of our lives.

If that future could include a baby for her, why not also Werner Media for me?

"Yes, I do want that, but..." She tilted her head up toward me. "But I don't care who runs the company. That's not lasting. I'd rather have the shares back. That's what I really want, and all of this just reminds me that the reason they're gone is because of me. And I can't change that."

The weight of her guilt was so heavy, it felt like I carried it too. God, I wanted that gone for her. I wanted her pain erased. I wanted the man who'd encouraged her to play these games in the first place to have to pay for these mistakes the way she did.

He would, eventually. I was determined.

I was also determined to get her company back for her, in whatever way I could.

I cupped the sides of her face. "It won't be like this forever, bird. I'll take over the company, I'll show Pierce he can trust me. Then, when it's time, he'll sell those shares to us. I promise you."

"No, Edward. Don't worry about that, please. Don't go head to head with Hudson. I don't want that."

"It won't be like that. Trust me. It will be friendly." Unless Pierce refused to keep it that way.

Before she could respond, Charlotte's voice sounded over the intercom. "Sorry to interrupt but Camilla is on the line. She insisted it was urgent."

I exchanged a glance with Celia before I pulled away and crossed to my desk. "Put her through," I said, my finger pressed on the intercom button. A split second later, the phone rang. I hit speaker. "What's up?"

"We have a problem," she said. "I'm in the elevator. Be there soon."

She hung up. Immediately, I buzzed Charlotte, telling her to send Camilla in when she arrived.

"Is it Ron?" Celia asked, her voice thin.

"I don't know what else would be urgent." If it were something at Accelecom, she would have brought her issues to me through different methods. If it were something to do with Freddie, she'd be with him, not coming into my office.

The tension built as we waited in silence, the seconds passing like years before Camilla knocked once and burst in.

"Is it Ron?" Celia asked at the same time I said, "What happened with Ron?"

My sister paused, taken aback by the barrage of questions. "Good. You're both here. This makes things easier." She tossed her purse on the sofa and crossed to my minibar where she took out a bottle of tequila and poured herself a shot, arguably a better means of coping than her usual means. She threw it back before turning to address us. "I heard from Ron."

Instinctively, Celia and I stepped toward her in unison, as if being nearer would encourage her to deliver her information more quickly.

"And...?" I prodded her.

"And it's all a big fuck-up," she said with despair. "He's having a 'party,' and he invited me and Leroy, which is all good. But the party isn't in the States. It's here. On Saturday night."

"Fuck. That's in two days," Celia said, aghast.

"Right. There wasn't a contingency for this. And it's not enough time to make one." She ran a hand through her hair. "I stuck to the plan, though. I told him that Leroy was interested and that I was sure he'd be there. I'm supposed to call back by five to tell him for sure."

I was already moving back around my desk to retrieve my cell phone from the top drawer. I pulled up Leroy's contact number and hit the call button, glancing at my watch as I did. It was half past one here, and Albuquerque was seven hours behind us. That made it...

"It's six-goddamned-thirty in the morning," Leroy said when he answered. "This better be good. I was just about to go for my run."

"It's not good, but it's important." I turned away from the women so I could focus on my conversation instead of theirs. "Ron reached out to Camilla. Party's on Saturday. Problem is it's here, in London. You can make that happen, can't you?"

I wasn't honestly sure that he could. Sure, Leroy could get on a plane and arrive in time, but Britain wasn't his jurisdiction. He couldn't make any arrests without coordinating with the local police, and with the short notice, an operation of that size could very well be out of the question.

But I wasn't ready to acknowledge the improbability. We'd worked too hard, invested too much time. This had to work.

"Jesus Christ," Leroy swore loudly in my ear. "This guy is good. He did this purposefully. He never said one word that this might take place off of U.S. grounds. He knew this would pose a problem."

"He is good, and that's why we have to take the bloody arse down. Tell me you can make it happen."

He groaned. "Fuck. Yes. I think so. I have to... Fuck." I waited as patiently as possible while he thought through the process. "Okay. I know some people at MI6. I'll contact them, see what we can do. This isn't their arena, but hopefully they can get us in touch with someone local. I'll give them your name and contact info, since I'll be on the soonest flight I can book. They may need to arrange some of this shit with you while I'm up in the air."

I could hear typing in the background, Leroy on his computer, likely pulling up the contacts he needed as we spoke.

"That's good. That's all good." If I said it enough, maybe it would decrease the size of the boulder in my stomach. "You'll get on a plane, I'll wait for the cops to call. What else do you need me to do?"

"I'm going to be honest, Edward. This is going to be tough. There might not be time for warrants. I don't have authority. I might not even be given permission to go to this shindig with immunity."

Panic crept into my voice. "You have to be here, Leroy.

It's your name on that invite list. You're the one he trusts."

"I know, man. And I'm going to be there. I'll deal with the red tape afterward. Meanwhile, I need to get things rolling. I'll call you back when I have some more news."

"All right," I said, calmer now that he'd assured me he was seeing this through. "Talk later."

I hung up and turned around to find both my sister and my wife looking expectantly toward me.

"Call Ron back," I said, sounding more calm than I felt. "Tell him Leroy will be there."

She started to cross to the couch, reaching for her purse, but I wasn't done. Leroy had me worried. If he couldn't get permission to put this together, if he didn't have authority, there was a good chance he'd call everything off.

Even if he didn't, I didn't feel good about having all our eggs in one basket. Leroy was the one who had developed trust with Ron, but so had Camilla. Like hell was I letting her walk into that party, but she might be able to add another name to the invitation list, if the name was someone that Ron knew for absolute certain wasn't an undercover agent of some sort.

"And one more thing," I said as Camilla brought her mobile to her ear. "See if you can get me on that list as well."

TWENTY-ONE

CELIA

I stood in front of the door to the library for several seconds, my hand on the knob. Then changed my mind and headed back down the hallway toward the stairs. Once I reached them, I changed my mind again. I'd tried to hold my tongue, but this was too important, and if I didn't speak now, it would be too late.

Determined, this time I didn't pause at all. I threw the door open and marched in.

"Don't do this," I said, my eyes pinned on Edward.

He was standing in front of his desk, one hip leaning against it. From his open mouth and the position of his hands, I guessed he'd been mid-sentence when I interrupted.

He looked at me for a solid two seconds before turning his focus back to the others—Leroy who was perched on the arm of a chair, Camilla who was pacing by the fireplace, Dominic and Felisha, two police officers, seated on the sofa.

"—send the signal for the bust to take place?" Edward continued with whatever question he'd begun before I entered.

Following his lead, the others ignored me as well. "The situation has to progress far enough that they'll be 'caught in the act' when we arrive," Felisha said.

"I can give the signal," Leroy said. "But if I'm unable to, for any reason, I'll ask you what time it is. You can naturally look at your watch and hit the button then."

I'd been in the room earlier, not for long because it made me anxious, but long enough to hear about the watch that they'd given Edward with a button that would send an alarm to the police. Leroy and Edward wouldn't be allowed to bring their phones in, and they might even be screened for a wire. The watch, though, should pass inspection.

Should being the key word.

Should being the reason I had anxiety.

Should wasn't definite, and with all the talk of how sophisticated Ron's operation was, there was no telling how he'd handle someone found to be operating undercover. What would happen if Edward and Leroy got caught?

"Edward, don't do this," I pleaded. "Leroy already offered to do it alone. It doesn't have to be you."

Except for a glance at me before Dominic spoke, I was again ignored. "Fortunately, since we were already watching Garrick Till, we know the best ways to approach. We'll be inside within minutes after you send the alarm."

Garrick was a long-time friend of my uncle's, apparently, and, though Ron was the official host, the party tonight was taking place at his house. I'd never heard his name until this week, but, unbeknownst to Till, he was well-known by the local authorities as a possible sex offender. They'd been trying for months to nail him with something but hadn't been able to infiltrate his circle. Their investigation was the only reason this sting was able to come together on such short notice. They'd already had the primary evidence gathered when Leroy had reached out. Getting the needed warrants hadn't been a problem at all.

I'd been flabbergasted as the details about Ron's circle had unfolded over the last two days. I'd always believed the man who had groomed me and abused me had only been able to do so because he'd had access to me. When I was no longer sent to spend time alone with him, I was convinced his behavior had come to a forced end.

Instead, it seemed I'd only been a small part of his sick network. I likely wasn't even the beginning. His methods had been too exact. He'd become an expert well before I came into his life.

Every new thing I learned confirmed one thing—Ron Werner needed to be taken down.

But that didn't mean that Edward had to be the one to do it.

I changed my tactic. "Leroy, tell him. Tell him this is stupid. What if Ron already suspects Edward? What if he discovers the watch before they get in?"

"It's seven twenty-three," Leroy said, disregarding me. "We should get going soon."

"I'll go up and get changed." Edward strode past me and out of the room.

Felisha, most likely pitying me, stood and walked to me. "There's no way anyone will suspect the watch signals the police to come, but, if they do, the worst that will happen is they'll confiscate it before he goes in. In which case,

Leroy or Edward will flash the lights. We'll be watching, and we'll see it."

Her words didn't comfort me. It only brought up a whole new slew of what-ifs, but I had no interest in discussing them with her. I turned away from her only to find Camilla waiting at my side.

"Ron didn't flinch at all when I asked to put Edward on the guest list," she said. "He doesn't suspect. After getting him to Exceso, he trusts me. I understand why this might be hard for you. I don't know if Edward ever mentioned, but Frank, my husband, was abusive. I knew I needed to leave him, but I stayed eleven years because I believed I loved him. What I'm saying is it's okay to have complicated feelings about your abuser. It's natural."

I was sure my expression was one of horror. There was too much to process. Her husband had abused her? She thought I wanted to stop Edward because I had "complicated feelings" for Ron?

"That's not—" I shook my head and left it at that. I didn't have time for this. Turning again, I hurried out after Edward.

In our bedroom, I found his shoes kicked off by the door and his jacket thrown on the bed. I headed toward the closet and found him in his boxer briefs, about to put his leg into his tuxedo pants. He glanced up at my arrival, then, like downstairs, went back to what he'd been doing.

"Don't go tonight. Please," I begged. When he didn't look up again, I snapped. "Do not just ignore me, Edward. That's not fair."

He finished fastening his pants then put his fists on his hips and sighed. "You should consider going to Amelie for a while. There will most likely be press clamoring to talk to anyone related to your family. Might do you good to stay away from the chaos."

Ordinarily, I liked the way he looked out for me. Tonight, when he refused to let me look out for him, it just pissed me off. "Don't treat me like I'm a fragile fucking flower."

His eyes flashed with anger. "Then stop acting like a fragile fucking flower."

Oh, it was on now. I took it as progress. Fighting was definitely a step up from being ignored. "It's not fragile to want my husband to stay safe. It's smart. Usually I don't have to explain intelligent behavior to you."

He pulled a white dress shirt out of his drawer, shaking it out before shoving an arm in the sleeve. He was calmer when he spoke. "There's nothing unsafe about what we're doing tonight. Our plan is solid. We've worked hard to gain Ron's trust, and it's paid off. I promise you."

"You can't promise that when you don't know. You can't have any idea what you're getting into. What if they take the watch? What if you don't have access to the lights? What if you can't get word to anyone?" My throat burned, I was so worked up. "Don't do this. It's too risky. Let the experts take care of it. It doesn't have to be you."

"You're really asking me to walk away from this? After everything that I've done to get here? After all the time and energy and years I've put into avenging my family?" He took a step toward me, his voice sharper. "After what he did to *you*? You're lucky I don't insist on murdering him with my bare hands. If you're worried about the risk, that's the biggest one I'll be facing, because believe me when I say that it will take a lot of restraint not to do just that."

He fumed, his nostrils flaring. "And you're worried about me being safe? I guarantee you that I'll be a whole hell of a lot safer than the little girls he plans on parading out tonight to a room full of predators. Little girls as innocent as you once were. How safe are they?"

I wanted to be strong.

But I couldn't help it—I burst into tears.

In an instant, his arms were around me. He hadn't gotten to buttoning up his shirt yet, so I pressed my cheek against his warm skin and let all the anxiety, all the fear, all the tension come out through my tears.

He rocked me, his voice soft and soothing. "We're so close to having this be over, bird. I want to be there when it is. I *need* to be there. I need this motherfucker to know that I'm behind this. That this is for us. That this is for you."

I hated it, but I got it. How many times had I imagined doing horrible things to my uncle? Or my father for not believing me? I'd even started to fantasize what my father would say when this all went down. It was sure as shit I'd tell him that Ron was in jail because of me. I suspected that would be the best part of all this.

Could I ask Edward to give up the best part for him? When he'd emphasized so many times that he was sure this would be the only way he'd truly be able to heal?

The tears fell faster. "You're going to see things, Edward, shocking things, and you're going to know how it happened for me. I don't want you to see that. I don't want you to know."

"Oh, bird." He forced my chin up so he could look into my eyes. "It doesn't matter what I see. Nothing that happens tonight will change that terrible things have already happened to you. If I know more of the details of that, or if I don't, it doesn't change that I am bloody deep in love with the woman those terrible things turned you into. Let me prove that love to you. Let me be there to see his face when they nail the bastard."

My breath shuddered as I drew it in. "Okay."

He swiped a tear from my cheek with his thumb then kissed my forehead. "Thank you." Then his lips found mine, and he kissed me with his gratitude.

He pulled away reluctantly. "I have to finish dressing now."

I nodded, then left him in the closet. The outburst having drained me of all my energy, I only made it to the armchair in the bedroom before I had to sit. As Edward said, all of this was almost over. After all the years I'd spent believing Ron would never be punished, he was finally going to have to face his wrongs.

It was exciting, in a way. And overwhelming. Was this really part of the healing process? Was this a necessary step? Would I be free of his hold on me once and for all after tonight?

I closed my eyes, trying to imagine that relief. Instantly, I was taken over by a memory from the distant past. The first party that Ron had brought me to, not the one where he'd auctioned parts of me off to the highest bidder, but one that had occurred the year before. He'd dressed me in a fancy gown, one much too mature for a girl of twelve. My breasts had only started to come in, and the bodice of the dress gaped, showing my nipples if I wasn't careful. I remembered being self-conscious about it, constantly trying to pull the dress up while Ron swatted my hands away.

"Leave it," he'd said. *"You're breathtaking. Let all my friends see how gorgeous you are."*

Then he'd paraded me through the den filled with men in tuxes who gave me similar compliments as I passed. I was instructed to address each one as *sir*, told to thank them for their praise. Told to not look away when someone pulled out his cock and stroked it in my presence or when one of the scantily clad women put it in her mouth while the man stared at me with a heavily lidded gaze.

I opened my eyes and shook the memory from me, swallowing the bile that had formed in the back of my mouth. These thoughts still haunted me. Less than they once had, but they still popped up now and again, when I least expected it. I was pretty sure that no matter what happened tonight, even if Ron was put away for the rest of his life, the past would still linger. I wouldn't be magically healed. Vengeance couldn't undo what had been done.

But Edward believed it could. Maybe believing would be enough to make it true for him.

So when he came out of the closet looking crisp and dashing in his tux, I ignored the knot in my stomach, ignored how he reminded me of the men from that party in the past, and smiled appraisingly up at him. "Good luck," I said. "I hope it's all that you need it to be."

And if it wasn't, I wondered what it would take, what he'd have to do. Wondered how far he'd go to reach the ending he desired.

I stayed sitting there for a while after he left, not thinking about anything while the sun set out the window, spreading orange and pink rays across the wall. It was almost dark when I finally stirred from my daze. I stood and flipped on the overhead light then picked up Edward's shoes and jacket and carried them to the closet. After putting the shoes on their space on the shelf, I took the jacket to the bag designated for drycleaning, remembering to check the pockets before I dumped it in. There were only a few items this time—a pen, a small stack of business cards, a piece of stationary folded into a square.

Being nosy, I unfolded the paper, and when my eyes found Camilla's signature at the bottom, I decided to read the entire thing.

Eddie,

I haven't always been enthusiastic about your schemes, even when they've been orchestrated for my benefit. I want you to know that I do support you, that I appreciate what you're doing in the name of our parents, and that I'm forever grateful for what you've done for me. After what we did to Frank, I didn't think that I'd ever be able to say that, but you were right—his death was the best thing to happen to me. I'm lucky to have you on my side.

Camilla

With my heart in my throat, I read it again. And a third time. I thought about what Camilla had said earlier, that Frank had been abusive. I thought about the odd ways she'd talked about her husband's death in the past. Thought about Edward's admission to having no boundaries.

Then I sank to the floor in shock.

Because I was pretty certain that I'd just learned that Edward killed Camilla's husband.

TWENTY-TWO

EDWARD

Leroy and I arrived separately to the party. My driver had taken him and dropped him off while I'd driven myself, leaving about ten minutes after he had. It was likely an insignificant detail that few people would pick up on, but we decided it was better to take every precaution.

"No cameras or recording equipment of any kind are permitted," the security guard at the door said. He gestured to a row of containers laid out on a long table behind him. "You can leave your phone in one of the boxes."

I retrieved my mobile from my jacket pocket and set it in an empty container. It wasn't secured the way belongings were at The Open Door in the States, but I imagined the trust level at these things was already high. Guests in attendance were confident that others weren't going to turn them in for illegal activity. Stolen devices seemed a trivial concern under the circumstances.

No one realized that all of these items would be confiscated before the night was over.

Leroy had warned me about that prior, so the mobile I checked in was a dummy. Mine was tucked safely in the glove box of my BMW.

"Spread your arms, please," the guard said next then waved a wand metal detector across my body. When nothing set it off, I was allowed past the entry. All of this before even giving anyone my name.

Two men in tuxes greeted me as soon as I stepped into the hall. One asked for my ID and then scanned a copy with his mobile when I handed it over.

"He's on the list," the other confirmed before making eye contact with me. "Follow me, Mr. Fasbender."

He led me down the hall, stopping when the walls opened up to a game room on our left. "The bar is self-serve," he said. "You can make yourself a drink and mingle with the others in the billiards room. We won't escort anyone into the ballroom until everyone has arrived."

I nodded and stepped over the threshold, scanning my surroundings. Immediately, I spotted Leroy, gathered with a trio of men by the liquor. Across the room from him, I saw another man I knew, Jeffrey Varga, one of the owners of Mills and Varga, the pathetic little network that had briefly employed my daughter.

Thank God I'd rescued her from that establishment. I'd thought Jeffrey was smarmy because of his pathetic business practices. I never would have guessed his wretchedness extended to his sexual behavior as well.

He lifted his glass when he saw me, and I forced myself to return a smile. He likely wasn't the only prominent man I would encounter this evening. It gave me a strange sort of high realizing I would be the downfall of these nasty predators.

At that thought, my smile turned genuine.

"I don't believe we've met." A portly man, old enough to be my father, extended a clammy hand in my direction. "Garrick Till. This is my house. You haven't been here before. May I ask who vouched for you?"

I wasn't sure whose name to give. Camilla's? Leroy's? And while the answer would be just as baffling if I'd come as a true guest, not knowing made my pulse speed up.

Before I could form a response, a hand clapped at my back. "Leave him alone, Garrick," a male voice said beside me. "I vouch for him. He's family."

"Ron," I said, somehow managing to keep the tightness from my voice. "I'm glad to know you consider me family, as we've had so little time to get acquainted." My skin crawled under the flat of his palm, and it took everything in me not to shudder.

"Nonsense. What else would you be? Though, if I'd known we shared the same interests, I would have made it a priority to get to know you sooner. I'm surprised our paths hadn't crossed before Exceso."

"My interests aren't quite so narrow in focus," I said. "All sorts of taboo catch my attention. This particular arena hasn't been one I've been able to delve into before now, I'm afraid."

"You're in for a real treat, I'll tell you. Hope you brought your checkbook." He dropped his hand and nudged Garrick. "Edward Fasbender. Owns Accelecom, and guess who he married. Celia."

Garrick's brows rose. "*Your* Celia?"

No, not his fucking Celia. Possessiveness boiled up inside me like lava.

"Yes, *my* Celia," Ron said with a disgusting chuckle. "I think you remember her fondly."

Garrick's eyes sparked. "That I do. Tightest virgin I've ever had around my fingers, that one. I'm sure you don't mind me telling you that. We're all accustomed to sharing here."

My vision went red. Garrick Till had to be one of the five who had bought my wife when Ron had auctioned her off to the highest bidders, and I wanted him dead. Fuck the mission for the evening. I was three seconds from lacerating his carotid artery with my fingernail.

Fortunately, an almost imperceptible jab at my side stopped me before I attacked. "Ed Fasbender," Leroy said, a warning in his tone only I would be able to detect. "I thought I saw you come in."

"That's right, you two already know each other," Ron said. "Camilla introduce you?"

I shook my head, remembering our story. We'd decided beforehand it would be easiest to keep details straight if they were close to the truth. "I'm the one who introduced my sister to Leroy. Met him on Exceso. When was that, 'Roy? Eight years ago now?"

Leroy pretended to think about it. "Sounds about right."

"He had the best damn collection of porn I'd ever seen at the time, and it's only got better since."

"I've seen it," Ron said excitedly. "Mine isn't quite as extensive, but I encourage you to check it out." He pointed at a bunch of photo albums strewn across the farthest billiard table. "That wife of yours used to be a good little model. Hope she's still rewarding you with what I taught her."

I was going to be ill. Not only was he a bloody sick

bastard, but he was proud of it. If I could ensure he got raped in prison, it still wouldn't be what he deserved.

"Has he seen our star of the night yet?" Garrick was an equally despicable monster.

"Ah, let me show you." The rule banning recording equipment obviously didn't extend to Ron who pulled a mobile phone from inside his tux jacket. After a few taps, he tilted the screen toward us. "Aster. She's as much of a flower as her name. Absolutely stunning girl."

The picture had three figures dressed for a night out—Ron, a dark-haired woman around the age of forty, and a young girl, the mirror image of the woman, who couldn't be more than twelve.

I could hear the blood rushing in my ears as anger flushed through my body. What horrors had that girl already been through at his hands? Did the mother have any idea what he was doing? How the fuck did she allow Ron to be alone with her daughter?

Leroy, trained to be better at this than I was, had the appropriate response. "Nice. The mother a friend of yours?"

"I've been seeing her casually," Ron said. "She's good enough at the role play, but, obviously the highlight of dating her is Aster."

"Lucky asshole," Leroy said conjovially. "Mother isn't going to be a problem tonight, is she?"

"Definitely not. Roofied her up about an hour ago. She'll be out until morning."

Again, Ron sounded like he was boasting. He fit right in with some of the depraved men I'd met on Exceso, but none had ever been so revolting. I knew it was because of Celia, that I cared more because I loved her and knew what he'd done to her. That knowledge made me disgusted with myself as well. After this, I vowed, when I was sure all the men here had thoroughly paid for these crimes, I'd be sure to invest in going after more of the evil fucktards that I dealt with. That was a promise.

Garrick flicked his wrist to look at his watch. "'Bout time to start, Ron."

Ron looked at the time on his mobile before tucking it away. "I'll go up and get her ready. Meanwhile, men, I hope you get some time with my albums. Oh, and Edward, there are some women of the night waiting in the ballroom, all of them paid to do whatever you're up for, no matter how taboo. Be sure to know that anything you do with them, as everything that happens here, will stay confidential."

He winked, alluding to the secrets he expected I was keeping from my wife, then merrily left the room. Garrick wandered on as well, needing to refill his drink.

I exchanged a glance with Leroy. Were we monsters for letting any of this happen at all? The police had emphasized the need to catch Ron and Garrick in the act, meaning we needed to not only let Aster be presented before signaling the raid, but we also had to let her be violated. Could I really do that? How much could I stand? Could the collection of porn be enough to nail Ron right now? Hell only knew what would be found on the guests' mobiles.

My gaze shifted toward the albums.

"Ten year max," Leroy whispered, reading my mind. "Not nearly enough. I'm going to go check them out, see what we have." He paused, and I knew we were both thinking about the pictures that he'd see, the ones that were very possibly of Celia. "Don't look at them, okay? You know enough. This doesn't need to haunt you too."

If it happened to Celia, I wanted it to haunt me too. She was certainly haunted. It wasn't fair that she had to endure that alone.

But she wouldn't want me seeing that like this, surrounded by men who got aroused by her young image. If there were indeed pics of her, she'd find out when the images were sorted and documented in the future. I couldn't protect her from that, but I could protect her from the crude things that were said by those viewing them if I wasn't there to hear them myself.

"I'll make myself a drink," I said, deciding that was a better way to spend the next few minutes. Maybe the alcohol would burn away the rotten taste in my mouth.

It was almost ten minutes later when Garrick gathered the guests together. There were twenty-six in all, twenty-four men who would be charged at least with indecency of a minor before the night was through. Some would be hit with more depending on how the rest of the evening played out.

The thrill of that knowledge—along with the cognac—was the only thing propelling me out of the game room and into the room that was set up to look more like a pleasure den than a ballroom. Comfortable sofas and chaise lounges were scattered throughout the space, beautiful women perched on several. Baskets littered the room, filled with what looked like lube and condoms. A table hugged the back wall with a variety of pleasure toys laid out, including two child-size sex dolls. The lights were on, but dim, and in the middle of the entire room was a makeshift stage, circular with a red sex chair positioned front and center.

The entire scene could have come out of a really good sex party, one that I would have been glad to attend, if it weren't all focused around a prepubescent child.

A fucking sex chair for an eleven-year-old. The girl wasn't old enough to know they existed, let alone how they were used. I bit down to keep myself from vomiting and ended up tasting blood when I snagged my tongue.

"Can I help you with something, sir?" A topless woman who looked too young to be legal wrapped her arm around my bicep. "We could find a cozy spot to sit. Up near the front, maybe?"

I couldn't do this. I couldn't be in here, casually flirting with a possibly unwilling sex worker so that no one would question my desire to be at the party. I needed a few minutes. Or thirty. Needed to get my head in the game.

"You could help me find a WC," I said. "I should freshen up before the evening gets more fun."

"Right this way, sir." She led me to a bathroom set just outside the ballroom. "Come and find me when you're back. I'd love to help with that fun you talked about."

She licked her red lips and batted her long lashes, an expert at both, making me wonder if she'd been superbly groomed or if she was a very skilled call girl. God, I hoped it was the latter.

I also hoped she'd been paid well, and in advance, and if she was here voluntarily, I hoped she didn't get in too much trouble for her part in the evening. Prostitution might be illegal, but in this pedophiliac environment, her profession felt as innocent as church.

Not that churches were necessarily innocent these days. But that was a crusade for another day.

Inside the bathroom, the door shut and locked behind me, I let out a long breath of tension. When my lungs were completely empty, I drew the next breath in with a measured inhale, counting each meditative in and out until I got to ten. I felt better when I got to the end, more focused. Centered. My reasons for being at this den of evil were sharply pinned in my mind. This was for my family, for the father I lost, for the life I could have known, for the sister who bore the brunt of the fallout.

And this was for Celia, heart of my heart, the child that Ron ruined and the woman I loved so much I'd ruined her more. Tonight would be a victory in her name. I could practically taste it.

As I returned to the ballroom, I gripped her name in my mind, holding it like a talisman. She was my motive and my drive and I could endure all of this and a hell of a lot more for her.

The room had settled in my absence, electric anticipation charging the room as Ron made his way up to the stage, Aster at his side. She wore a button-down white satin nightgown, her chestnut hair braided to the side and resting over one shoulder. She clearly felt intimidated by the crowd, and the way she clung to Ron suggested she considered him her safety, as though she trusted that he would protect her from any harm.

I had thought I understood his relationship with Celia, but until then, until I saw the way Aster looked at the predator at her side, I hadn't really seen the whole picture. He hadn't just violated her in unimaginable ways, he'd also fucked with her mind. He'd convinced her that exploitation was what love looked like. Fuck him for everything he'd done, but fuck him most of all for that.

And fuck him for whatever he was planning to do to Aster.

He introduced her to the crowd, interviewing her with questions that seemed almost innocent until viewed through a predator's lense. Questions about what toys she liked to sleep with and what her favorite sweets were to lick.

I hung at the back of the room, near the wall, unable to force myself in closer. I was antsy, my eyes drifting repeatedly to my watch, not looking at the time, but at the button that would bring this whole circus to a close. Reminding myself over and over that the charges against these arseholes needed to stick, that whatever would happen to this girl, it would have been a whole hell of a lot worse if Leroy and I weren't there.

After what seemed like a year, after Ron paraded Aster through the crowd then back to the stage, he finally got to what he called the "good stuff." "Aster, sweet flower, come hop up on this seat so all my friends can see how beautiful you are. We're going to show them the most beautiful parts of you, the parts that are our special secret, remember? These are my bestest friends, so it's okay if we share with them."

I tensed, my breath no longer moving evenly through my lungs. I wanted to look away, but my eyes were locked on the child's, part of me willing her to fight him off, part of me hoping she would cooperate so that we could hurry up to the part where she was rescued.

Apparently groomed well enough beforehand, Aster got up on the sex chair, putting a foot in each stirrup, her legs barely long enough to reach. The position would open her up, expose her innocent private parts to the men once she was undressed.

And there was no way Ron wasn't going to undress her.

When my hand reached toward the watch, Leroy caught my eye. With one sharp shake of his head, he warned me it was too soon.

Fuck. I couldn't stand it. I couldn't stand it for Aster, and I couldn't stand it for Celia. The two wrapped themselves as one in my head, though they looked nothing alike. Each thing Ron said to this girl, I heard the imaginary child voice of my wife in response. Each errant caress, each overly fond stroke of her skin, I saw the stain his touch had left on Celia, invisible bruises that could be seen decades later.

Ron stood in front of Aster and began unbuttoning her gown, coaxing Aster too quietly for me to hear in the back. When he was finished, he pushed the nightie off her shoulders and stood aside to reveal the girl's undeveloped chest and white cotton panties.

I stared at the side of Leroy's head, willing him to push the button. It was supposed to be his call, and I trusted him, but after his years in this line of work, he was immune to this shit. He could tolerate it longer than I could. For too long, in my opinion, considering Aster was almost naked.

Leroy didn't flinch, didn't make a move to even check the time.

"Aster, I'm going to share a secret with my friends tonight, and then they're going to share a secret with you," Ron said. "Would you like that? Do you like our secrets?"

"Yes, sir," she said, her voice too small and high pitched to be thought sexy.

Yet, as I looked around the room, several men were already reaching for their cocks.

"I knew you would enjoy this, my sweet girl. First, let me give you a hint about the secret they're going to share with you. Remember that feeling I told you about the other day? The one that takes hold of your body with a rush and makes you feel so so good, the best you've ever felt? Remember how I told you I sometimes have that feeling about you when I'm touching myself and you said you wanted me to show you that feeling too one day?"

The girl's cheeks went red as she gave a single nod. I could feel my own face going red with anger, hot and potent and ready to destroy.

"That's not how you respond to me, young lady," he said, his tone suddenly sharp as he flicked the skin on the inside of her thigh.

She flinched at the pain then corrected herself. "Yes, sir. I remember."

"That's a good girl," he purred. "You're about to get your reward."

He turned again to speak to the crowd. "Gentlemen, Aster has never experienced an orgasm. Never been stroked by a grown man's hand. Never been tasted." He let his words sink in, the declaration causing an excited stir in the room. "Who here would like to be the first to show her the ecstasy of pleasure?"

Hands raised, voices shouted out starting bids.

And I pressed the button on the watch.

It had to be enough, with the testimony of myself and Leroy and the girl, and there was no way I could let any of those men touch her like that. No way in hell. I'd do whatever I had to in order to keep their dirty paws off of her.

Anxiously, I tapped my foot as the bids increased, willing the police to hurry up and bust in. I'd been warned it would take them a few minutes to approach, but I hadn't realized the minutes would crawl by at an excruciatingly slow speed.

"Aster, love," Ron said when the bidding stalled out.

306 | LAURELIN PAIGE

"I need you to take off your panties so my friends can see your pretty pussy. Can you do that?"

"Yes, sir," she said, then began to shimmy out of her pants.

I lurched forward, wanting to stop her, wanting to stand in front and hide her from lecherous eyes.

An arm shot forward, barring me from going any closer.

"I hit the button," Leroy whispered. I hadn't even noticed him come over.

"I did too," I admitted. But the cops still weren't here and Aster was now naked with the auction at a stall.

"Going once," Ron said. "Twice."

I did the only thing I could do. "Seventy-five thousand," I shouted, not sure if we were bidding in dollars or pounds. It didn't matter. The money would never be paid. This was a stall tactic and nothing more.

"Eighty," came the man with the previous high bid.

"Eighty-five," I said.

"Ninety."

"One hundred." The two of us were in a bidding war, which was fine with me. I'd match him as high as he'd go.

"Gentlemen, please remember," Ron said. "If you don't get to go first, you can certainly be second. Do I hear higher than one hundred thousand?"

The other man was silent.

"Going once, twice." The obligatory pause. "Sold to Edward Fasbender."

"Keep stalling," Leroy whispered with a smile, clapping his hand across my back as though to congratulate me.

Jesus, where were they?

Somehow refraining from looking over my shoulder, I walked forward, taking my time to engage with each debauched man who had a lewd comment to share as I approached the stage. It took everything in my power not to cover Aster up when I got there. I did manage to stand in front of her, blocking the crowd's view while I spoke to Ron.

"Should I write the check first?" I r eached i nto my jacket pocket, looking for my billfold.

"I think you're good for it," Ron said, his face flushed with exhilaration. "Let's not waste time with the housekeeping. I'm ready for the show."

All the ways I wanted to hurt him flashed through my mind in the space of a few seconds. I wanted to take his eyes out with my teeth. I wanted to rip his intestines out through his arsehole. I wanted to break his erect cock with my hands then press on his balls with the heel of my foot.

I smiled at him. There was a commotion out in the hall-way, and I knew what was coming next. "I'm ready for the show, too," I said. "I think it's going to be a good one."

Then, right on cue, the task force was upon us, shouting out commands, guns pointed. I turned to Aster, hand-ing her the discarded pants and helping her cover up before passing her off to Felisha who was designated to take her away.

By the time my attention went back to Ron, he was on the floor, his hands pinned behind his back while an officer cuffed him. I was seconds from being cuffed as well—I'd been warned that Leroy and I might even be booked before Dominic got to us. I could spend the night in jail, for all I cared. Nothing would take away the glory of this mo-ment, of watching Ron's horrified face while he was read his rights.

It was over.

It was finally over, and I was higher than I'd ever been. This moment was karma and justice and, yes, it was revenge, but it was the most deserved of any I'd ever administered, and the power that stirred in me was beyond intoxicating. I was no longer human—I was a god, doling out Ron's reckoning as though I were sitting on a throne on Judgment Day.

"This is for what you did to my father's company," I told Ron, making sure that he knew without a doubt that this came from me. "But most of all, this is for Celia."

His horror turned to outrage, the look of murder sharp in his eyes.

And I laughed, amusement bubbling up through me like champagne despite my arms being wrenched behind my back and slapped with metal cuffs. I was untouchable. I was without bounds. I was on cloud nine.

It was over, and, deep in the marrow of my bones, I knew it had only just begun.

TWENTY-THREE

CELIA

"You're still up?" Edward asked as he walked into the bedroom just after four in the morning. He'd entered the house so stealthily, I hadn't even heard him moving around downstairs.

I sprang up from the armchair I'd been sitting in. "Of course I'm still up! Did you think I'd be able to sleep?"

Honestly, I hadn't even tried. I'd taken a shower and changed into loungewear simply so that I could appear to have made the effort, knowing Edward wouldn't want me staying up all night, but I never even made it under the covers. There was every chance he'd want to punish me for it, and I didn't care one bit.

It wasn't punishment on his mind, though, when he strode to me and wrapped me in his arms. He held me like that, his face pressed into the crook of my neck, his embrace so tight it was almost uncomfortable.

I tolerated it for about fifteen seconds.

Then I couldn't stand it. "What happened?" I asked

impatiently, needing to know everything.

I tried to push him away so I could see his face when he answered, but he only gripped me harder. "I'll tell you. Just...give me a minute. I need to hold you first."

Understanding rippled through my chest sending goosebumps down my arms. Whatever had occurred, it had been awful. Of course it had been. I lived with the memories all the time. I was used to them. They were second skin, so embedded in the fabric of my being that I sometimes forgot how brutal they were to look at head-on.

I reached my arms around Edward's back to hold him closer. "Okay," I said soothingly. "I'm here. It's okay."

Time passed without measure while we clung to each other. What he'd witnessed, what I'd discovered about him earlier—none of it meant anything in the moment. It only mattered that we loved each other—in good and bad, in dark and light, within boundaries and beyond. Everything outside of that was insignificant.

But moments only last so long.

And eventually, his grasp loosened, his breathing steadied, and slowly, he untangled himself from my arms.

Then, we were no longer alone, our recent discoveries about each other as present as though they were beings in the room with us.

I hugged my arms over my chest, suddenly cold. "If you can't talk about it right now, I understand. But I need to know—did we get him?"

His chest lifted and fell before he answered. "We got him."

I wanted to believe it too badly. I needed to be sure. "He can't talk his way out of this? You're certain the charge will stick?"

"There are several he'll be facing after tonight. Too many witnesses and evidence against him. He won't get bail. He'll serve time. No doubt in my mind."

Relief threaded through me, overwhelming and euphoric. Not the relief I'd imagined, like a tight muscle suddenly becoming unknit or a heavy weight being taken off my shoulders. More like a release from a tether, like the flight of a butterfly bursting out of its cocoon or the rising of a phoenix from a fire.

Tears sprang to my eyes, the ecstasy so unbelievably potent. I'd never realized how captive I was to my uncle, after all these years. After all the work I'd done to break loose. His freedom had been my tether. Now, with him behind bars, I was finally unleashed. I wouldn't have believed it could make such a difference to my existence.

Edward had known, though. He'd said this would matter, and he was right.

Did that justify all his acts of vengeance?

The thought threatened to ruin the glory of my liberation, and I shoved it away.

"Thank you," I said, focusing on the good. "Thank you for doing this, Edward. I know it was for you, too, but I'm grateful beyond words."

Hands in his pockets, he leaned against the wall, looking so tired that he needed the structure to keep him standing up. "It was primarily for you, bird. Especially after tonight. After what I saw, after knowing what it must have been like..."

He trailed off, and what he didn't say—what he was *unable* to say was more telling than if he'd used words. The party had to be agonizing. Whatever those men had done, whatever Ron had done...

"You don't need to say," I told him. "I know."

"You do. You know."

His gaze locked with mine, so full of sympathy for what I'd gone through in my past. So full of compassion. So intense, I had to look away.

I perched on the arm of the chair, thinking about the terrible things Ron had done that hadn't been done to me. "This was meant to heal you as well. Did it do that? Is it what you wanted it to be?"

"Yes." He nodded. "It's more than I wanted it to be."

This relief was almost as intense as the first. "I'm so glad, Edward. Now we can move on and put all these schemes behind us." Yes, I was grateful he'd done this, but I was equally grateful that his distractions could be done.

But his response put me back on edge. "I don't know about that."

"What do you mean?" I asked, digging my fingernails into the upholstery because I was afraid of the answer.

He smiled suddenly. "We found the fifth man, Celia. All of them were there. The ones who were still alive. We have them all now."

Over the past year, with my help, Edward had discovered the fourth man who had purchased me at auction had passed away. The fifth we had yet to identify.

Those men were the sources of my nightmares as much as Ron was, if not more. He'd given me whiplash with this change of subject, but I was happy for the turn. "Thank God for that. I can't begin to express how that makes me feel. *Thrilled* isn't the right word. *Relieved* isn't good enough either."

"I understand." He ran a hand over the scruff of his jaw. "To think how long they've been doing this...all those girls who will feel the same way you did when they find out about this bust. This will bring them so much peace."

"And all the girls you've saved from future harm."

"Yes, that." His smile slipped away into solemness, his gaze laser sharp. "I realized a lot tonight. I realized that these schemes are important. That they make a difference. And I realized that I have power. Because of my class, because I'm a man, because I have the stomach to fight the fights others can't fight. I can't retire from this work now, just because my own list has been completed. There are more battles, and I have a responsibility to wage them."

My mouth went dry as unease settled again on me.

"Okay. That's good. That can be...good." I didn't want to jump to conclusions, but I was sure I knew where he was headed. All I could do was try to steer him another way. "There are others who need help. People who need a social justice warrior. Our resources could be extremely valuable. We can reach out to different organizations, see who needs money and advocates and..."

There were so many ways we could contribute. My mind was spinning with possibilities.

"Yes, we can do those things too. But there are personal battles we still need to get through."

My heart sank. "I don't like where this is going."

He pushed off the wall and crossed to his dresser, undoing a cufflink as he did. "One of the men there tonight—I knew him. He's one of the owners of the company that Genevieve worked for before coming to Accelecom. I can't stomach how close he was to my daughter."

"I don't mean to minimize how that must have made

314 | LAURELIN PAIGE

you feel, but I'm sure he wouldn't have done anything to her. If he was there tonight, I'm guessing he has another type."

He set the cufflink down and started on the other. "Yes, I'm sure you're right. But other people's daughters aren't so lucky. It takes the people who are close to the predators to call them out. The reason we don't catch them in their horrible acts is that their friends keep their secrets. We can't be bound to those sorts of obligations. To be better, we have to be willing to expose what needs to be exposed."

"Edward…" Silently, I willed him not to do this, not to turn tonight into a crusade.

"Tell me his name, Celia."

My eyes closed briefly, and in that tiny space of time, I allowed myself to be disappointed. I'd hoped beyond hope that tonight would have taken him another direction. I'd allowed myself to believe he'd drop his pursuit of A's real name, that he'd let it go, that a change of heart might be possible. Finding that it hadn't happened was devastating.

But as soon as I opened my eyes again, I let that emotion pass so I could focus on the one that was necessary, the one that would give me fuel—anger.

"No," I said sharply. Then I stood and brushed past him to go to the closet.

Edward followed on my heels. "He's a predator of a different kind, but he's still a predator. You are well aware of the harm a man like him can do."

I pulled a sundress off a hanger and haphazardly folded it as I spoke. "He's not like that anymore. He's changed, and this is not your responsibility."

"You thought you were the only one with Ron, too. Do

you know how many victims he's had since you? You have journals upon journals of games you played with this shithead. You really believe he stopped when your friendship ended? You didn't stop."

I paused to glare at him. "Our friendship ended *because* he stopped. I was the bad guy in that scenario, Edward. *Me*. Not him."

"There's no way you can know that he really stopped." He took off his jacket and threw it on the closet island, ignoring my attempt to shift blame. "Even if he did stop, he has to take responsibility for what he did before. Not only his own victims, but yours as well, because he's the one who taught you. Tell me his name."

"I won't." I threw the dress into my open suitcase then reached for another off a hanger. I'd set the bag out earlier, when I'd realized what Edward had done to his brother-in-law, unsure how I should react to that knowledge.

All night, as I'd paced and waited for word, the luggage had sat untouched. The truth of it was that my husband scared me. But he'd always scared me. If I'd stuck with him before, there was no reason for that fear to suddenly drive me away.

Now, though, I was glad I'd set the case out for a different reason—because I was raging, and I needed space.

Apparently, Edward was too narrowed in on our fight to have noticed. "Stop stalling. You will tell me eventually. Get it over with and tell me now."

I spun toward him. "And then what? What will you do to him when you find out who he is?"

"Whatever is needed." He smirked like he was untouchable. Like he was omnipotent. Like he had every right to rule the universe, and if that meant taking extreme action, so be it.

It was too much power for a man to have. He believed in calling people out? Then, fuck if I didn't call *him* out. "Did you kill Frank?"

Something flashed across his eyes so fast I almost missed it. "What?"

"Don't play dumb. You killed Camilla's husband, didn't you? Do you want to tell me about that?"

"Not particularly," he said cooly, as though detached from the accusation.

His nonchalance flamed my fury. "I'm just supposed to give up A—a man who is a decent, respectable human, no matter what you think—when you still can't tell me all of your secrets?"

"The two aren't related in any way."

"Aren't they?" I threw the outfit I was holding in the suitcase. "Did Camilla know what you were going to do to her husband? I'll bet she didn't have a clue."

"You're guessing." But his tone wasn't so sure.

I pounced on his uncertainty. "She might be thanking you now, and that might justify your actions as far as you're concerned, but it doesn't justify them to me."

"Ah," understanding clicked on his expression. "You found her letter."

I'd given myself away, but it didn't mean I was wrong.

I doubled down. "It makes me sick, Edward. That you could take things that far. You said you had no boundaries, and I knew you didn't, and still I let myself believe you wouldn't do *that*. Now I'm facing the truth, and I'm horrified."

The corner of his mouth lifted into a sneer. "No you're not."

"Yes! I am!"

"You're telling yourself that you are, because you think that's what a decent person should think." He took an intimidating step toward me. "But deep down, you're not horrified at all." And another. "It excites you." He was right in front of me now, bending to my ear. "To know that I would go to those lengths for someone I love. To know the lengths I would go for *you*—you're turned on."

His breath was hot on my skin, and I shivered, not only from his nearness, but because he was right, as always. It did excite me. It did turn me on.

And because of how it made me feel, I was horrified.

This is where he usually won, where I backed down and admitted he knew me better than myself and his ego puffed up a little bit more because of his omniscience.

Not this time. He'd told me he needed me to give him limits, so this would be mine. I wouldn't fold.

"You're full of yourself." I pushed past him to go to the drawer where my underwear was kept.

He chuckled behind me. "Only the truth, Celia, remember?"

"The truth is that you're insane."

"Let's stop with the harsh words, can we?" His voice was softer but still patronizing. "Listen to me. You can't deny how tonight has changed things for you. It's given you an end that you so badly needed. You need this closure with A too. *We* need this closure. Then we can be free of the past, and we can have your baby—"

I cut him off sharply, my finger pointed at him. "You're

just as manipulative as anyone else. Hanging a baby in front of me like bait. You think I'm thinking about a baby right now? When I know how dangerous you can be? I'd be just as crazy as you are to even consider it."

Now wasn't the time to tell him what I'd already done. I couldn't even think about it myself.

Edward was silent. I could feel his eyes on my back as I dropped the handful of panties in the suitcase then reached for my shoes.

"You're packing," he said, after a beat. "Where are you going?"

"I'm going to New York. My parents are going to wake up to a scandal. I should be there." I didn't look at him, set more than ever on what I was doing.

"I'd feel better if you were here or Amelie. *Because* of the scandal. You don't need to be wrapped up in this, and you will be if you're with your father."

I slammed my pajama drawer shut, feeling a flicker of satisfaction when it banged. "What I need is to not be told what to do for half a minute. What if what I need is to be away from you?"

"Are you leaving me?" The question came out deep and provoking. Daring me to say that I was.

I didn't want to answer. It wasn't my intention to leave him, but I certainly wanted him to think it was a possibility. I wanted him to be scared that I could. I wanted him to have consequences that would mean something. I wanted him to have to fight—wanted him to *want* to fight—wanted him to want to *change* in order to keep me.

The truth wouldn't push him to that.

"I'm leaving this house," I said, trying to talk my way

around it. I pulled two more dresses off hangers and tossed them in my bag. "And I'm leaving without you, so I suppose I am."

"You know that's not what I was asking. You aren't leaving me, Celia." His declaration came out as a growl. "I won't allow that. Especially not over this."

His possessiveness usually made me melt.

Not this time. "Well, I'm not staying. And if you try to keep me hostage again, I can tell you sure as shit that that will be the end of us." I zipped up the suitcase. I didn't have everything I needed, but I was making a statement. Anything I'd missed, I could buy in the States.

I could feel Edward's brain calculating as I grabbed a jacket and slipped on a pair of shoes. I was calculating as well. It was best to leave now and not give him time to find ways to keep me. I didn't have a ticket yet, but I could buy the next flight out at the airport. If he didn't let me have a car, I could call a cab.

When I went to lift the suitcase off the luggage rack, Edward was suddenly there, taking it from me. "Perhaps you're right," he said, his tone even. "Perhaps facing this with your parents will be good for you. But you will come home to me."

I took in a shaky breath and wrenched the suitcase away from him. I was too upset, too pissed, too determined to let him do anything for me at the moment.

When I had it in my hand again, I felt emboldened. "We'll have to see how that goes, won't we?"

Then I spun my back to my husband and marched out of the closet, leaving him, not forever, but for now.

TWENTY-FOUR

EDWARD

The doorman hung up the phone and handed my passport back to me. "You're cleared to go up, Mr. Fasbender. Second elevator. Top floor."

I had held my breath while he'd called up to the Werner penthouse, half afraid I'd be turned away. After four weeks of nothing more than curt texts from my wife, I wasn't sure I'd be welcome at her parents'. Especially showing up unannounced and uninvited.

If Celia would have answered any one of the fifty-plus calls I'd made over the past month, she would have known I was coming. Though, if she'd answered, I wouldn't have had to make the trip at all because I would have demanded she return home. A month apart was far too long to be away from her. God only knew how I'd managed longer absences when she'd been on Amelie.

I was honest enough with myself to realize that I'd been in control of our time apart back then, and that having the power made it easier to endure. The realization only made these last few weeks harder to bear, knowing I was most likely alone in my misery, and that Celia had probably faired the month better than I had.

All that would be behind us soon enough, though I was fully aware I could still be turned away at the door.

I was alone in the lift. Once it was in motion, I turned to the mirror that lined the back of the car, surveyed my image, and frowned. I looked tired, like a man who had spent the last week in a plane rather than a handful of hours. My outfit was fresh, since I'd changed my clothes when I'd stopped by my hotel, but now I wished I'd cho-sen something more impressive than a T-shirt and jeans.

I sighed, and shoved a hand through my hair in a fruitless attempt to improve my appearance. When the car stopped, I looked no better than when I'd got in, but I took a deep breath to straighten my posture and took the few steps to the Werners' door with confidence.

My knock was answered by an apple-shaped woman dressed in clothes that suggested she was staff, but Madge was just behind her.

"It really is you, Edward," she said, blinking. "I couldn't believe it when the doorman gave me your name." She turned to the other woman. "Lupita, this is Celia's hus-band, all the way from London. Can you put on some cof-fee? Better yet, brew some tea."

I nodded in appreciation for the gesture, despite not having any interest in any type of beverage at the moment. Frankly, I was grateful for the hospitality simply because it meant I hadn't been banned from the family.

Lupita and I exchanged greetings, then, as she went off to her assigned task, Madge ushered me into the liv-ing room. "I apologize for the unprepared welcome. We should have had you on the door list. Celia didn't say anything about you coming."

My mother-in-law, though not overly warm in countenance, was much more congenial than the last time I'd seen her on my wedding day. The phone calls I had made to her while Celia had been on Amelie seemed to have earned her trust. That hadn't been my primary intention at the time, but it was a definite benefit.

"Celia didn't know I was coming, actually," I said, when she finally let me get a word in. "It's sort of a surprise visit." Having no idea what my wife had told her family about her stay or the state of our marriage, I decided the best move was to act as though everything was normal, avoiding the fact that I hadn't really spoken to her since she'd come to the States.

"How fun. I can't remember the last time Warren did something romantic. I keep telling Celia she snagged a good one. She best be treating you right." Her tone said she was fishing. Either she suspected a rift in our relationship or she just loved any sort of gossip, both seemed likely possibilities.

Whichever it was, I wouldn't give her the satisfaction of confirming anything. "I'm certainly lucky to have found her. Is she here?"

"Oh, yes. Lupita?" She caught the attention of the servant as Lupita set a tea tray on the sideboard. "Could you please tell Celia that Edward is here?"

"My pleasure."

I almost asked if I could just tag along, but I didn't get the chance.

"Edward Fasbender. In my own home. Who would have thought?" Warren Werner entered the room as Lupita left, his expression as smug as mine had likely been when he'd last been a guest at my house.

I bit back a grimace. "Warren. I hadn't expected to see you home this early in the day." I'd specifically chosen to come on a weekday, hoping my father-in-law would be at the office, not that he spent much time there in the last few years. Rumor was that he was running the company on a fifteen-hour work week. What I could do with that company...

The potential was endless.

"Been a bit chaotic at work. Get more done at home these days."

I hadn't failed to notice the reporters as I'd come in the building. I'd had my fair share in London as well. They'd been quite an annoyance back home, but I smiled when I encountered them today, knowing I had a hand in the irritation they must cause Warren.

"I am sorry to hear about your family troubles," I said, attempting sympathy that I hoped read sincere.

"It's been one helluva debacle, I'll tell you that. I got him a good lawyer. But if it turns out he's really done these things, there's nothing I'll be able to do to help him."

I wanted to punch the arse.

He was still trying to live in the dark. Had Celia even tried to talk to him again about her own history with Ron?

"It really is a surprise," Madge said, laying it on thick. "We had no idea. Celia used to be close to him when she was little. Never any problems at all."

I knew about the psychology of denial, but never had I seen it so blatantly displayed. I was angered by it, naturally, but some of that anger was directed at myself. I should have thought about what this environment might be like for Celia when she was very likely struggling with her emotions as Ron's crimes were shared all over the media. I should have been there for her. I should have come sooner.

I shouldn't have let her leave London in the first place. Not that she'd given me any choice in the matter.

"I'm sure it's been a difficult time for all of you," I said, resisting the urge to open their eyes to Celia's past horrors. She needed to be the one to talk to them, for her own healing.

"Excuse me," Lupita said, returning to the room. "Celia seems to be napping. Shall I wake her?"

Napping? My wife rarely slept during the day. "She's not unwell, is she?"

Madge made a dismissive gesture with her hand. "No, no. This whole nonsense has been exhausting is all. I think she's had trouble sleeping from it."

Again I kicked myself for having let her be away so long. Though, a small part of me hoped her lack of sleep might mean she'd been as miserable without me as I'd been without her.

Regardless of the cause, I couldn't disturb her, much as I was desperate to see her. I was just about to tell Lupita not to wake her when Warren answered for me.

"Let her sleep. Gives us time to talk."

Fanfuckingtastic.

"Should we go to my office?"

"I'm comfortable right here," I said. "Lupita's just served tea." As little interest I had in being caught in a conversation right now, I had even less interest in discussing business with Warren seated behind his desk. He already held dominion just by being on his turf.

"We can stay here then," he said, disappointment evident in his tone.

The women took that as a cue to disappear, leaving us alone.

Immediately, Warren headed to the minibar. "Can I make you a drink?"

I looked at my watch. It wasn't even two in the afternoon. "A tad early for me, I'm afraid." It was probably best to have a clear head around my former nemesis.

"Yes, I suppose it is," he said. He looked longingly at the tumbler in his hand then set it down. "I guess I don't need one either. Have a seat, will you?"

Another opportunity to hand over power that I refused to cede. "I'd rather stand, if you don't mind. Long flight and all."

"Right, right." He glanced at his armchair, considering. In the end, he stayed standing as well. "I imagine you're pleased with how our joint efforts are panning out in India. I'm quite pleased as well. I'm eager to see what else we can put together. Be a good chance to brainstorm face to face while you're here.

"Oh, and I know all this hullabaloo with my brother has put a damper on our stock prices, but they'll bounce back. I assure you. Ron hasn't worked with Werner in quite some years. We'll rise above his misdeeds, no problem."

I might have been impressed how he could be so laser focused on business despite his family turmoil if I weren't so disgusted with the way he spoke about his brother's sins. As though he'd simply been caught going a few miles over the speed limit. As if his crimes were only menial sins.

He defiled your daughter, I said to him silently as he spouted out potential ideas for future collaboration. *He vi-*

olated her and assaulted her, and you don't have the balls to confront it.

He was a coward and an opportunist and deserved to pay for those flaws. I'd hoped his brother's arrest would bring him sufficient turmoil, but seeing how minimally it had affected him, he would need to pay retribution in other ways.

Giving me control of his company would do just fine.

"I have another thought," I said, interrupting whatever he was saying—I hadn't been listening. "Instead of spending our time and energy on a trivial joint venture that ends up being quite meaningless in the big picture, why don't we do something that will have a significant positive effect on both our companies."

He frowned in annoyance, probably because he'd been quite proud of whatever idea he'd been presenting, but he took the bait. "You have something in mind?"

"I do. We should merge."

He visibly drew back. "You can't be serious." He studied me, looking for signs of my sincerity. Apparently finding it, he let out an affronted laugh. "Oh, hell no. You're family now, but you think that makes up for all the obstacles you put up for me in the past? It doesn't."

I smiled, imagining exactly how this would play out, which move I'd make, which move he'd counter with. I could see all the way to checkmate, and fuck if that wasn't thrilling.

"We've both done a quite many misdeeds in our rivalry," I said, using his word from earlier. "And yes, I do believe that should all be water under the bridge. Because we're family."

"That's a lot of nerve you got. This the real reason you

married my daughter?"

"It is not." Eh, it was mostly true. "I love your daughter very much. Speaking of Celia, it's really her decision what happens next at Werner, isn't it? It's because of my respect for you that I'm going this route instead."

My wife had been right in her accusations—I was manipulative. Maybe even more so than any other man in her life. Warren still believed the majority shares were in the family, that Celia had them in her name, and, though she'd signed over her voting power to him, that she had the potential to override any of his decisions if she took her vote back.

I was fully committed to exploiting that fact.

His face blanched, then he scowled. "Those shares aren't really hers. If I had to take it to court, I'd win."

I wasn't so sure of that. "No need to bring up talk of lawsuits. Celia has no plans to take advantage of those shares you gifted her, and neither am I planning to encourage it. If you took that as a threat, it's not what I intended."

No, it was exactly what I'd intended.

"I was merely reminding you the reasons you signed over those shares to Celia. Because you wanted to provide for your only child. Because you wanted the Werner legacy to remain in the family."

"Of course that's why I gave them to her," he said.

Which was an utter lie. He'd had thoughts of tax evasion in his mind when he'd done it, and nothing else, but I was purposefully playing to his sense of fatherly duty.

"You mentioned the current state of your stocks. I'm sure, as you said, they will recover, but what if they don't? Merging with a company that has a considerable share of markets Werner has no access to would give a meaningful boost to the bottom line. Not only will your stocks go up again, they'll skyrocket. Isn't that the legacy you want to leave your daughter?"

Warren glowered at me in silence. He was caught and he knew it. Zugzwang. Warren wasn't ready to trust me with his company, but it was the right move. Not only for his company, but for his daughter. To prove he cared about her. He'd failed her so completely in other ways. This was his chance to show she was his priority.

"Sorry to interrupt," Lupita said.

I waited until Warren's gaze moved to her before I moved mine. "What is it?" he snapped.

"Celia's awake now. I told her you were here, Mr. Fasbender, and she asked that you meet her in the conservatory. I can take you there when you're ready."

"Splendid. I'm ready now." I patted Warren on the arm, patronizing him purposefully. "No rush to decide right this minute. Sooner the better, though, probably, considering how far Werner has dropped. Thirteen points just today, wasn't it? Yikes."

Before he could say anything else I turned back to Lupita. "Where's the conservatory?"

It was tempting to feel self-righteous as I followed the servant down the hall. Warren would concede eventually. Unfortunately his motives were most definitely his own pocketbook and egotistical desire to have his company thrive, but he'd say it was for Celia, and that would mean something to her despite the lie.

Werner Media completely vanished from my mind, though, the minute I was out of Warren's sight. Celia was the only thing I was thinking about now. How close she was, how soon she'd be back in my arms.

My whole being vibrated in anticipation.

"Through there," Lupita said when we reached a set of open double doors.

I nodded appreciatively then stepped over the threshold, halting as soon as I did. Because there she was, standing at the window, looking out over Central Park, her hair tied in a messy knot, her skin pink from too much sun, her lips gripped in a straight line.

God, she was magnificent.

I could hardly breathe in the splendor of her presence.

She must have sensed my stare. I hadn't moved or made a sound when she turned and caught me looking at her.

Her eyes lit up—or I imagined they had, because I very much wished that she'd be excited to see me—and her chin quivered, as though she were about to speak, but she remained silent.

She remained on the opposite side of the room, as well, which was disheartening when I wanted so badly to touch her.

For that matter, I was still standing at the door. There was a chasm between us, wide and yawning, and I knew I had to be the one to find a way across.

But I was stubborn too. Stubborn in my belief that I knew what was best for her, and as much as I wanted us reunited, it couldn't be by surrendering my side of this fight.

Which left only the truth to close the gap.

"I am well aware that there are more than my feelings that matter in this, but for what it's worth, I've been a wreck without you." My chest shuddered with the act of

330 | LAURELIN PAIGE

being vulnerable, but I pushed on. "I don't sleep well without you in my bed. It's extremely hard to focus on anything at all, even the crossword, and my stomach is in constant knots when I'm not able to look after your care."

I took a timid step forward, approaching her as a hunter would approach his prey, despite not knowing who really held the power in the room. Was it her? Was it me? It was impossible to tell. "I know we both feel strongly about our current positions. You know who I am. You *know*, and I'm certain you don't expect me to be a different man. Likewise, I'm not asking you to lose any ground you've made by coming here. I'm simply asking if we might find a way to love each other past our differences. I'm better at your side, and I believe you're better at mine."

I waited for her to say something, ready to go to her as soon as she gave the sign. The seconds passed loudly, the ticking of the room's grandfather clock deafening in the silence. As I watched, her chest lifted, her mouth opened. Then it shut again without having said a word.

My pulse sped up as my heart plummeted in my chest. Was this it? Was it over between us? What would I have to do to keep her?

"Bird...say something. Please."

She did then, her voice carrying loud and clear across the invisible gorge, bringing me two words I'd never thought I'd hear a woman speak to me again. "I'm pregnant."

The Slay story concludes in Rising: Slay Four

With their marriage in a state of uncertainty, Celia and Edward's relationship is pushed to the limits.

ALSO BY LAURELIN PAIGE

Visit www.laurelinpaige.com for a more detailed reading order.

The Dirty Universe

Dirty Filthy Rich Boys - READ FREE
Dirty Duet: Dirty Filthy Rich Men | Dirty Filthy Rich Love
Dirty Sexy Bastard - READ FREE
Dirty Games Duet: Dirty Sexy Player | Dirty Sexy Games
Dirty Sweet Duet: Sweet Liar | Sweet Fate
Dirty Filthy Fix
Dirty Wild Trilogy: Coming 2020

The Fixed Universe

Fixed Series: Fixed on You | Found in You | Forever with You
Hudson | Fixed Forever
Found Duet: Free Me | Find Me
Chandler
Falling Under You
Dirty Filthy Fix
Slay Saga Slay One: Rivalry | Slay Two: Ruin
Slay Three: Revenge | Slay Four: Rising
The Open Door

First and Last Duet: First Touch | Last Kiss

Hollywood Standalones

One More Time
Close
Sex Symbol
Star Struck

Written with Sierra Simone

Porn Star | Hot Cop

Written with Kayti McGee under the name Laurelin McGee

Miss Match | Love Struck | MisTaken | Holiday for Hire

LET'S STAY IN TOUCH!

I'm on **Facebook, Bookbub, Amazon,** and **Instagram**. Come find me. I totally support stalking.

Be sure to **join** my **reader** group, **The Sky Launch**, facebook.com/groups/HudsonPierce

Check out my website www.laurelinpaige.com to find out more about my books. While there, sign up for **my newsletter** where you'll receive a **free book every month** from bestselling authors, only available to my subscribers, as well as up-to-date information on my latest releases.

Only want to be notified when I have a new release? Text **Paige** to 21000, and I'll shoot you a text when I have a book come out.

About the Author

With millions of books sold worldwide, Laurelin Paige is a New York Times, Wall Street Journal and USA Today Bestselling Author. Her international success started with her very first series, the Fixed Trilogy, which, alone, has sold over 1 million copies, and earned her the coveted #1 spot on Amazon's bestseller list in the U.S., U.K., Canada, and Australia, simultaneously. This title also was named in People magazine as one of the top 10 most downloaded books of 2014. She's also been #1 over all books at the Apple Book Store with more than one title in more than one country. She's published both independently and with MacMillan's St. Martin's Press and Griffin imprints as well as many other publishers around the world including Harper Collins in Germany and Hachette/Little Brown in the U.K. With her edgy, trope-flipped stories of smart women and strong men, she's managed to secure herself among today's romance royalty.

Paige has a Bachelor's degree in Musical Theater and a Masters of Business Administration with a Marketing emphasis, and she credits her writing success to what she learned from both programs, though she's also an avid learner, constantly trying to challenge her mind with new and exciting ideas and concepts. While she loves psychological thrillers and witty philosophical books and entertainment, she is a sucker for a good romance and gets giddy anytime there's kissing, much to the embarrassment of her three daughters. Her husband doesn't seem to complain, however. When she isn't reading or writing sexy stories, she's probably singing, watching shows like Game of Thrones, Letterkenny and Discovery of Witches, or dreaming of Michael Fassbender. She's also a proud member of

Mensa International though she doesn't do anything with the organization except use it as material for her bio. She currently lives outside Austin, Texas and is represented by Rebecca Friedman.